READERS ARE OBSESSED WITH LAUREN NORTH'S THRILLERS

'This book **floored** me'

'Full of **intrigue, suspense, twists** and **turns**'

'**Wow** – that's the first word that comes to mind'

'Had me **hooked** from the opening pages'

'**Addictive** and intriguing'

'A **thrilling** read that will leave you **breathless**'

'Lauren North is really developing into a **must-read author**'

'Both heart-rending and **powerful**'

'Utterly **brilliant**'

'A **riveting** read I couldn't devour fast enough'

'One of my **favourite** books this year'

'The absolute definition of a **page-turner**'

'If I could give it **more than 5 stars,** I would'

Lauren North writes psychological suspense novels that delve into the darker side of relationships and families. She has a lifelong passion for writing, reading and all things books. Lauren's love of psychological suspense has grown since childhood, and from her dark imagination of always wondering what's the worst thing that could happen in every situation.

Lauren studied psychology before moving to London, where she lived and worked for many years. She now lives with her family in the Suffolk countryside. Readers can follow Lauren on Twitter @Lauren_C_North and Facebook @LaurenNorthAuthor

Also by Lauren North

SAFE AT HOME
THE PERFECT BETRAYAL
ONE STEP BEHIND

All the Wicked Games

LAUREN NORTH

PENGUIN BOOKS

TRANSWORLD PUBLISHERS
Penguin Random House, One Embassy Gardens,
8 Viaduct Gardens, London SW11 7BW
www.penguin.co.uk

Transworld is part of the Penguin Random House group of companies
whose addresses can be found at global.penguinrandomhouse.com

First published in Great Britain in 2022 by Penguin Books
an imprint of Transworld Publishers

A CIP catalogue record for this book
is available from the British Library.

ISBN 9780552177962

Typeset in 11/13.5pt Sabon by Jouve (UK), Milton Keynes.
Printed and bound in Great Britain by Clays Ltd, Elcograf S.p.A.

The authorized representative in the EEA is Penguin Random House
Ireland, Morrison Chambers, 32 Nassau Street, Dublin D02 YH68.

Penguin Random House is committed to a sustainable
future for our business, our readers and our planet. This book
is made from Forest Stewardship Council® certified paper.

For my dad

Don't start what you can't finish.
It's one of life's rules, don't you think?
As fundamental as a commandment.
I bet it's even in the Bible somewhere,
right next to that bit about 'do unto others'.

But here's the thing – you can't mess with
people's lives and expect them just to forgive
and forget. That's not how this works. There have
to be consequences. People have to pay for their
choices. Quid pro quo.

So just you remember, when all this is over, who
started this game – because I'm the one finishing it.

Chapter 1

Cleo

Now

It takes three words to shatter the safety glass of my oh-so-perfect world.

Rachel is missing.

My feet stop dead on the pavement. Shoppers coming from both directions step around me, knocking my shoulders. Someone tuts.

Don't they get it? I'd move if I could. But there's a weight on my feet, a whopping great steel anchor pinning me to this one paving slab outside M&S on Southampton High Street.

I read the text again.

Beth Winslow, Fri 15 Jan, 10.21 a.m.
Rachel is missing. Have you seen her? We're really worried.

3

A cavern rips open inside me. It's panic. It's fear. It's guilt. Oh my God, the guilt. Like fire and ice burning my insides. It's everything I work so hard to keep squished deep down in the darkest of corners.

My chest tightens. I reach my fingers into the pocket of my raincoat, wriggling and pushing beyond the folds of fabric and the packet of tissues, until I touch the thin metal chain of the attack alarm that is always there.

'Cleo,' a voice calls out. I turn my gaze to Gemma, waving her free hand at me over a group of pushchair mums. Gemma's heart-shaped face, her smile, is a safety beacon. All I need to do is follow. Except I can't.

'I'm going on,' she calls, lifting two bulging M&S bags in the air. 'I got the last Percy Pigs.' She laughs, and sixty seconds ago I would have laughed too, before chasing after her with my own haul of Marmite and Maryland cookies, and the five little pots of honey-flavoured lip balm from Boots that save my lips from the constant air conditioning of the ship. 'You coming?'

My eyes flick to my watch. I have an hour until staff boarding. Two hours until I need to be in my maroon pinafore with the lime-green collar, greeting passengers with a welcoming 'this is your 108 days of paradise' smile.

'Be right behind you,' I manage to reply.

Gemma nods and disappears and all I can think about is you and how much this guilt burns.

I find a bench away from the main high street. It's one of those modern concrete slabs with no back, and when I sit down the January cold bites through my jeans. My fingers are numb; the tip of my nose stings. I long for a winter coat. A bulky parka with a faux-fur-trimmed hood instead of the little pocket mac that is so easy to stash in my backpack wherever I go. It doesn't seem possible that I was in Barbados a week ago.

I pull up Beth's number, but my finger hovers a moment too long, and just for a second I imagine myself boarding the *Enchantress* without a backwards thought to you.

Just like last time, then. Your voice comes from nowhere. It's so real, so you. It's like you're standing right there, clinging to my arm and whispering in my ear, like you've done a thousand times before.

The guilt morphs – hot lava flushing my cheeks, my body. Images of the woods flash through my mind.

The moment passes. I draw in a shuddering breath and expel it like smoke from a cigarette. We never could get the hang of smoking.

Your sister answers on the first ring. A furtive 'Hello?' Her voice is so like yours that I have to scrunch my eyes shut tight against the hurt.

'Beth, it's me.' And then, because it's been five years since we last spoke, and because we are strangers now, I add, 'It's Cleo.'

'Cleo? Oh my God. Have you seen Rachel? Is she with you?'

'No.'

'When did you last talk?'

I pause then, the answer jagged in my throat. 'Not for a while.'

The silence that follows is laced with disappointment. I picture Beth sitting on the worktop in your mum's kitchen, pushing her hand through her dark hair over and over, the same way you used to do when you were annoyed. I picture her scowl – the narrowed eyes she saved just for me.

'No, that's not right,' she says. 'You were texting each other. You met her last Friday night, didn't you?'

'What? No, I didn't. I . . . I've been away.'

Another silence draws out between us and I feel her hatred burn down the phone. Your sister never liked me, did she? I tried not to mind. I put it down to jealousy. Our closeness, the bond we had that she'd always wanted with you, but never quite achieved. But after everything that happened with Luke Richards, that dislike became a gnarled, thorny hate.

The way she looked at me in the hospital, it was like she could see straight through me. She could see my secret, knew I'd lied to the police; to that detective, Anik; to you.

Five years on, her hate for me is just as sharp.

'But why would Rachel say you were meeting when you weren't?' Beth asks, her voice still accusing.

'I don't know.' The question rings in my mind and I swallow back the mounting guilt. You texted me last month. Early December:

Can we talk? It's important!!

I slipped my phone into my pocket, telling myself I'd reply later, but I never did.

It wasn't me texting you, Rach.

So who was?

Icy fingers trace across my skin. There is only one person I can think of. His name whispers through my mind. *Luke Richards. Luke Richards. Luke Richards.*

'What's going on, Beth?' I ask. 'What happened?'

'I told you. She's missing. She went out last Friday night to meet you – or that's what I thought, anyway – and no one has seen her since. That's why I'm calling

6

you. I've tried her phone a thousand times but it's switched off.' Her words come fast, panicked. 'She's been missing a week.'

A shudder races over me.

'A week? Why hasn't it been on the news?'

'Because the police aren't taking it seriously, that's why,' Beth half shouts in my ear.

'Who was the last person to see her?' I ask.

'I don't know. Her landlord, Simon, got in touch. He was the one who said you were meeting Rach on Friday. You know him, right?'

'Simon?' I frown. 'Does Rachel still live in the house share?'

A pause. 'You didn't know?'

'No.' Images of our past threaten to take over. I force myself to stay in the present, fixing my gaze on a couple walking fast, their suitcases dragging behind them, wheels clattering.

'I should go,' I say, my thoughts pulling back to the *Enchantress*. 'I'm sorry about Rachel. Let me know she's OK.'

'Wait,' Beth says. 'I'm sorry, OK? I know I'm being a bitch to you. I'm upset and I'm worried. Don't go. Simon said she never came back that night,' Beth continues. 'He messaged me on Facebook and asked if I'd heard from her. I don't know what to do. I've been calling people all week. I tried her work colleagues and your old housemates, Lisa and Katie. No one has seen or heard from her.'

Memories crawl, poison ivy, over my skin. Remember that summer between our first and second year that we spent in Bristol staying at your mum's? Working behind the bar at Revolution, counting down the days until we could get back to London and the future

7

that seemed so bright. I was part of something when I was there.

Two passing seagulls caterwaul above my head, reminding me that I'm part of something here. A new life I happen to like very much.

'After what happened . . .' Beth's voice trails off and the relief that it does is almost breath-taking. I can't listen to the end of that sentence. 'I don't know what to do. I don't know any of her friends. I'd go to London and look for her myself, but it's Mum, Cleo – she's sick.'

'I'm sorry. What—'

'Dementia. It's early stages, but she gets so confused if I'm not here for her. There's no one else I can ask. I can't leave her. She keeps asking to talk to Rachel. It's so hard. I've been putting her off, but I don't know what to do.' Beth's voice is a squeak of emotion. She's crying.

'I think Rach is in trouble,' Beth continues. 'I think it's happened again. The last time I spoke to her she was walking home from work and something scared her. She said someone was following her. She ran to the house while I stayed on the line and I could tell she was petrified. She laughed it off when she was safe again. I asked her what had happened and she said she'd seen the cowboy, which I didn't understand, and when I asked her what she meant, she told me not to worry, that it was nothing. But whatever she saw, it really scared her.'

Every muscle in my body tenses. *The cowboy.* Beth doesn't know what she's said; she doesn't know that 'the cowboy' is the name you used for Luke Richards. Shit!

I can't process this. He can't be back. It's been so long.

I leap up and pace beside the bench, heaving in the cold air and the smell of the sea.

'Cleo?' Beth's voice is shaking now. 'What do we do?'

'I'll help.' The words are out before I can stop them. 'I'll make some calls. I'll ring you back.'

I check the time. Forty minutes until I need to be on board.

I think of the girls on our make-up course. Would any of them know where you are? I doubt it. It was always us and them.

Which leaves Simon. Bloody hell, Rach. I can't believe you still live there. How can you bear it?

He answers on the fifth ring. 'Yep.' Just that one word grates on me. Same old Simon. What did I ever see in him?

'It's Cleo. Cleo Thomas.'

There's a pause, a silence on the line that makes me lift the phone from my ear to see if we're still connected. We are.

'Cleo,' he says eventually. 'It's been years. Still waxing bikini lines for wrinkly old cruisers?'

His words sting, but I have no retort.

I see him in my mind – those sharp features, the small eyes and the eyebrows tilting up at the ends, that brooding attractiveness. God, he could be so rude, though.

It didn't stop you.

I wish it had. That was a mistake.

I wonder if he still works crazy hours, ignoring his tenants for weeks on end. I wonder if he still has moments of being a massive arsehole.

'I'm calling about Rachel,' I say. 'What's going on?'

He sighs. A proper long 'do I really have to waste

my time talking to you?' kind of sigh. I guess I have my answer to the arsehole question. 'Like I told her sister, I've not seen her since last week.'

His words hit with the same shock as Beth's text. I long to be on the ship, for none of this to be happening. My eyes search the nearby shoppers, fixing on a man across the street. He has his back to me. Thin frame. Cropped blond hair. My pulse drums in my ears.

I don't breathe. I don't move. My legs are jelly, my feet cement, as I wait for Luke Richards to turn around and see me. And then he does and I catch the profile of his face.

'It's not him,' I say, heaving a breath.

'What was that?' Simon asks.

'Nothing.' I shake my head, wishing I could free my thoughts from the panic. 'Beth said you reported Rachel missing to the police?'

'Of course. Not that it's done any good.'

'So they'll find her, then. I'm leaving today. I can't . . . I'll be away for four months.' I want to help you, Rach. I do. Please believe that. But I can't; it's too much.

'Fine. Whatever you want.' There's an abruptness to his tone that makes my jaw clench. 'You called me, remember?'

'Because her sister is worried.'

'So am I, but I've got a meeting. Have a nice life, Cleo.'

'Wait,' I say, before he can hang up. There's a silence and I feel his annoyance vibrating in my ear. 'I'm sorry, OK? For how I left things with us.'

He laughs, a barking 'ha'. 'We slept together a couple of times five years ago, Cleo. There was no "us".'

'Good, then,' I snap, remembering how infuriating Simon is, how cutting his blunt honesty can be. 'Is there anything you can tell me about Rachel, anything that might help Beth find her?'

'One thing.'

'What?'

'She was doing it again.'

'Doing what?' Even as the words leave my mouth, I know. A dread is creeping over me, a scream lodging in the back of my throat.

'She was playing your game again.'

I feel myself falling. Plunging into ice-cold water. Drowning. I pull the phone from my ear, ignoring the tinny sound of Simon's voice calling my name.

Chapter 2

Rachel

Five years earlier

The brush tickles the top of Rachel's cheek, feathery light in a way that makes her squirm. She's the make-up artist, not the model, but this is what they always do on Fridays. They sit on the bed in her room, they drink their cheap toilet-cleaner white wine – £6.98 for a litre and a half of Frascati Superiore from Mr Hakimi's corner shop – and they practise their make-up techniques.

It's always Rachel's room, not Cleo's. Rachel's is bigger and warmer, despite the fact that it's downstairs and right by the front door, which is always crashing open and shut when their housemates troop in and out.

They used to hang out with the other housemates, back when they first moved here. They used to cook meals together and spend all night in the kitchen. Freddie on the top floor, always complaining how hot it was in his room. Lisa, Katie and Cleo in the middle,

Rachel at the bottom. They had parties sometimes too, until Simon would shout at them to shut up because he had to work in the morning. Those were the best days. But then Freddie moved back home and Lisa and Katie fell in love and got a place together in Clapham and everything changed.

New people came in and they tried to be friendly, but no one stays long any more. Not that Rachel can blame them. Now it's Efe on the top floor, who doesn't speak much English. Then a stoner in Lisa's old room, who always forgets to shut the front door properly, and Jess, who steals their milk and never replaces it.

The house is run-down, battered by the rolling turnover of tenants who don't care. Rachel's room is shit too, even with the photos on the wall and fairy lights draped over the mirror. The double bed is cheap and lumpy, and the bedside table, wardrobe and drawers are all painted a mucky brown that's chipped in places to show plywood underneath. The armchair in the corner is in no better shape and used solely to throw her clothes on at the end of the day. There's a random sink in the room with a cold tap that only gives out hot water, no matter how many times Simon tries to fix it.

The room looks better at night, like it is now, when the soft glow of the lamp hides the patches of mould creeping up the walls and they've been in the house long enough not to smell the damp any more.

'Will you sit still!' Cleo's voice is stern but her lips twitch and they laugh. 'You are the worst model.'

'OK, sorry. It's taking forever.'

'I've got to get the blend right.' Cleo studies the eighteen-colour palette in her hand. It looks straight out of a Halloween dressing-up kit, with gleaming white, yellow, and then reds and blues and blacks. 'You can't rush it.'

'Can I just check my phone?' Hope balloons in Rachel as she reaches towards the bedside table.

'Definitely not.' Cleo bats her away. 'It's sat right there. We'd have heard it.'

'Maybe I should text him again.' The hope disappears. She sighs at her own lameness, hating herself for liking Nick so much, for being this desperate. Something flickers inside her. A question. A worry – what is she doing here? Darkness clouds Rachel's thoughts, inky black. It sinks through her, heavy and hollow all at once. She can't carry on like this. The thought pushes into her head along with another – something needs to change.

'Hey,' Cleo says. 'Rach, are you OK? Really?'

Rachel takes a breath and expels the thought before it can properly take hold and plunge her into its depths again. Then she forces a smile, drinking the last inch of wine from her glass. 'Yeah, I'm fine.'

'He isn't worth it,' Cleo says, squeezing Rachel's shoulder. Rachel can't tell her the truth, that this feeling inside her is more than Nick. It's more than anything.

'I just don't get how this keeps happening to me. I made Nick take me on five dates before we slept together, and only then because he said he was falling for me. I really thought he was different, you know? But he was just the same as the others. The minute men sleep with me, they lose interest. I don't get it.'

'It's shit,' Cleo says, the brush tickling beneath Rachel's eye again. 'But like I've said before, you're a magnet for commitment-phobes.'

'You say that, but remember Tom? I dated him in

14

our second year. Remember how I bumped into him at Abacus Bar on your birthday night a few months ago? He told me he was engaged and so I asked him out-right what it was about me that stopped men wanting a relationship. Remember what he said?'

Cleo nods. Of course she remembers. Rachel has told her fifty times, but she says it again anyway because the wine is slinking through her veins and ranting makes her feel better.

'He told me that I looked like I was up for it. I think he's right. I think I've got "one-night stand" printed on my forehead in invisible ink. Or it's my nose. It's a bit squished, isn't it? A bit piggy.'

Cleo huffs and looks for a second like she's going to smack her. 'You do not have a piggy nose, and you do not have a sign over your head that says "sleep with me and dump me".'

'It's all right for you. Every guy you date wants to take you home to meet his mother.'

'Which I hate just as much as you hate being ghosted.'

'It's not the same.'

'I know.'

'Maybe I should be a redhead, like you?' Rachel fid-dles with the ends of her dark-brown hair, and there it is again – the despair, the burning need to change something. Anything.

'Dark hair suits your complexion,' Cleo says, before fixing Rachel with a wicked grin. 'Could you be crap in bed?'

She laughs. 'No way. I am awesome in bed.' Rachel reaches up to prod her friend but Cleo yelps and waves her brush in the air, and as they collapse into giggles like they're schoolgirls, Rachel thinks how good it feels to have this friendship. It's the only good thing about her life. Before moving to London, the closest thing she had to a best friend was her big sister, but that was always Beth bossing Rachel around, thinking she knew best.

'Stay still. I'm almost done.' Cleo leans close and Rachel can smell the tang of wine on her breath and the lingering scent of the sickly perfume that's kept below the make-up counters at Selfridges. The one they're expected to spritz all over – hair, neck, body – before their shift starts. Even after a double shampoo and a generous dollop of shower gel, Rachel can still smell it.

'There.' Cleo stands back. 'I just need to add a touch of translucent powder, and . . .' She dabs at Rachel's left eye a final time. 'Done.'

Rachel leaps up and looks in the mirror by the door, gasping at her reflection. 'Oh my God. My eye looks actually swollen. I look like I've gone ten rounds with Mike Tyson.'

Cleo's grinning face appears beside her in the mirror. 'It's all about adding the darker colours to the soft areas and leaving the bony parts skin tone.'

'You are a genius.' She stares again at her left eye. The bruise is deep purple in places and yellow in others, and even though Rachel knows that Cleo has done this, she still can't believe it isn't real.

Rachel lifts a hand to touch her eye but Cleo smacks it away.

'You'll smudge it,' she shrieks.

Rachel turns to face Cleo and grins. 'You are totally going to make it. I just know it. This time next year, you will be painting bruises on Daniel Craig's face.' Rachel means every word. It's her own future she's not so sure about.

'And you'll be doing Shane Richie's make-up for *EastEnders*.'

'Or *Coronation Street*. I'm happy with any soap, actually.' Rachel laughs, but inside, her stomach twists.

They stand for a moment staring at their reflections, the desperation wafting around them as thick as the store perfume. A weight returns to Rachel's chest. Like a metal chain being wrapped around her heart. That feeling again of sinking into the darkness. Her eyes move to Cleo, absorbing the glow of her friend, the energy Rachel wishes she felt.

'You OK?' Cleo asks, their eyes meeting.

'Yeah,' Rachel says, repeating the word in her head until she can almost believe it's true. 'We totally need to show this to someone.' Rachel points at her face. 'Test it out.'

'Who?' Cleo frowns as she draws on the start of a bruise around her lower lip.

Before Rachel can answer, the front door slams and there's movement in the hall. She grips Cleo's arm and they fall silent, eyes finding each other. Simon is back from another work trip.

'We should say hello,' Rachel whispers.

'Don't,' Cleo hisses, reading her mind. 'He already thinks we're nutters.' Cleo raises her eyebrows and narrows her eyes exactly like Simon does when he looks at them, making Rachel snort. 'Plus, he knows we're make-up artists. He'll know it's fake.' Cleo pulls a face. 'And we said we wouldn't keep bothering him.'

'But I want to ask him about the hot water again. I can't keep having cold showers.'

'You wouldn't have to if you got up earlier.'

'Like that's ever going to happen.'

'True. But let's leave him now. He's such a grump.'

'You wouldn't say no, though, would you?' Rachel winks then smiles, pretending to be happy, to be playful. Fake it till you make it – isn't that what people say?

Cleo pauses. 'I . . .' Then she shakes her head. 'Nope, and neither would you.'

'Lucky he's not interested, then,' she says.

'Lucky we said he was off-limits. We'd never let a man come between us,' Cleo replies, and Rachel smiles at that because Cleo is right. Nothing will come between them, but Rachel throws the door open anyway. 'Simon,' she trills, voice loud in the big hallway.

He steps back, eyes narrowing first on Rachel, then on Cleo appearing beside her with a sheepish smile on her face.

'Been playing dressing-up again?' he says, half amused, half something else.

There are dark smudges under his eyes and a line of stubble on his face and yet he is still achingly hot.

'It looks good though, right?' Cleo gestures to Rachel's face.

Simon flicks another look at Rachel before returning his attention to Cleo. 'Yes, it does.' He nods. 'I'm knackered. I'm going to . . .' He points at his door further down the hall.

'Sure,' Rachel says, disappointment prodding her insides. What did she think was going to happen? 'By the way, any chance of a bit more hot water in the mornings?'

His eyes linger on Cleo before he walks away without a glance at Rachel. 'Any chance you could let me walk through the door on a Friday night without jumping out at me?' he calls over his shoulder. 'Do you have any idea how many hours I've worked this week? How much pressure I'm under?' He shoves his key into

18

the lock and pauses. 'But yeah, I'll look at the boiler settings over the weekend.' And with that he's gone, disappearing into his own flat with its living room and kitchen separate from theirs. Rachel has never seen inside Simon's part of the house, but she's certain it's better than the rest of the house too.

Rachel closes the door, deflated, empty.

'What a grump,' Cleo says. 'Hey, are you sure you're all right tonight? You seem a bit—'

'Totally fine,' Rachel lies before Cleo can finish her sentence. 'I was just thinking that we need new people to see us. People who don't know we're make-up artists.'

'We can't go to the pub like this, if that's what you're thinking.' Cleo frowns. 'We have no money, for starters.'

A familiar frustration slices through Rachel.

'Hey, we've got that wedding tomorrow.' Cleo's voice is still low, but soft now too. She knows what Rachel is thinking. 'Cash in hand. We should treat ourselves to a takeaway. Chinese?'

'I hate weddings,' she groans. 'They make me feel like a sell-out.'

Cleo rolls her eyes, returning her gaze to the mirror.

By the time she's finished making herself look as beaten up as Rachel, the wine is almost gone, but Rachel doesn't want the evening to end yet. She doesn't want to lie on the bed with Cleo and watch a stupid Friday night comedy.

'We need to test this out,' Rachel says again.

'How?' Cleo shrugs.

And then it hits her. An idea so perfect Rachel can't believe she hasn't thought of it before. A smile stretches across her face. This is going to be so good.

'Why do I suddenly feel nervous?' Cleo turns to her, arms folded. 'You've got that look in your eye, Rach.'

'What look?' She raises an eyebrow.

'It's the same look you got when you tipped a pint of blackcurrant cordial over that bloke after he groped me on the dance floor at that club – what was it called, that place?'

'Strawberry Moons. And that was so funny. The look on his face.'

'Sticky.'

'Exactly. It was worth the life ban. Plus, you're too much of a goody two-shoes to have done it yourself.'

'Oi!' Cleo laughs. 'But that's the look, anyway. Like you're gunning for something.'

Rachel laughs, and for the first time in ages she feels exactly that. Gunning for something.

This is what she needs, what she's needed for so long – to do something different. Be someone different. She doesn't want to be the twenty-four-year-old girl who gets ghosted. The girl with £38 in her bank account to last nine days. The girl who has to pretend to her best friend that she's happy and normal because telling Cleo the truth is just too damn hard. Cleo is gunning for something too, even if she's looking at Rachel with weary concern, always so sensible, but Cleo is just as desperate as she is to do something.

'Trust me. This will be fun,' Rachel says as she throws open her wardrobe.

Chapter 3

Cleo

Now

My lungs burn from running and there's an ache stretching down my legs as I reach the station. I scan the departures board and press my phone to my ear. There's a train leaving for London in five minutes. I have to be on it.

You wouldn't play our game without me. You wouldn't play, full stop.

I did it before. Your voice in my head is dancing with mischief and suddenly I want to slap you. I want to shake the sense right into you.

'Hello?' a voice says in my ear.

'Donovan, it's Cleo,' I say, still breathless with panic and exertion.

'What's wrong?' Donovan asks, and the kindness in his voice makes me want to crumble to the ground and cry. What the hell am I doing? Racing to London to find someone I've not seen for five years, all because . . .

because I need to know you're OK, Rach. I need to know you haven't been playing.

Beth's words ring in my head. *'She said she'd seen the cowboy.'*

Christ, I hate that nickname.

I reach the self-service ticket machine and start to jab at the screen.

'Family emergency,' I reply. 'My mum's had a heart attack.' No pause, no stuttering. How easily the lie comes. We had a lot of practice.

'Oh Cleo, I'm so sorry.'

Tears sting my eyes at how genuinely worried Donovan sounds and for a moment I think of my mum, my lovely mum, who pretends so fiercely that she doesn't mind that her only daughter never comes home.

'What do you need?' Donovan asks.

'Just a couple of days,' I say. 'To check she's OK.' Thoughts of my mum evaporate and my head fills once more with you.

There's a pause and I hear the tapping of keys and picture Donovan's broom-cupboard-sized office on the crew deck, him peering at staff rotas, juggling people and times in his head. Crew life on board is a delicate ecosystem. There are almost nine hundred crew for the two thousand passengers that will spend the next four months on board the *Enchantress*. Staff range from cleaning crew to chefs to the talent – the singers and dancers. Keeping everyone happy is Donovan's job.

As Crew Manager, he's our mum, our dad, our best friend. He's the one who'll kick us up the arse or give us a hug, and who always knows which one we need. He knows who is sleeping with whom, who is home-sick, who wants a promotion. He's one of us, but stands apart, and he is very good at his job.

22

'There's a flight leaving from Heathrow to Bermuda a week on Sunday. You can meet us there before we depart for Florida.'

Nine days. It's more than enough; it has to be.

'Thanks. I'll be on it. Email me the details and give my job to Gemma. She's ready to be Spa Manager.'

'I know. Don't worry about us. Do you need anything from the ship? I can get it couriered to you.'

I look down at my old jeans, and one of Gemma's hoodies. All I have on board is a few summer outfits, my uniforms and some toiletries. There isn't space for anything else. I have my bag with me. A light rucksack with my purse, my make-up bag, my passport – carried out of habit for all the times we're at port. 'Thank you, but I'm fine.'

'What about a sub?'

I close my eyes. His kindness is killing me. For a split second I think of turning around, jumping in a taxi for the docks. Donovan, Gemma, the crew, the ship; they are my family now, my safe place. Leaving them tears me apart.

'No.' The word is barely a whisper. 'I've got savings.' A lot of savings. It's free room and board on the ship, and while most of the crew will go home after the ship returns to port, spend time with families, take a break, I will jump on another cruise, whatever I can get. God, how we used to long for money to spend. Always just a little bit more.

'Keep in touch. I'll be thinking of you,' Donovan says.

We say goodbye and I feel Donovan's concern lingering around me as my feet pound the platform, reaching the train with twenty seconds to spare.

The train pulls away and I find a seat by a window,

close to the doors, and position my body so I can watch the half-empty carriage. My heart is racing. I'm sweating. Legs jittering. My eyes move across the seats, searching, always searching. There's a teenage girl listening to AirPods, head bobbing gently to a beat only she can hear. Behind her is a man in a suit, hunched over, laptop balanced on his knees. Across the aisle is a mother with two children bickering over who gets the window seat.

I call Beth and tell her I'm on my way to London. She sounds relieved and asks me what I'm planning to do. I tell her I'm planning to find you. When we hang up, promising to text or speak every day, I scroll through my phone contacts, searching for anyone who might know something. Only one name stands out – Detective Anik Saha – and just like that, I'm being dragged back to that hospital cafeteria, the smell of baked beans and fried eggs clogging my senses, and the lukewarm hot chocolate I couldn't pick up to drink because my hands were shaking too much. Detective Anik Saha, with that sharp black goatee and those piercing eyes, sitting opposite me.

A spark of something burns in the pit of my stomach. It's been so long since I've thought about that time, and especially about Anik. There was so much going on, so much to process, and yet when I think about him, I think about the warmth of his hand resting on mine and how safe it made me feel.

The train picks up speed and as another train passes, going the other way, I feel the jolt of movement against my shoulder. It's enough to dislodge another memory. I scrunch my eyes shut as I hear the thwack of the fist. I see the open car door, feel the rush of air.

I gasp for breath and blink back the surroundings of the train as the memory recedes.

'Cool it,' I whisper to myself as I try to remember the breathing techniques from that therapist, Ingrid. I only saw her a few times, but I can still hear her strong Swedish accent and how she said everything in that no-nonsense way of hers. *In through the nose . . . one . . . two . . . three. Out through the mouth . . . one . . . two . . . three.*

Did you ever go to see Ingrid, Rach? Has she fixed you in a way she couldn't fix me?

'You must deal with your PTSD, Cleo. It won't go away on its own,' she told me when I said I was leaving. 'Running away is not the solution.'

More memories fly through my thoughts like wispy white ghosts. You and me, lying side by side on your bed in the dark. All the things we needed to say stretched out in the silence, like elastic pulled too tight, ready to snap back at any moment.

'It wasn't your fault.' Your voice was robotic, empty.

'Your sister thinks it was.'

'She's wrong.'

'I'm sorry.' My voice cracked again, the tears wet on my face. I wanted so badly to tell you what I was sorry for, but the words stuck in my throat.

Chapter 4

Rachel

Now

There's a dripping tap.

Drip. Drip. Drip.

Drip fucking drip.

It's driving Rachel insane.

She can stand the locked room, the pitch-black, no windows, no clue what day it is, what time; she can stand all of it, but not that constant dripping.

Rachel crawls across the floor, patting each space with her hands, checking it's clear. There are forgotten nails on the floor, the dirt and grime of neglect. She finds the wall and pats her way up it, swiping her hand in the dark for the light cord. She knocks the plastic end and it swings away and she has to start all over again until it's in her hands and she gives it a tug.

A bare bulb illuminates the ugly yellow bathroom suite – a sink, a toilet, a bath with a crack down the side. There's a bundle of duvets on the floor where she sleeps, and bags of food in the corner that have been

26

left for her. It's nothing glamorous. Crisps and pre-packed sandwiches, some little boxes of cereal. Oh, and a massive box of prescription sleeping tablets. As if she would take one. She needs to keep her head straight. She needs to think.

Rachel blinks and rubs at her eyes as she looks in the mirror. They're puffy and sore from too many tears. She tries to keep her focus on her eyes but, as always, her gaze moves to her scar. An icy chill shoots through her body. Memories of the woods flash in her mind.

'*You wanted this.*

'*You liked playing games with people, didn't you?*'

She scrunches her eyes shut, forcing his voice out of her head and wishing she had her make-up with her. It's been five years and she still can't look at her scar without everything from that night rising up to the surface of her thoughts, chilling her to her core until she's trembling with fear all over again.

It was all supposed to change soon. All that money she's saved. All the years she's spent in that shitty house share so she could save and save for the very best Harley Street plastic surgeon to fix her face. She paid the deposit last month. They're expecting her call to book the surgery and instead she's living in this hell.

Drip. Drip. Drip.

How much longer? The question whips through her until tears sting at her eyes.

There's a pang in the pit of her stomach. Being here is so different from last time, but it's the same too, and makes Rachel think of Cleo. She thought nothing would come between them – no man, no job – but in the aftermath of what happened to them, there was only darkness. They came between each other. A sob catches in Rachel's throat. She can't believe this is happening again, but this time, she's all alone.

'Oh my God.' Her voice is a hoarse croak. She runs the tap, slurping water from her hands. It's cold, and droplets roll down her top and on to her bare skin.

'I'm OK,' Rachel tells herself. She's really OK. It's like prison; solitary confinement. She can stand it as long as she doesn't think about Beth and her mum.

The light starts to hum. It does that after a few minutes. An annoying, high-pitched electrical whining sound that gives Rachel an instant headache. She turns off the light and crawls back to her covers in darkness.

She can stand a lot of things. Just not that dripping tap. Not the visits. That's the only time Rachel worries she won't be able to carry on. When the door opens and she's led into a bedroom with a mattress on the floor and she knows what's expected of her.

Afterwards, she washes herself in the cold water of the sink and wonders how many days it's been, how many more she has left.

Chapter 5

Cleo

Now

My feet move on autopilot, carrying me towards the Underground. Only when I'm boxed in, bodies pushing, train rattling from one stop to another, do I wish I'd taken a taxi. The noise, the crowds, the stink of body odour and stale food make my stomach turn.

When I climb the steps at Bethnal Green I breathe in big gulps of air that smells of petrol fumes and the fried-chicken shop on the corner.

Roman Road is achingly familiar. There's the red-brick library on the right and the little park where we used to sunbathe in the summer. The old fire station on the left is still a Buddhist centre, by the looks of it. And there's the school with the high metal fence, the market stalls in the small square.

I keep walking. Left, then right, then left again. Past Mr Hakimi's corner shop with the bright-blue awnings and the same outdoor display of foreign fruits and vegetables that I remember. I've travelled the world four times, I've been to every corner of the Caribbean, I've wandered local markets in every port and I still can't name half of them.

I turn on to Lockton Road and take in the long row of Victorian houses, some semi-detached, some terraced. All with faded brickwork and bay windows. Grey has become popular since I left. The once-white or yellow porches are now all shades of that dull colour, but it's still a typical London street with the mix of some owned, some rented. Families and house shares, students and those like we were, the just-starting-outers, all mixed in together.

Your little red car is parked opposite the house and I stop when I see it. Pete the Peugeot. You called him an old rust bucket five years ago and yet he's still here.

Then I'm outside number seventy-two. Three steps up to the same mud-brown front door. Same scuffed brass doorbell with the sharp, trilling ring.

The door flies open a minute later and I find Simon standing barefoot in jeans and a black polo shirt. I almost gasp at the sight of him. He looks the same. Exactly the same.

That thin nose, those eyebrows. And his dark hair, swept back from his face. I notice a touch of grey at his temples. He's only five years older than us, but always seemed so much more grown-up.

Still got the hots for him, then? I hear you cackle.

Oh, Rach! I thought you'd have moved on. I imagined you in a studio apartment or a ground-floor flat with a courtyard garden where you'd sit on warm evenings. But somehow, it's no surprise that Simon is still exactly where I left him.

Was it his aunt who left him the house, or his gran? We couldn't believe it when he told us. Fancy inheriting this huge house at the age of twenty-five! And instead of selling it and buying something swanky, instead of using the money to travel the world, or renting out the rooms to his friends, he converted the living room and part of the downstairs into his own apartment and rented out the rest of the house to strangers, leaving them to their own devices while he worked every hour of the day in IT for an investment bank, spending half his life travelling to other offices around Europe.

'Can I help you?' Simon asks in his public-schoolboy voice. A familiar impatience in his tone.

'Simon, it's me.'

'I'm sorry. Who?' He narrows his eyes and frowns.

'Cleo.'

'Oh, you look . . . different,' he says and then, out of nowhere, he smiles. He actually smiles, and it's the weirdest thing, reminding me of those times when I would slip into his room and straight into his bed. The thought sends a red heat creeping up my neck.

The smile only lasts a moment and then it's gone and that same old impatience is pulling at his features. He peers at me again and I shift my feet. 'I thought you were leaving for a cruise. Have you had surgery?'

I shake my head. 'It's the hair,' I lie, touching my blonde pixie cut that sweeps across my forehead. My face has changed too. The dark eyebrows I'm forced to paint on every morning because of all the times I pull at the hairs without realizing. The contouring I add to my face, creating the perfect blend of shadow and light so my nose looks thinner, my cheekbones more defined. Although that's less of a problem now. It turns out anxiety, paranoia, PTSD, whatever it is that sears through me day after day, is a great calorie burner.

'Do you want to come in?' he asks, motioning me inside.

I step through the open door, catching the smell of the old carpets and the lingering whiff of the kitchen: burnt toast and dirty dishwater. The world tilts and I have the strangest sense of stepping back in time. My eyes draw to your bedroom door right there on the left and I wait for it to open. I wait for you to be standing before me, waving a bottle of wine and beckoning me into your room.

Let's play.

I take a breath and then I get it, I get why you stayed. This place was our haven; no one could get to us when we were inside these walls. This is your bubble of safety, just as mine is the *Enchantress*. And even though the smell is worse than I remember, the walls grubby, the air cold, I feel it too. I feel home.

Then the front door slams behind me, throwing the hallway into gloom, and I spin around, the fear grabbing me tight as I scramble for my alarm.

Chapter 6

Rachel

Five years earlier

Rachel is so bored. So fucking bored and miserable. She can feel her brain rotting from the inside out every second she spends in this place. Her back aches from the effort of standing, shoulders back, head high. No slouching on the make-up floor. Not unless she wants Mandy on her case again.

She swears that woman went to French finishing school, tip-tapping around the place in her insanely high heels like she sodding well owns it. Mandy is only a few years older than them but acts like she's hit the career jackpot, like they should all be striving for her job.

Why did Rachel bother to get out of bed this morning? She hadn't wanted to. Hadn't been able to for ages, in fact. She'd lain awake listening to Simon in the room next door to hers, getting up, leaving the house. Then Cleo making her breakfast. Rachel had told herself to move, to get ready for her shift. She'd told herself over and over to do it, but the darkness had been so heavy, and if it wasn't for the fact that Cleo had burst in and pulled the covers off her, and that Rachel has already called in sick twice this month, she'd have stayed where she was.

Rachel sighs and wishes she was back in her bed, or anywhere, actually. Anywhere but here. She glances at her watch. Still another six hours to go.

Six hours of this.

Fuck! She hates Mandy. She hates this job. She hates this life.

A woman approaches Rachel's end of the counter. Rachel glances at Cleo restocking the mascara. Cleo gives her a nod, eyes urging her on. *Think of the commission*, Cleo's look says, and Rachel does.

'May I help you with anything?' Rachel says, her voice silky smooth, but still the woman jumps. She straightens up, assessing Rachel with pursed lips that show the fine lines of a smoker's mouth. The woman's foundation is a shade too dark and the liquid has dried in the lines. It ages her.

She's holding a bottle of £50 foundation in her hand. 'I just popped in for this.' She waves the bottle in the air.

Rachel plucks another bottle from the shelf. 'Might I suggest a slightly lighter shade for your skin tone? If you have five minutes, I can show—'

'No, thank you. I like this one.' She steps back, choosing to walk around to Cleo's till to pay, but not before looking down her nose at Rachel like they all do in this hellhole of a store.

And then it's back to doing nothing. Staring at passing shoppers, trying to guess how much money they have in their bank accounts. It's always more than her.

The run-up to Christmas will start soon enough. Double shifts, later opening hours. More money. And at least it will be too busy to think. Empty time is dangerous. It allows the darkness to loom over Rachel like a huge beast, a giant from a long-forgotten fairy tale, threatening to stomp her into nothing.

Rachel hears Mandy before she sees her. The tap of her heels hitting the hard floor.

'Cleo, Rachel.' She gives a little one-two clap of her hands. 'You've got your breaks now. I'll man your counter.'

'Great sales this week, Cleo,' Mandy trills before her eyes fall on Rachel with the look of a disappointed mother. 'Rachel, darling, perhaps you could smile a little more? Be a bit more . . .' Her forehead pinches and she makes a face as she searches for the right word. 'Welcoming.'

Rachel forces a smile, a retort forming in her thoughts, but then Cleo is by her side, steering her through the displays towards the staffroom where their homemade ham sandwiches are waiting for them. Warm by now. Soggy. Rachel would kill for a Pret.

She has a sudden urge to cry. The way that customer looked at her, the same way Mandy does, everyone does, like she's dog shit on their shoe. One day she's going to get Mandy back for being such a cow to her.

'You OK?' Cleo asks.

'If you count a desire to jump out of the third-floor window as OK, then, yep, I'm fine.' Rachel smiles to show she's joking.

They push through the staff-only doors and into a corridor. The subtle lighting from the shop floor is replaced with dull strip lights that don't reach the dark-grey walls, the dusty floor. Could this be the most depressing place on earth? Feels like it.

The staffroom is also grey, with a wall of orange lockers, a sofa, a table and chairs. No window. No natural light.

Rachel drops on to one of the chairs as Cleo rummages for their lunch. 'Mandy has it in for me. She's desperate to fire me.'

'No way.' Cleo shakes her head, throwing Rachel a foil-wrapped sandwich. 'You know more about the products than any of us.'

'Last month she told me to stop smiling because a customer complained I looked smug. And now I'm supposed to smile again. I swear, I have one of those faces, Cleo. I'm unlikeable. Men and women both just want to throw me under the bus. The only difference is men want to shag me first.'

'Hey, I like you, and for the record, I'd never throw you under the bus. Now, come on, don't take everything so personally. My sales are only up because that teenager came in for her birthday with her mum and she said she could have anything she wanted.'

'How much did she spend?'

'Seven fifty.'

'Shit. That's more than our rent for a month.'

'Yep. That's exactly what I thought.'

'Maybe you should move down to my room and we'll share? Think what we could do with the extra money.'

'Things aren't that desperate yet. And besides, you snore, remember?'

'Only sometimes.'

Cleo laughs. 'Yeah, if sometimes means all the time.'

'Have you looked on JobServe this week?' Rachel

already knows the answer. Scanning the job websites is an obsession they share.

Cleo nods and rolls her eyes.

'Subway artist,' they say together.

'Seriously,' Rachel huffs. 'How can making sandwiches be an art form, and how is it the only job on there for us?'

'Something will come up. We just have to wait.'

'But for how long? You realize we've been here for nearly two years? I don't have another year of this in me. I want my shot. I'm sick of my life.'

'Thanks very much,' Cleo laughs, taking a bite of her sandwich.

'Not you,' Rachel says, unwrapping the foil packet and prodding at the squished-up bread. 'You're the only thing that keeps me from stabbing Mandy with one of her high heels.'

'She's not that bad. Come on, it's Friday. That's got to cheer you up.'

Rachel smiles, and for the first time all day, it doesn't feel fake. Friday night at last. 'Who are you going to be?'

Cleo smiles. 'Claire?'

'Boring.'

'Cassie?'

'Better. I'm going for Roxy.' A giddiness nudges out the darkness. It's been three weeks since Cleo painted the bruise on Rachel's face. Three weeks since that first game, and still the buzz of excitement is there.

'Roxy?'

'As in "Roxanne". My mum listened to that Police song over and over when I was, like, eight. I used to wish she'd named me Roxanne.'

'You know that song is about a prostitute, right?' Cleo grins.

'I do now,' Rachel laughs, 'but little eight-year-old me didn't.'

'Let's be like those girls who came into the shop the other day.'

'Which ones?' Rachel asks.

'The ones that had "Daddy's money" written all over them.'

'They were absolute bitches,' Rachel groans. 'You, you there.' She clicks her fingers, mimicking their nasally posh voices. 'Get me this one to try.'

'And be quick, we don't have long,' Cleo adds in her own haughty voice.

'This is going to be perfect. I'm totally going to let off steam. Did you hear one of them talking about going on a spa day because her job is so stressful? I asked her what she does and it turns out she's a club promoter. As if that's a proper job. She just invites her friends to go out with her every night.'

'What if we meet someone from the last few weeks?' Cleo raises her eyebrows. She's still smiling, but there's worry there too. Always the good girl. 'Can you imagine seeing those psychology students – Denise and Alex – again?'

'God, they'd kill us! But we won't.' Rachel laughs, thinking of the first time they played and feeling that same something lift inside her.

Chapter 7

Cleo

Now

'Wow, Cleo.' Simon steps back as he sees the horror on my face. 'Are you OK?'

'Yes, sorry.' I free my hand from my pocket. It's clammy and hot despite the cold of the hallway.

Simon leads us past your door to the back of the house and the communal kitchen that overlooks the unkempt garden. Clearly, Simon hasn't bought that lawnmower in the years since I left.

The kitchen is just as I remember. There's a spray of black crumbs on the worktop, splats of something orange on the floor. I wonder if Mrs Carrington from three doors down still comes in to give it a cursory clean once a week.

My eyes fall to the washing-up in the sink and the mug balanced on top. Plain white. Chip in the handle. Bold black writing.

I don't like morning people, or mornings, or people.

An ache hits my chest. I gave you that mug one

39

Christmas, the year we had to be at Selfridges by six a.m. and you barely opened your eyes on the tube ride in.

Simon clears his throat. 'Must be weird being back.'

'Something like that.' I tear my eyes away from the mug and move to lean against a counter, before thinking better of it as I spot a splatter of congealed food on the cupboards.

'So, what happened?' I ask.

He checks his watch a moment before he answers. 'It's like I told you on the phone. I saw Rachel last Friday. She was all dressed up. Said she was meeting someone for a drink.'

'You told Beth that Rachel was meeting me.'

'No. I said I wondered if she was meeting you. She didn't say.'

'And you were here when she left?'

'For once, yes. I'd been working in Jersey all week but I caught an earlier flight home. We're in the middle of an office move,' he explains. 'So I'm back and forth constantly at the moment. Talking of which, I'm really sorry, I know you've only just got here, but I'm working from home today and I have a call in ten minutes.'

The words are out of my mouth before I can stop them. 'Hey, I didn't ask for Rachel to disappear. I'm trying to help here.'

He raises an eyebrow. 'I know. But I didn't ask her to disappear, either. I'm the one who contacted her sister and her office and reported her missing to the police. Not that it did any good.'

'Some things never change.'

'What does that mean?' he asks.

'It means you never have time for anyone but yourself,'

I huff, wishing I didn't sound so much like a petulant child.

We fall silent and when Simon speaks again, his tone is softer. 'I tried to be there for you after the attack, Cleo. You pushed me away and then you left without saying goodbye.'

'I . . .' The heat returns to my face. I want to tell him he's got it all wrong, but he hasn't. 'I'm here for Rachel. What happened between us—'

'Was a very short fling that happened five years ago,' he finishes. 'Cleo, I'm not still hung up on you. If you must know, I'm engaged. I met someone at the bank. Her laptop broke in the middle of an important client meeting and I swooped in to save the day,' he adds, his face lighting up. 'Liz has been living in Jersey for the last few years, but she's moving back to London in the summer.' He pulls out his phone and shows me a photo. It's a selfie of Simon, his smile wider than I've ever seen it, his arm around a blonde woman with a pretty face and sparkling green eyes. 'I took it on the beach in Jersey just after Liz agreed to marry me. I'm going to sell this dump and we're going to get a place together. People only want to stay here short-term now – a month or two. The level of admin is ridiculous, and let's face it, I'm a crap landlord.'

I smile at that last bit and something shifts between us – a truce. 'I'm glad you're happy,' I say.

'I am. And I'm glad you're here. Rachel needs you.'

'I don't know how I can help,' I admit. 'I'm supposed to be on a cruise right now and I've come all this way. I have nine days until I need to fly to Bermuda to rejoin the ship. Is there anything else you can tell me?'

'Not really. I usually see her going out for a run on Saturday morning, but—'

'Running?' But you hate exercise.

'Sure. Every Saturday. Normally, she runs for a couple of hours. Then she knocks on my door for a quick chat. She keeps an eye on the tenants and house when I'm away. I assumed when I didn't see her that she'd had one too many and slept in, or maybe even stayed over somewhere. When she wasn't home by Sunday morning, I tried calling her but her phone was off. And then on Monday I called her office to see if she was there, but she wasn't. Monday night I found her sister on Facebook, but she hadn't heard from Rachel either, and so I reported her missing to the police that night.'

'It wasn't me she was meeting. We weren't in contact.'

'What? But I'm sure Rach told me you were planning to meet each other in London.'

I shake my head. 'I . . . I don't get signal on the ship and the staff Wi-Fi is patchy.' My voice trails off. The worst excuse.

'That's weird.' He runs a hand over his hair. The movement causes his T-shirt to rise up, showing an inch of toned stomach. 'Rachel definitely said you'd texted from a new number on Boxing Day and you were planning to come back to London.'

Unease trickles through my body again. There is only one reason you would tell Simon and Beth that we were talking – because you thought we were. And there's only one person who would do that – Luke Richards. It's exactly the kind of game he'd play.

A weakness hits me with a slow tremor, a rattling hunger. I've not eaten since breakfast, and that was only a banana and a cereal bar. I feel so empty.

'I should go,' I say.

'OK.' Simon nods. 'Where are you staying?' he asks.

An image flashes in my mind – the *Enchantress* cutting through the open sea. The spray of salty droplets in the air, the hum of excitement and possibility from the passengers. The longing is acute.

'I don't know. I don't know why I came, to be honest.'

'You came because you know better than anyone what she used to be like.' Simon is tiptoeing around it, but I know what he's talking about. He's talking about our game.

'You said . . . you said on the phone that she was playing again. How do you know?'

'The walls are pretty thin,' he says with a shrug. 'I'm not a great sleeper and over the last few months I've heard her moving around at two, three in the morning. She was talking to people a lot. I heard her tell someone her name was Roxy.'

Oh, Rach. Oh no. Panic squeezes my chest.

'Your old room is empty at the moment if you want to stay here?' Simon continues. 'I'm pretty sure your stuff is still in the cupboard under the stairs.'

'My stuff?'

'The things you left in your room when you moved out. Rachel boxed it up when it was clear you weren't coming back. She paid your rent for an extra month, too. She was sure you'd come back.'

You did that? Guilt – a bitter bile – burns inside me. I had no idea. If I'd known, I would've . . . I could've . . .

The words trail into nothingness in my thoughts. The truth is it wouldn't have changed anything. If I'd known you'd done that, I'd have told you not to. I'd have told you to bin everything. But that's a lie too, isn't it? The truth is I wouldn't have answered my phone if you'd called.

Simon eyes me expectantly and I find myself nodding. I don't know why I'm here or what I'll do now. I don't know if staying is the right thing either, but the *Enchantress* has left port and I'm stuck here. At least if I'm staying in this house, then I'll be the first to know if you come back.

I knew she'd come. How could she not? It's all about finding the perfect bait.

A lonely woman desperate to fall in love.

A best friend riddled with guilt.

It's all too easy.

Oh, the game is on now!

Chapter 8

Five years earlier

'Good stalls today,' Rach says as we reach the end of Brick Lane Market, veering away from the final plot with its open suitcase filled with worn trainers. There's something flat in Rach's tone that sends worry worming through me. I want to ask her if she's OK, but she always makes this big thing of rolling her eyes and saying yes, like I'm being an idiot for even asking. Work is miserable. I get it. But it feels like more than that.

'Yep. Except that man.' I nudge Rach's side and grin as I tilt my head towards the suitcase.

'God, yes,' Rach smiles. 'Who would buy one old red trainer?'

'Someone like that couple with the shoe fetish we met the other night.'

Rachel barks a laugh and I push my worries aside. 'They were funny.'

'And weird.'

46

'Very weird, but they lapped up Roxy and Cassie.'

'You love unleashing your inner bitch in Roxy, don't you?' I smile.

'I'm not so sure there's much "inner" to my bitch, to be honest.'

I laugh at that and loop my arm through hers as we turn around. The graffiti at this end of the road is new. It's a cosmic universe with a woman's head in the centre, and has yet to be tagged or defaced with posters advertising clubs and shows. It's stunning, and raw too. There's something so harrowing in the woman's face, like I can feel her pain.

We wander back down the road. No rush. A Saturday when neither of us is working is rare. No wedding make-up or charity event this week either, and however much I would love the extra money in my account, I'm grateful for the day. It's been months since we were last able to do this and there's an almost holiday feel to the air around us, helped by the weak winter sunshine and crystal-clear skies.

'I'm glad I got this belt,' I say, swinging the flimsy blue carrier bag in my hand. 'It's going to look great with my red top and jeans at the housewarming party on Friday.'

'Friday?' Rachel pauses. 'I thought Lisa and Katie's party was Saturday.'

'Definitely Friday. Lisa told me it's so they have all weekend to recover and clean up, which sounds like typical Lisa.'

I wait for Rach to comment but she's quiet.

'Hey,' I say. The worry returns and I give her another nudge. 'What's up?'

'Nothing. I guess I'm just not sure if I'm up for a party. We could stay in and play our game instead.'

47

I stare at Rachel's face for a moment. She smiles and raises her eyebrows in a 'what?' expression and I don't know what to say, except that staying in is the last thing Rach needs right now.

'Rachel, come on. We can play anytime. I know it's a laugh, but this is a real party. Real people. New people. Lisa said Katie's inviting a load of her work friends and they're all men.' I sing-song the end of my sentence, knowing Rach never misses a chance to meet someone new.

'All right, all right, but no ditching me when someone sweeps you off your feet.'

'As if.'

We start to walk again, Rachel leading me towards a stall with vintage jewellery on a black tablecloth. The gems glint in the sunlight. 'I really love that,' she says, pointing at a black-and-silver beaded choker.

I lean forwards and peer at the tiny handwritten tag. 'It's forty-five pounds,' I hiss. 'That's too much.'

'I know,' she groans, 'but it's exactly what Roxy would wear.'

'Yes, but Roxy is also rich. You are Rachel and you don't have the money.'

'God, you really were the head girl of your school, weren't you?' Rachel grumbles, but her tone is playful.

'No, actually, I wasn't. Alison Smith got Head Girl. I was Head of Prefects.'

'What a surprise.'

We laugh and I pull us away to a stall selling second-hand bags. We've already looked once but we look again anyway. There's a leather clutch bag I like the look of, but it's more than I'm willing to pay and the zip looks a bit battered. It's a far cry from the bright leather and tight stitching of the items in Selfridges.

'They're not exactly Michael Kors,' Rach says out of the corner of her mouth as we continue to the next stall, this one selling intricately painted tote bags. I buy one in a blue floral print for my mum's Christmas present, and then we keep moving.

We're nearing the start of the market when Rachel's phone rings from her pocket.

'Beth,' we say in unison, sharing an eye-roll.

Rachel pulls out her phone and shows me the screen as Beth's name runs across the middle. She sighs but answers anyway.

'I'll go ahead and grab some bread,' I mouth, knowing my presence beside Rachel will only annoy Beth. I've only met Beth twice in the years I've known Rachel. Two times too many for Beth.

I try to see Beth's point of view. In her eyes, I'm the one stealing Rachel away from her. I'm the one keeping Rach in London, chasing dreams Beth doesn't believe in. I'm the one who Rachel confides in now. I get all that, but the snarky comments still hurt. All of her 'Why are you here?' and 'No one asked you' snipes that get under my skin.

'Hi,' Rachel says as she answers. 'How's it going?'

There's a pause before Rachel speaks again. 'Yeah, it's nice here too. No, it's just me. I'm walking home from the shops.'

Rachel slows down, waving me ahead, and I go, my mind on cheese on toast for lunch and a Saturday afternoon film on Rachel's bed. A half-hour walk later, I pick up bread and another pint of milk from Mr Hakimi's shop, along with a bottle of wine, and it's as I'm turning on to Lockton Road that I walk straight into the path of Simon.

We collide in a bump of bodies and apologies, both of us leaping back. I pull a face and Simon laughs, his eyes crinkling at the sides.

'Hey,' he smiles, pushing a strand of dark hair away from his forehead. 'Been shopping?'

I hold up my two carrier bags. 'You guessed it.'

'Anything nice?'

'I'm not sure I'd count bread and milk as nice, but I did pick up a new belt.'

'Well, I look forward to seeing it.' He pauses, drawing in his lower lip in a way that pulls my eyes to his mouth.

'Off anywhere fun?' I ask, eyeing his shirt and trousers. It's one of the few times I've seen him without a tie.

He laughs. 'The office. Where else?'

'Ah, sorry.'

I'm turning to go when Simon calls me back. 'Hey, I meant to ask – are you going to Katie and Lisa's party next week? I'll probably head there straight from work, but I thought we could share a taxi back later, if you fancy?'

'Um . . . maybe. I think Rach and I were talking about the night bus.'

'A taxi would be easier,' he says, his brow lines pinching as though I've said something wrong.

'And more expensive,' I retort.

He laughs. 'I'm paying.'

'OK, then,' I reply, dragging out the words. There's something odd about Simon today and it takes me a moment before I realize what it is. He seems happy.

'So you're definitely going?' he asks, and this time

when he looks at me there's a spark between us that fizzes in my stomach.

'I wouldn't miss it.' I smile.

'See you there, then. I'm looking forward to seeing the new belt.' We lock eyes and there's something mischievous in his gaze, something flirty, and I find myself wondering what it would feel like to kiss him.

'Sure.' I start walking before Simon can see the blush creeping over my cheeks.

What the hell was that? I think back to the looks we've shared recently, just a second here or there when something has passed between us. I've ignored them so far. We can flirt all we want but nothing will happen between us. Simon is off-limits.

'Hey.' Rachel jogs up behind me as I reach the front door. 'What's so funny?'

'What do you mean?'

'You're grinning.'

'Oh, nothing.' I shake my head.

'Did you see Simon just now? He totally blanked me.'

'Me too,' I lie.

'Grumpy bastard.' Rachel holds up a polka-dot paper bag. 'Don't be mad, but I went back and got that necklace.'

'Rach!'

'I haggled,' she says, her bottom lip jutting out in a way that makes it impossible to stay mad at her. I know it will be me covering our shopping next week, but if this necklace makes her happy and takes the flatness from her voice, her mood, her everything, then it will be worth it.

'Shall we play our game? I really want to try being Roxy again.'

'Sure. But I need food first. Let's play tonight. I got us a bottle of wine.'

'Sometimes, Cleo Thomas, I bloody love you.' She dances into the kitchen and hooks the choker around her neck. 'What do you think?'

She turns towards me, her grin wide. The necklace is more beautiful now it's on. The silver catches the light and the black makes her eyes look darker, fiercer. 'You look great. You look like Roxy,' I add. Another niggle of worry creeps into my thoughts.

Chapter 9

Cleo

Now

There's pressure from all around me. A dead weight. Cold everywhere. I can't breathe. I can't open my mouth. My eyes itch with something and I scrunch them tight. I try to move my hand, reaching for my alarm, but my arm is pinned to my body.

I'm trapped. I can't breathe.

I open my mouth to scream but no sound escapes. I taste it then – bitter, gritty dirt.

I'm buried alive. I'm choking, suffocating, dying.

I wake with a jolt, throwing my body upwards, hands flapping in the air, pushing away the earth that isn't there.

I'm shaking all over. I can still taste it in my mouth: that grainy feeling against my teeth.

I wait to feel the soft hum of the ship's engine, the almost imperceptible movement of the ocean around us. The safety of being adrift in the world. It's amazing how quickly I get used to the faces of the guests, how quickly I stop looking for that one face among them.

But then I catch the glow of the street light through the flimsy curtains, the soft orange that illuminates my room, and I remember my impulsive race to London. I remember Simon pulling three cardboard boxes out from the cupboard beneath the stairs before leaving me to carry them up to my old room.

I dumped them in the corner, only bothering to open the one with *bedding* written in your swirly handwriting. I remember locking the door to my room and calming myself down, before eating half a pack of Maryland cookies and wondering what the hell I'd done coming here.

As I fight to push the nightmare away from my thoughts, I swig from my bottle of water, washing away the taste in my mouth. How many times have I had this nightmare? A thousand at least. I remember waking like this just after it happened. Same bed. Same nightmare. I remember hearing your screams pierce the silent night and me rushing through the house to get to you, to wake you up and hold you.

How different your screams sounded when they were directed at me.

Ingrid's voice breaks through the memory. 'Something terrible happened to you and your friend,' she said in one of our sessions. 'You both have a long road of recovery ahead of you, but in order to begin the journey of healing Cleo, you must first separate your emotions from Rachel's emotions. They are so enmeshed,' she said, entwining her fingers as though to prove her point.

I turn on to my side and reach, like I always do, for my phone. The white light stings my eyes as the screen comes alive and I find the website I always scroll through. Don't laugh, Rach! It's a survivalist website. Some whacky guy who thinks the world is about to end and has written pages and pages of worst-case scenarios and what to do. Floods, fires, earthquakes, droughts, deadly viruses, but it's only the burial that interests me and I jab a shaking finger at the page.

What to do if you're buried alive:

1. Don't panic.
2. Slow your breathing.
3. Carefully move your hands towards your head.
4. Try to make some space around your face for oxygen.
5. Start to push the debris towards your legs, keeping as much space around your face as you can.
6. Work slowly, pushing your hands up until they reach the surface.
7. Once your head and arms are free, shout for help or start to dig yourself out.

I know it's all bullshit. What this guy doesn't say is that his seven simple steps are for those lucky enough to be buried only a little way under. Too deep and there would be no space for air and I'd suffocate just like I do in my nightmares. But I love how simple he makes it sound. How easy it would be to escape if lightning were to strike twice.

I read the words over and over until my eyes ache from tiredness and my phone feels too heavy in my hands.

My eyes close and I'm just drifting off somewhere when a noise pulls me back. The front door opening and shutting. Footsteps on the stairs.

I listen, curious about the other housemates. How well do they know you?

You never used to like people much. Big girly groups, all the 'love ya's and 'hun's, air kisses and sharing clothes. I wasn't much better. I never had the patience for the drama of those girls on our make-up course, but I think I'd have been friends with one or two of them if we'd not had each other. Them and us.

But we got on all right with our old housemates. The first lot when we moved in. Freddie and Lisa and Katie. Lisa and Katie got married. Did you know? They sent a wedding invite to my mum's address a few years ago. I wonder if you got one too, if you went.

The creak of the stairs stops and I listen for the sound of the bathroom across the landing – the click of a light, the tap running – but nothing happens.

Minutes pass and I'm starting to think I imagined the noise of the stairs when there is another creak. This one close, this one outside my door.

My heart starts to pound. Every muscle in my body tenses as I listen to the silence ringing in my ears. There is someone on the other side of the door. I can't see them. I can't hear them. But I can sense them there. Still. Thinking. Wanting to get in.

I stare wide-eyed and frantic at the door, suddenly sure it will fly right open, the lock unable to stop whoever is on the other side.

There's another part of me, though, deep down, that even in my panic knows I'm being paranoid. This will be like all the other times, and any second now I'll realize I was wrong and give a shaky exhalation.

Then the door handle moves. Just a fraction at first. Then another. My hand slips beneath my pillow and grabs my alarm. My mouth is suddenly dry and I can't swallow. It's the nightmare all over again, but it's not earth pinning me down, it's fear. I watch the handle inch slowly down, down, down. There's a soft nudge as the catch moves all the way back, but the lock stays put, the door remains closed. For a fleeting second I wonder if it's Simon, wanting to check on me, but surely he'd knock? And it's the middle of the night.

There's a pause and then the handle is moving again. Up and down three times, but still the lock stays closed.

Time passes. Seconds? Minutes? I don't know. I hear nothing for a long time. And then something. This time the movement is above me. Steps padding softly in the loft, belonging to whoever just tried to get into my room.

Chapter 10

Cleo

Now

I fall asleep in the early hours, stirring what feels like minutes later to the rattling hum of the old extractor fan in the bathroom across the hall.

Remnants of last night – the nightmare, the moving handle – flood my thoughts and I'm instantly awake, heart thudding in my chest. Who tried to get into my room? Who lives on the top floor? I need to speak to Simon.

I stare at the ceiling, following the swirling pattern of the Artex, breathing in for five and out for eight until the fear dissipates, and all the while I hear Ingrid's voice in my head.

'Tell me what you remember about that night, Cleo . . . Tell me how you survived . . . Tell me why you taste dirt in your nightmares.'

Every time she asked, I'd whisper or shout or cry, but my answer was always the same. *'Because of the graves.'*

The extractor fan stops and a few minutes later I catch the rise and fall of your housemates' voices. Do they know you better than I do, Rach? The pang of jealousy comes from nowhere.

When I first started working on the cruises, I would lie awake at night, listening to the soft breathing of my roommate and pretending it was you, your room we were in. I'd pretend we were still those girls working at Selfridges, still best friends. I'd pretend Luke Richards didn't exist and we'd never played our games.

Instead, I'd tell you about my days. The times we docked when I was too trapped by the anxiety to leave the ship – my bubble of safety. I'd tell you about the passengers and the crew. How on the crew party nights, the girls would line up and I'd pull out my make-up case and do face after face and it would feel so good.

And yeah, I thought about you living in London in an airy ground-floor flat, but I never thought about your friendships, the people you would rely on who I wouldn't even know. Does that make me selfish? I think so.

The voices carry up the stairs and I leap out of bed and throw on yesterday's clothes before unlocking the door and chasing after them.

'Hey,' I call, grabbing the banister as the front door opens with a blast of cold air.

There are two women standing in the hall below, and as they turn to face me I feel suddenly exposed. Sleep-deprived and no make-up. I don't need to look in the mirror to know how dreadful I look.

They are younger than us. Mid-twenties, I guess. Both dressed in high-waisted jeans and flat winter boots, big coats. Large handbags are slung over their shoulders. One is half a foot taller with bushy black hair tied into a ponytail. The other is curvy with blonde hair and a thick rim of eyeliner.

'Hi?' the taller one says, her face questioning, in the polite way people do when they don't want to be rude and ask, 'What do you want?'

I smile my most welcoming of smiles. My 'come into the spa and we'll make everything better' smile. 'I'm Cleo.'

The taller woman nods. 'Lexy,' she says, pushing the door shut. 'And this is Faye.'

'Can I ask a quick question?'

Lexy shrugs. 'Sure. Are you new here? If it's about the heating, we've already asked for it to be on longer.'

Some things never change.

'I used to live here, actually. I'm looking for my friend, Rachel. She lives there.' I point to your door and feel that odd sense of déjà vu, that strange, desperate hope that if I stand here for long enough, you'll appear.

There's a pause, a beat of silence in which Faye looks to Lexy, eyebrows raised, eyes wide. She swallows and her mouth opens like she's going to reply, but Lexy nudges her side.

'We haven't seen her for a while.' Lexy gives a 'what more is there to say?' head-shake. 'Simon asked us if we'd seen her the other day, but we haven't.'

'We've not been here that long. Just a few weeks,' Faye adds. 'We're only here until the flat we've bought is ready to move into. We spend most of our time in our rooms.'

'We'd better go.' Lexy motions towards the door.

The déjà vu returns, but this time it's not you, this house – it's Lexy. I stare at her face, wondering if we've met, but the feeling is a wisp of smoke I can't grab hold of.

'Have we met before?' I blurt out the question and immediately regret it.

'I don't think so,' Lexy replies.

'Sorry we can't help,' Faye says as Lexy steps out of the door. 'We don't really know Rachel, but you should talk to the guy in the loft room the next time he's here. I saw Rachel talking to him on the day we moved in and it looked like they were arguing, but I might have been wrong.'

Something close to a scowl crosses Lexy's face and she grabs Faye's arm, yanking her out of the door.

'We're going to be late. Good luck finding your friend,' Lexy shouts before slamming the door.

I stand in the sudden silence, my mind processing the exchange with your housemates. There was something off about it. The look on Faye's face when I mentioned you, and the way Lexy grabbed Faye's arm when she was talking to me. It felt like . . . it felt like they know something more.

Why didn't Lexy want Faye to mention the other housemate – someone you've argued with? I heard him in the loft room last night, just after someone tried to get into my room.

I race up the stairs two at a time, but I don't stop when I get to the top. Instead, I grip my alarm in my hand and cross the upstairs hall, past my room and up the narrow staircase to the loft room.

I reach the top step and freeze. Something is very wrong here.

Chapter 11

Rachel

Five years earlier

CamChat loads and Rachel hovers the mouse over the 'chat' button. No login, no username. Just them and thousands of random people from all over the world. Cleo is by the mirror, adding another layer of gold glitter to her eyelids. She's wearing a bright-red lipstick which should clash with her hair but doesn't. Nothing clashes on Cleo.

'Come on, let's play.' The excitement is humming through Rachel as she reaches for her glass of wine. It's the first time in days that she's felt anything but the darkness. Her nails are black, matching the gems on her choker. She's wearing her absolute favourite black top. It clings to her chest, showing cleavage and just a touch of the lace on her bra.

It's been fun getting ready. Like a proper night out, without worrying about how much money they have, chatting up men they don't like so they'll buy them drinks and using water bottles to sneak vodka into clubs. It's so much better this way.

'I'm ready.' Cleo turns, plonking herself beside Rachel on the bed and leaning over the laptop to fill up their glasses with the last of the bottle.

The slogan appears, drifting down from the top of the screen and settling in the middle. 'Have fun. Make friends. Fall in love. The safe place to meet new people,' they say together in cheesy American accents.

'Do we want to add any filters?' Rachel asks.

'Like what?'

'Going Out? Fun? Clubbing? I don't know.'

Cleo swallows a mouthful of wine before asking, 'What do the filters do again?'

'They narrow down the chats so we're more likely to meet people we have stuff in common with.'

'Oh, OK, then. Let's do Clubbing and Going Out.'

The buzz hits Rachel's stomach as she adds in the filters and clicks 'chat'. The first screen is a man with a guitar singing a love song. He's not looking at the camera, not even caring he's being watched.

Rachel glances at Cleo. 'Skip,' they say at the same time before she presses the button.

Then it's a bald man with a ginger beard who reminds Rachel of a character in that Guess Who? game she used to play with Beth.

'Hi.' Rachel simpers the word.

He smiles but stays silent.

'Where are you from?' Cleo asks.

He nods. 'Yes.' The word is heavily accented and Rachel doesn't need to look at Cleo to know they're skipping this one too.

There's a pause and the screen turns black as they

63

wait for the next chat to load, and then there's a bedroom, a bed, a man's torso, stripy blue-and-white boxer shorts. His head is out of shot and Rachel is about to say hi when his hand moves to his dick and Cleo reaches across her and skips.

'Don't worry,' Rachel says for herself as much as for Cleo. 'We've only just started.'

When the screen changes again it's a living room. There are three guys in their twenties sitting on a sofa drinking cans of Stella. They're cute, sort of. Too fake-tan try-hard pretty-boy for them, but the boys light up when they see their faces and Rachel just knows they're perfect.

Here we go.

'Hello, ladies,' one of them half shouts. 'I'm Toby, this is Jack,' he says, patting the shoulder of the boy on his left. 'And this is Chris.' He taps his can of Stella against that of the boy on the right and they all smile.

'Hi.' She grins. 'I'm Roxy. This is Cassie.' Just saying their fake names sends a shiver of excitement through her.

Cleo gives a little wave of her fingers before examining her nails as though she's bored, but that's just part of the game.

'Where you from?' Toby asks, clearly the ringleader.

'London,' Cleo replies, pretending to mask a yawn. 'You?'

'Not far away. Brentwood, in Essex.'

'What do you do?' Chris asks – or is it Jack? Rachel has already forgotten which is which.

'We work in club promotions,' Cleo says and then she laughs. 'Although most of the time we just invite our friends on nights out.'

Rachel laughs too. Laughs at the stupidity of it, of how insanely different their real lives are, and how in this moment it doesn't matter. They're Roxy and Cassie. They have money and power and can do whatever the hell they like.

'What, like nightclubs? That's so cool.'

'Beats being a bricky,' Chris says, before receiving an elbow from Toby. Rachel shares a look with Cleo. Maybe they're not the only ones playing this game.

'Can you get us in somewhere cool? Like, somewhere the celebs go?'

Rachel laughs again, throwing her head back and swishing her hair in the way she's seen those rich girls do. 'Yes and no. Yes, we can get people into the clubs we promote, and yes, you'd probably recognize quite a few of the clientele, but I'm sorry—'

'We'd struggle to get you boys in,' Cleo finishes with another bored sigh. 'It's only for a certain type of person.' Cleo gives her best pitying look and Rachel snorts another laugh.

God, this is fun. Their good bitch, bad bitch game is totally going to mess with these boys.

The faces on the screen fall – one, two, three – and they look like lost little boys. Hurt and confused.

'Now, hang on, Cass,' Rachel says, taking a sip of wine. The chill has subsided and it hits with a sharp tang. 'Maybe these boys are the right kind of people.'

'Yeah.' Toby nods. 'We are.'

'Prove it.' She runs a hand over the beads of her choker.

'How?' Jack frowns and leans towards the screen and for a moment Rachel thinks he's going to skip them, but then Toby shoves his hand away and they wrestle briefly in that way boys do.

'You know,' Rachel says then, turning to Cleo, 'we have got spaces tonight.'

Cleo frowns and shakes her head. 'Yeah, but, come on.' She tilts her head at the screen and raises her eyebrows. The boys shout in protest.

'Give us a chance,' one of them says.

Cleo's look isn't acting. She's telling Rachel to cool it, but that would be boring and Saturdays are not for boring.

And so the game begins. Toby, Jack and Chris rush in and out of the room. An ironing board appears in the background and they walk around in Calvin Klein boxer shorts, sucking in their stomachs and acting like they've forgotten the camera is there. More Stella is drunk. And every now and then they appear with a shirt option that Cleo boos.

The put-downs are easy. 'That one makes you look fat.' 'That looks really cheap.' 'I thought you said you had nice clothes.'

Half an hour later Rachel can practically smell the aftershave wafting through the screen as all three boys pile on to the sofa once more. They actually look pretty good. Tight black shirts and jeans, hair styled, eyes bright with possibility.

'You don't look too bad,' Rachel says.

'Hey.' Cleo turns to her. 'We need to get going.' She makes a show of looking at her watch and picking up her bag. 'The club opens in half an hour.'

She reaches across the screen, ready to skip, but Toby shouts out. 'Hey, wait, Cassie, Roxy, come on. Do we pass or what?'

Cleo starts to shake her head but Rachel has a better idea. 'Actually, you do. Are you sure you want to come tonight?'

She can feel Cleo's eyes on her but doesn't care.

Toby's face lights up. 'For real?'

'Yeah.' Rachel grins. 'We'll get you into our club. VIP. A few free drinks. It'll be a laugh.'

'Sweet,' Chris replies and Rachel almost feels sorry for them. Almost.

Jack leans towards Toby, mumbling something to his friend, and the reply nearly makes her crack up. 'Ask your mum to lend you some.'

'Look,' Rachel sighs, her best bored bitch face on. It's not hard. It's the same face she has to fight against every time she's at work. 'If you're not interested—'

'We are,' they say, three desperate little puppies.

'All right, then. Meet us outside Green Park tube at ten thirty, OK? Don't be late.'

'Where we gonna stay after?' Jack asks, still hesitant. 'The last train is at one.'

'You can crash in one of our spare rooms.' She smiles invitingly at the camera, knowing how Toby will read it. It's enough, and a second later they're on their feet again.

Cleo grabs Rachel's arm. 'Come on. We need to go.'

'So, you're coming?' Rachel asks.

The boys nod, already pulling on their shoes, patting their pockets. 'On our way.'

Rachel skips the chat and the screen turns black as they collapse on the bed in a fit of laughter. 'Oh my God, that was so funny.'

'You don't think we took that too far?' Cleo asks when they can speak again. 'You don't think they'll actually come, do you? They really believed our story.'

Oh, they'll come. And there's something about the thought of those three boys standing outside Green Park tube on a Saturday night in the cold pissing rain, waiting for two girls who don't even exist, that fills Rachel with a sort of glee, a power. But she shrugs and says, 'Maybe,' because she can tell Cleo is worried.

Cleo bites her lip. 'But—'

'Look, those guys would've been showing us their dicks if we hadn't taken charge. They were losers, Cleo.'

'But Rach, they were broke. You could tell. They're going to get stranded in London tonight.'

'Who cares?'

'Hello?' A voice breaks through their conversation and Rachel glances at the screen. There's a man's face. The room around him is dark and he's wearing a baseball cap low on his head.

'Weirdo,' she mutters, skipping him without a second glance.

'Do you think that guy heard what we said?' Cleo asks. 'We used our real names and we talked about our game.'

'No way. The screen only just loaded. Anyway, what does it matter? It's not like we're going to see him again after I change the filters. It's totally random.'

'I guess it doesn't matter.'

'God, this is fun.' Rachel slugs back the last of her wine and waits for the next chat to load. Finally, she's enjoying herself. Finally, her life has purpose. She knows it's nuts to think that way, but it's how she feels. It's everything to her right now.

Chapter 12

Cleo

Now

The door to the loft room is wide open, the room beyond empty. The curtains are half drawn, adding a grey gloom, and there's a strange feeling in the air, as though someone was just here. But that can't be. There's only one way in and out of this room and if anyone had left it, I'd have met them on the stairs. The realization crawls under my skin, prickling and cold.

I take one step and then another, until I'm standing in the middle of the room. It's small, but warm. This really is where all the heat hides.

The furniture is basic. There's a wardrobe in the corner and a chest of drawers by a bed. The mattress is bare, and when I silently inch open each drawer, I find them empty. The only sign that someone lives in this room at all is the padlock on the wardrobe, a chunky metal thing with a four-digit lock.

Where is the man Faye saw you arguing with? Who

came up here last night? Who tried to get into my room?

I hear it then – the whisper of his name in my thoughts. *Luke Richards*. He's connected to whatever has happened to you. And yet I'm chasing the shadow of your housemate. I need to get a grip and think clearly, logically. For starters, I can ask Simon about who lives in this room.

An hour later, after a lukewarm shower and doing my make-up, after knocking on Simon's door and finding no answer, I step out of the tube at Oxford Street. I have eight days to find you, and the first thing I need is a change of clothes. I can't live in the same knickers and Gemma's old hoody for a week.

The pale-blue sky and cold air give the impression of freshness despite the exhaust fumes from the steady flow of cars, taxis and buses. There are people everywhere. So many people. All hurrying between shops as though the January sales will end at any moment.

It's still early. I didn't think it would be busy yet. My plan to grab a few essentials and go – in and out before the Saturday crush – seems ludicrous now.

I spot a Pret and push my way inside, ordering a coffee and a bagel. I eat it so fast it sticks in my throat, forcing me to sip my scalding hot coffee to wash it down.

By the time I'm back on the street, the caffeine is jumping through my body.

I stride towards River Island. It's been years since I was last here, but the familiarity of the street, the shops, the hum of London around me feels nice. The store is huge: rails and rails of clothes. I take my time, running my hands over the silks and nylons, touching clothes I know you'd love.

We used to love this shop, but as I pull out another top with no sides I realize the clothes are way too young. I guess we're not twenty-four any more.

I try Zara and Mango, the stores we only ever browsed. I feel a sudden urge to buy something just because I can, but I see nothing I want. I'm only here for a week.

It's another few minutes walking among the swelling crowds before I find myself outside Selfridges. That vast corner building we used to loathe is now oddly comforting. I step inside, catching the sickly sweet smell of the perfumes. Make-up girls hover around their counters like bees around a hive, and a stab of longing plunges through me. We hated this job so much. Hours on our feet, being treated like shit and paid even worse, and yet, looking back, our lives seemed so simple.

They weren't.

I know. Rose-tinted glasses and all that, but we were OK, weren't we? Until we started playing the game.

It feels quieter in Selfridges than on the rest of Oxford Street. Maybe it's the space. Six floors and wide aisles. Or maybe it's the familiarity – the yellow banners, everything just so.

I grab some underwear, a pair of jeans and two jumpers. At the last minute I pull a thick parka jacket from the sales rack. It's dark green and one size too big but I don't care. There's no point taking it with me to Bermuda. I pay without looking at the cost and wonder if you can do that now too, or is money still tight? I wonder a lot of things about you as I move through the store.

Simon mentioned an office job and I wonder what you do. All I know is that it's not in make-up.

Memories punch into my head. The hospital. The gaping wound of our friendship.

'Where were you, Cleo?' Beth's voice was snappy. 'Rach needed you.'

'I was . . . I couldn't . . .'

'It's OK,' you said, taking my hand and shushing Beth. But we both knew it wasn't.

My gaze travels across the shop floor, searching for something real, something I can cling on to. I don't want to remember any more. I spot the fire exit sign, a green beacon, and wait for the memories and hurt to fade.

Then someone moves in the corner of my vision. It's just a second, but I see it. I see him. That blond hair, gelled and brushed – like Draco Malfoy, I said once, and you rolled your eyes, jumping to defend him like you always did.

I turn towards the movement, but he's gone. Hiding behind a rail of clothes. Spots dance across my eyes. Air stops hitting my lungs. I step backwards, knocking into someone.

'Watch it.' The voice is sharp, angry, and I spin around, the apology ready on my lips, but it's him. Luke Richards.

A violent tremor takes hold of my hands as I grab the alarm in my pocket and yank the chain free.

Chapter 13

Cleo

Now

One hundred and thirty decibels of noise reverberate across the shop floor. Everyone turns. Eyes bore into me. They think I'm crazy.

I blink. Once. Twice. Three times, and the man morphs before my eyes. His face is all wrong and the hair I thought was blond is grey. It's not him, Rach. It's nothing like him.

As I continue to stare, dumbfounded and frozen, he scoops a crying toddler into his arms. Her face is screwed up, tears leaking from her eyes like rain down a windowpane, but I can't hear her wails above the screeching siren of my alarm.

It's deafening – a jackhammer to my brain. Every thought of you shatters into a million tiny pieces. All I hear is the noise. All I see is my own fear.

And then I gasp, breathing again. I swallow and taste the dirt.

A shop assistant approaches my side and reaches

out a hand. I jump back, knocking against a display of shoes that clatter to the floor.

Still the siren wails.

I stare down at my hands, chain in the left, alarm in the right. I try to push them together, but I'm shaking too much.

A security guard appears at the top of the escalators. Head, then gut, then two stubby legs. He bowls towards me, hand resting on the radio on his hip like it's a gun.

'Come on,' I mutter, voice lost to the wailing siren.

Then, finally, the chain connects. The alarm stops. The silence is just as deafening and startles the toddler out of her crying. She stares, snivelling in her father's arms. His face is a mix of anger and pity as he places a protective hand on his daughter's head and moves away.

'Sorry.' My voice is a whisper that even I don't hear. The alarm is still ringing in my head, but I start to move. Shoppers step back, keeping their distance as though I'm contagious, and if I had a drop of energy left, I'd tell them they can't catch this, it's been given to me, punched right into me, branded, stamped, never to be removed.

But I have nothing left. My head is spinning as I stumble from the shop. My early resolve to think clearly is gone. I've been in London less than twenty-four hours and already I'm a mess.

The street outside is heaving. More and more people, walking five across, shopping bags bulging. There is no escape. I'm trapped. My nerves jangle. There is only one way out – the road. I dodge the shoppers and move to the edge of the pavement just as a black taxi pulls up and a woman steps out, holding the door open for me. 'Do you want this one?'

I throw myself in, slamming the door behind me, muffling the street noises.

'Where to?' the driver asks.

I pause for a moment. Where am I going? A hotel? A B&B? The airport? I think of all the faces I'll see – always his face, his eyes on me. And then I realize there is only one option. 'Lockton Road, Bethnal Green,' I reply. The house is the only place I feel safe right now, and where else can I go that will help me find you?

I stagger into the house and up the stairs, passing your door without a glance. My legs are weak, body trembling with a current of panic, but I don't stop until I'm in my room, the door locked. I don't stop until I've flung open the boxes of my old life that you so carefully packed away for me, shaken every last thing to the floor.

There are scarfs I don't remember owning. Perfume and half-empty bottles of moisturizer. An entire carrier bag filled with used make-up brushes tumbles out.

I pick up an old CD case of Feist. The plastic is cracked down the side and the disc is missing. I think I left it in your room. It seems like such an old technology now. There are a dozen yellowed paperbacks I can't remember reading. And my portfolio. I run a hand over the black leather cover, feeling a stab of bitter nostalgia.

My fingers rifle and rake through the contents of my old life as I sob, a mess of snot and tears. I feel like I'm looking for something – a connection to the person I used to be, the person who could leave the house to shop for knickers and it be nothing. No big deal.

But that girl is lost. Gone. Only I am left.

I hurl myself at my locked door as another wave of panic attacks my body. I scramble with the lock before throwing it open and sprinting towards the bathroom, vomiting first before twisting around as my bowels release. It's the ugly side of panic attacks, the aftermath that's rarely mentioned. When I'm spent, empty, I crawl into the bed, crying fat tears of mortification and fear.

I should never have come back.

I can't save you, Rach.

I can't even save myself.

Does she think people feel sorry for her?

*Does she think people can't see
through her little act?*

*This is another game to her. Pulling that attack
alarm right in the middle of the shop. Genius!*

But this time the rules have changed.

I'm the one in control.

*Soon, oh so soon, the three of us
can really start to play again.*

Chapter 14

Cleo

Five years earlier

The beat of The Killers thuds from a speaker on the opposite side of the room. It's so loud I can feel the vibrations humming through the wall behind me. I take a sip of warm white wine and check my phone for a text from Rachel. She should be here by now. I'm the one who had to work the later shift, changing in the toilets and almost dropping my sodding ankle boot in the loo.

This isn't even fashionably late any more. It's just late.

I send her a 'where are you?' text before looking around the room. It's a nice-sized flat in an ex-council block a short walk from Clapham Junction and the park. It's exactly the kind of flat I desperately want to get with Rachel, even though I know it's out of our price range.

There are groups of people in twos, threes and fours, chatting, laughing. I should mingle. If Rachel was here, that's exactly what we'd be doing, pulling each other along and finding the cutest guys to flirt with.

A man with shoulder-length brown hair turns in my direction and holds my gaze a moment too long. He's sort of cute in a shaggy kind of way, but there's no spark and I push off from the wall in search of the kitchen and another drink before he decides to talk to me.

The kitchen is just as busy as the living room. It's a long, narrow space with bodies leaning on every available counter, everyone talking at the tops of their voices. I squeeze through the people and find Katie in the middle, mixing a bowl of red punch.

She's wearing hot-pink leggings and a vest top, her blonde hair tied into a bun with what looks like a thong. I know she hasn't spent a second thinking about her appearance, which is probably why she looks so utterly cool. I feel suddenly uncomfortable in my jeans and belt.

'Cleo,' Katie shouts over the noise. 'You must drink this. It's my secret recipe.' She pushes a plastic tumbler towards me and I take a reluctant sip, grimacing as the vodka scorches the back of my throat.

I spot Lisa on the small balcony laughing at something. She catches my eye and waves manically as someone leans across me and takes a cup. 'Hey,' Simon says, his mouth close to my ear.

'Hi.' I cough slightly, taking another sip of punch to mask my surprise. I knew he'd be here, I just wasn't expecting to find him standing so close to me.

'I think the secret recipe is a seventy–thirty ratio of vodka to cranberry,' he says and I laugh.

'Plus a dash of orange-and-mango squash,' Katie laughs. 'Hey, Cleo, where's Rachel?' she asks me.

'She should be here any minute,' I say, checking my phone and finding a reply.

Not feeling up for it tonight. Sorry!!!! xx

Oh, Rach! I press the phone to my ear as I call her. I think back over the last few weeks. Shifts at work. Vegging out in front of her little TV. All the times I've pulled her out of bed in the mornings and jollied her along. It's like a cloud has been hanging over her. Only when we play on CamChat is she different, and it's that thought, that realization, that worries me most of all.

She doesn't pick up and I start to text a reply when Simon leans closer and sees the message.

'Looks like it's just you and me. Come on, let's make a proper punch and get drunk,' he says, before nudging Katie to one side. 'Move aside. Let the masters work.' He gives me a wink as he rolls up his shirtsleeves. 'Cleo, you're on crushed ice. Katie, have you got any Worcestershire sauce?'

I slip my phone into the back pocket of my jeans, deciding to reply later, as Katie hands me a bag of ice from the freezer.

'What are we making?' I ask as someone pushes by and I fall into Simon, catching the scent of his aftershave – woody and enticing.

'We are making my own version of a michelada. It's got the best kick to it.'

'And that's a good thing?'

He leans close, scooping my hair behind my ear in a way that makes desire fizz through me. 'A very good thing,' he whispers.

Time speeds up and it's gone midnight by the time I realize three things:

One: I'm drunk. Very.

Two: I've crossed the flirting line with Simon, and based on the kiss we just had on the balcony, we can no longer be considered friends.

Three: I'm a terrible friend. I've not texted Rachel back and now I'm breaking our pact. Even in my brain-fuzzled state, I know I'm in trouble. Not just because the hangover tomorrow is going to kill me, or because I'm being a terrible friend, but because of the fourth thing. The very important fourth thing I'm struggling to admit to myself – I properly, hands down, no doubt about it, have the hots for Simon.

He crosses the room towards me, two more cups of something in his hands. 'Don't worry,' he says as he approaches. 'It's water.'

'Thank you.' I smile and gulp it back in two mouthfuls.

'I don't mean to be presumptuous,' Simon says, throwing an arm around me. 'But would you like to come back to my place?'

I tip my head back and laugh. 'How can I say no to that? I mean, I do live with you.'

'Let me reword it,' he continues, kissing my neck. 'Would you like to come back to my bed?'

I swallow as heat burns inside me, and before I can think about it, I nod, and he takes my hand and leads me into the night.

It's not until lunchtime at work on Saturday that Rachel and I get a chance to talk.

'You look proper shit,' she grins, sidling up beside me at the counter.

'Thanks. I feel it.' I dab at a film of sweat forming on my upper lip and scoop my hair away from my face.

'I guess it was a good night, then?'

'Very.' I suck in my lips, fighting the smile creeping across my face. My head is pounding, my mouth is furry and there isn't enough water in the world to take away my thirst, but all I can think about is the achy feeling of my body, the lingering buzz of Simon's touch and how, even though I'm exhausted, half asleep on my feet, all I want to do right now is climb back into his bed.

'What time did you get back? I didn't hear you come in.'

'It was late,' I reply, dodging her question. Now is the time to tell Rachel that I got a taxi with Simon. Now is the time to tell her everything. But somehow the words won't form. 'What happened to you?' I ask instead. 'You totally ditched me. I wish you'd come.'

Rach's face falls; she looks sheepish. 'I know, I'm sorry. When you didn't reply to my text, I thought you might be mad at me.'

'I'm not mad. I just want to know why you changed your mind at the last minute. What did you get up to?' I know the answer before she tells me.

'CamChat.'

'Rach, that's not real life, you can't—'

'It's no big deal,' she says. 'I didn't fancy going to a party, that's all.'

I'm about to say something more when Mandy appears on the floor. We busy ourselves with stocking the lipstick as she approaches, tottering in her sky-high heels.

'Rachel?'

'Mandy, hi.' Rachel turns around, a tight smile fixed on her face. I keep my back to Mandy, hiding how crap I look today.

'I do appreciate the effort it takes to put on make-up, and you're clearly very skilled, but perhaps a little softer around the eyes tomorrow, please?'

'Of course,' Rachel says, the two words ringing with annoyance I hope only I hear.

'And that necklace – it's rather vulgar for Selfridges. Please remove it during your lunch break.'

She strides away and only then do I realize, in my hungover state, that I've not taken in Rachel's appearance. Mandy's right: her make-up is heavier than normal. Her eyes are inked in smoky black liner, her lips dark, almost purple.

'Shall we play tonight?' Rachel asks, her fingers fiddling with the beads of her choker.

'I'm not sure I'm up for it. I'm exhausted.' It's the truth, but it's more than that. It's Rachel going on CamChat without me. It's her change of make-up, her necklace choice, how she's looking just like she does when she pretends to be Roxy. The thought is unsettling. It feels wrong that the lies, the game, the fakeness, seem to be the only thing making her happy.

'OK.' Rachel shrugs before being pulled into a makeover by a tearful woman in her fifties, and whatever moment there was to talk about Rachel looking more like Roxy, her going on CamChat without me, Simon and what happened between us last night, is gone.

Chapter 15

Cleo

Now

I wake in the afternoon, groggy, exhausted. As I reach for my water, I find my attack alarm wedged so tightly in my hand it's left grooves in my skin.

Memories of Selfridges pierce my thoughts. I really thought it was him, Rach.

I struggle to my feet and get dressed, pulling off the tags of my new clothes as I go. The coat is chunky and warm like a hug. The panic I felt earlier is no longer shooting through my veins. It's not gone, just smothered by a restless sleep.

But the determination is back. Think, plan, take control. I didn't see Luke Richards in Selfridges, but I know he's involved. Who else would do this? Who else would you call 'the cowboy'?

I need more information. I need to speak to the detective investigating your disappearance. Beth said the police aren't taking it seriously, but maybe that's because they don't have all the information. Beth would've told them about the time you were scared walking home, but she didn't know who you'd seen. She didn't know the nickname you had for Luke. I have to tell them, make them see what's really going on. They'll have to take it seriously then.

Hunger rattles through my body as I leave the house. I dig in my backpack for the last two cookies. I know, I know, I can't live on cookies alone. But that's the thing about five years of crew life: I'm out of practice in thinking about food. We have our own chef, our own restaurant. It's nothing like the fancy dining rooms above deck, but every meal is supplied. All I have to do is turn up during my break or after my shift and collect a plate.

I promise myself I'll do better. I'll stop at Mr Hakimi's shop after the police station and get some supplies.

I quicken my pace as I reach Roman Road. It's barely three p.m. but the sky has clouded over and the sunlight is fading from beneath a thick blanket of grey. The air is icy cold, stinging my face. It'll be dark soon. The thought sends a shot of worry through my body that makes me want to spin on my heels and hurry back to the house. But I'm out now and I want answers.

The old red-brick police station is where it's always been, tucked behind the new fire station on the main road. I'd half wondered if it would have moved, or merged with the station in Bow, but it's still here and I push open the heavy glass door into an empty waiting room. There are two rows of blue plastic chairs on either side and a high front desk at the end. A chair creaks as I step forward. 'Good afternoon.' The voice is male and scratchy with age. A second later the officer's head and shoulders appear from behind the desk. He has thinning grey hair next to wisps of faded orange sideburns that curl and poke in different directions.

'Hello. I'd like to speak to someone about a missing persons case, please. Her name is Rachel Winslow.'

'Do you have information regarding the case?' the officer asks, eyes travelling over my face, and I have to fight the urge not to fidget beneath his gaze.

'Yes.' Sort of.

He points me to the chairs and I sit for long enough to see a woman report a lost purse, and a homeless man who's been mugged.

'Again, Brian?' the desk officer asks, his tone firm but kind.

'Don't know why it keeps happening to me,' comes the gruff reply.

'Take a seat. I'll get you a cup of tea.'

'Thank you.'

It's then that a female officer in uniform appears from a doorway and looks right at me. She's late-twenties, like us. The collar of her shirt shines a bright white next to the jet black of her short, straight hair.

'You have information on a missing persons case?' she asks.

I leap up and nod, and she leads me to a small inter-view room that looks like it's been taken straight out of a TV crime drama. Grey walls and a scuffed grey table bolted to the floor.

I half expect her to offer me terrible coffee served in a plastic cup to complete the look, but she doesn't.

'I'm PC Emma Leighton,' she says, scooping her hair behind her ears before opening a small notebook and noting down my name and address. 'Can you start by telling me what your connection is to Rachel Winslow?'

'I'm her best friend. I came back to London when I heard she was missing.' My cheeks flush with heat and beneath the table my legs jiggle. It's not a lie, so why does it feel like one?

'And what information do you have?'

Oh God. I can't do this. Why did I think I could? How can I begin to explain about CamChat, what we did?

An expectant silence stretches out and I know I need to say something. 'She had a . . . sort of boyfriend five years ago. His name was Luke Richards. He . . . wasn't a nice person.' Bile burns the back of my throat. I pause. The air is heavy with expectation but I can't find the words. 'There's a police file on what happened,' I say eventually. 'There was a detective – DS Anik Saha. He could help.'

'So you think this boyfriend has had something to do with Miss Winslow's disappearance?' PC Leighton makes a note before her eyes are back on me.

'Yes. Her sister told me she'd seen him following her.'

'We don't have a record of this information from her sister.'

'I know. It's because Rachel didn't actually say she'd seen him. When she told Beth – her sister – that she'd seen him, she called him "the cowboy", and her sister didn't realize that it's a nickname she had for Luke Richards. If I could speak to the detective investigating Rachel's case, I might be able to help. Rachel liked to chat to people on a website called CamChat. I think it might be connected to her disappearance.'

'I'm the duty officer assigned to Rachel's case.'

I frown. PC Leighton looks competent, but she's definitely not a detective.

'But Rachel hasn't been seen for over a week. Why isn't there a detective looking at her case? Why isn't this all over the news? Surely she should get more than this?'

'It comes down to the level of risk assigned to each missing persons case. High risk being a grave concern for their safety, and that's when you would see a national media campaign and a dedicated task force. The initial enquiries conducted by my colleagues suggested quite clearly that Rachel is low risk.' PC Leighton's words are slow and precise, as though she's explained this many times before.

'But how? No one has seen her.'

'There could be a very simple reason for that. Are you aware that Miss Winslow mentioned planning a holiday to her sister, and subsequently booked two weeks' holiday from her job, telling her colleagues she was going away?'

I shake my head. This can't be right. 'But nobody knows where she's gone.'

'That's true, and it's important to understand that we are still treating Rachel as a missing person, but it's not uncommon for people to turn their phone off during their holidays.'

'So you're doing nothing?'

'We're keeping an eye on the situation and we will escalate Miss Winslow's case if she doesn't return by . . .' PC Leighton checks her notes, 'a week on Monday – the twenty-fifth of January. I assume she didn't mention a holiday to you?'

'No, she didn't. What about her bank account? Surely that will tell you if she's on holiday?'

'We've not progressed to that point in our investigation. The current hypothesis is that she is on holiday.

Our investigation will not progress until there is evidence to the contrary.'

A frustration floods my body. I came to London to help, to find you. I came to the police for answers, but they have none and I don't know what I'm supposed to do now.

'I guess I'll have to go out and find some evidence for you, then,' I snipe, regretting the comment instantly, but still it hangs between us.

'When did you last see or speak to Miss Winslow?' PC Leighton asks, ignoring my outburst. Her notebook is open. Pen poised. I'm suddenly too hot in my coat.

'It was a while ago,' I admit, trying to calm myself down. 'But I'm worried about her.'

'Try not to be. She'll most likely turn up in a week's time, surprised at all the fuss. That's what normally happens in cases like this.'

I nod, feeling scolded. Stupid. The desperate urge to leave the police station, London, England – the whole sodding lot – throbs through me as PC Leighton leads me back to the waiting area. I have my bag and my passport with me. I could go to the airport right now and never look back. I picture myself checking in to an earlier flight to Bermuda, lying on a sandy beach, the hot sun beating down on me as I wait for the *Enchantress* to arrive.

Are you lying on a beach somewhere, Rach? Backpacking through a jungle? Exploring castles in Scotland? Are you safe and happy? Why the hell didn't your sister tell me about your plans to book a holiday?

The moment I'm outside the police station, the cold air whipping at my face, I call Beth.

'Cleo. Have you found her?' Beth's voice is just as desperate as the last time we spoke.

'I've just spoken to the police,' I say by way of reply.

'Oh.'

'They don't even think she's missing – that's why they're not interested. Why didn't you tell me?'

'Because it's bollocks, Cleo. Rachel mentioned something at Christmas about wanting to book a holiday, but she didn't actually say she was going to. And there's no way she would've left for two weeks without telling me first. We speak every few days. She'd know how worried I'd be. And why isn't she answering her phone?'

'I can't believe you didn't tell me this.'

'I know, I'm sorry, but the police are wrong – that's why I didn't tell you. It doesn't make sense that she'd go on holiday without telling me.'

'Are you sure about that?'

'Yes,' Beth replies, but there's less certainty in her voice now.

'I'm sorry, Beth, but I'm going to go. I'm supposed to be working on a cruise right now. I don't know what else I can do. The police think she's on holiday. She booked time off work, for God's sake.'

A silence stretches out between us before Beth speaks again. 'Please, Cleo. She's not on holiday. I know it. I can feel it. Something is wrong. You have to find her. Don't you think you owe her that?' There's a sudden sharpness to Beth's voice, her words cutting into me – shards of broken glass – and I flinch, ending the call before she can say any more.

'Don't you think you owe her that?'

The fiery ice of my guilt ignites inside me, just like it did in Southampton.

Beth's words hurt because they're true, and she has no idea how right she is, but that doesn't mean I have the first clue what to do now.

According to the police, you booked two weeks' holiday. You told your colleagues you were going away. And sure, it's weird you didn't tell Beth, but that doesn't mean you're in danger.

I came back because of guilt, because I thought you were in trouble, but the only person in trouble is me. The anxiety, the memories – they're no longer buried but swimming through me. And the longer I stay here, the harder it is to keep control.

Chapter 16

Rachel

Five years earlier

The moment the web page loads, the tingling in Rachel's stomach spreads through her body. Glittering, unstoppable. She settles against the pillows and, for the first time all week, she feels her shoulders relax. She is Roxy now.

The screen turns black, then the word *CamChat* floats down from the top.

She glances at Cleo, grinning beside her, and they clink their glasses. It's the second glass on an empty stomach and Rachel loves the heady road to drunkenness ahead of them. There's another bottle in the fridge. So what if they eat beans on toast tonight, tomorrow? So the hell what?

The cursor lands on 'chat' but Rachel hesitates for a moment, savouring this feeling, letting the shit show of her week drain away. Mandy was an absolute bitch about her make-up. The snooty cow hasn't stopped picking on her this week. If Rachel spends too much

time restocking, then she's not looking out for customers. If she doesn't restock the make-up, then she's
daydreaming. It's school all over again. One rule for
everyone else, one rule for her, and she can never, ever
get it right. She can never win.

Cleo is the only reason Rachel hasn't told Mandy to
shove the job up her arse. Cleo is the only thing making it bearable, the voice of reason and hope.

'Ready?' Rachel asks.

'Ready,' Cleo says, and Rachel pretends not to hear
the reluctance in her voice.

'Let's play.'

Rachel clicks the touchpad and their faces appear.
The laptop is cheap, the camera a bit crap, but even
with the pixelated screen, Cleo's bright-red hair is the
first thing anyone will notice, followed by the swish of
their black eye make-up, and Rachel's cleavage in a
tight purple vest top. It's her third-date top, her best
night-out top.

A second later their screen shrinks into the bottom
left corner and the buzz inside her intensifies. The
image that loads is a man alone in a bedroom. The
camera is directed down to his legs and an ugly cock
he's currently rubbing.

'Oh my God,' Cleo shrieks. 'Skip.'

A giggle bursts out of Rachel and she clicks 'skip',
but not fast enough to stop the screen blurring.

'Did he just . . .' Cleo makes a face.

'Yep. Clearly we helped him finish.' They burst out
laughing.

'Gross.'

'So gross.'

The next screen is a teenage boy with a strong South
African accent. 'Hey, pretty girls, where you from?'

Rachel senses Cleo about to speak but she skips anyway.

'Hey,' Cleo says. 'Why did you skip?'

'I just wasn't feeling that one.'

Rachel skips the next few chats – an older woman and then a group of teenage girls. She's not sure what she's looking for. Last week, the week before that, these people would've been perfect, but Rachel wants something more now. Bigger.

It's only when the next face appears that Rachel finds the perfect chat. It's a man – pasty skin, bald with a patchy beard. He licks his lips when he sees them.

'The things I would do to you two,' he says, voice gravelly, low.

Cleo's hand shoots towards the keyboard but Rachel moves the laptop away, out of Cleo's reach, and ignores her frown.

'Like what?' Rachel asks.

The man's eyes widen – surprise and delight. His tongue runs slowly across his lower lip, back and forth, and then he answers, his words graphic and disturbing. Rachel hides a shudder and forces herself to smile.

Cleo tugs at her arm. 'What the hell?' she whispers. 'Skip him.'

'In a sec,' she replies, and to the screen she says, 'Where do you live?'

'London.'

'Me too.' Rachel grins, and this time it's real. 'Are you one of those guys who's all talk, or are you going to come and show me in person?'

'I'll show you, all right.'

'Come over now, then.' Rachel reels off the address before skipping him and collapsing back on the pillows

94

with a shaky sigh. Adrenaline pumps through her body. That was exactly what she needed. Payback!

'Rach, what was that?' Cleo's voice rings with alarm.

'Just a bit of fun.' She gives a nervous laugh, feeling light, almost dizzy. But it's a good feeling. Anything that isn't bleak misery is good, surely?

'Was that address made up?'

'No.'

'Whose, then?'

'It was Mandy's.' Her eyes catch Cleo's and she waits for her friend to laugh, but Cleo is still frowning.

'Rach, what have you done? That man was a nutter. What if he actually goes round there?'

'Then Mandy will get a fright, which is what she deserves after the way she's treated me this week.'

Cleo sucks in her lips. She's not happy and her worry is a buzz-kill.

'Mandy's married, right?' Rachel says.

Cleo nods.

'So she's not home alone. All that's going to happen is that some weirdo is going to knock on her door.'

'Hey?' a voice calls out from the laptop.

They jump, their eyes moving to the screen where the next chat has already loaded. There's something familiar about the bedroom, those magenta curtains and the Salvador Dalí art posters on the wall. It's only when Rachel's gaze lands on the girl leaning close to the screen that she knows who she is. Denise. Shit! There's a movement in the background and Rachel spots Alex coming into view. It's the girls from their first week.

Everything stops. Rachel holds her breath. Why are they seeing them again?

It's random. A totally random interface with over a million users. It's not possible to see the same people twice. A chill races over her body. This can't be happening and yet it is.

Cleo gasps from beside her. 'Shit.'

'Hey, Rachel, Cleo. That's you, right?' Denise frowns, her eyes moving between them.

'Skip,' Cleo hisses, her cheeks flushing a shade lighter than her hair.

Rachel taps the touchpad, but she can't find the cursor. Her finger swirls around and around. Where the hell is it?

'It is you.' Denise sits back and Rachel spots her grey Bristol University hoody as she folds her arms. 'What the hell? What happened?'

'I know what happened,' Alex calls out. 'They were faking it.' She takes a seat beside Denise and it's just like that first time they loaded CamChat and found two girls who bought hook, line and sinker into their game that they were two sisters living together, one with a violent boyfriend who would hit them both. Denise and Alex were so sweet, so desperate to help them. They even phoned Alex's brother in London to come and help. Rachel and Cleo shouldn't have used their real names, though.

God, they look pissed. Really pissed.

'You can't mess with people like this,' Alex says, her voice sharp, her tone cutting. 'You know my brother drove around South London for over an hour, knocking on doors, looking for you? Someone called the police on him. What kind of people are you? Life isn't a game, you know?'

Tears swim in Alex's eyes and Denise touches her arm. 'Forget it, Alex. One day someone is going to teach them a lesson and they'll get what's coming to them.'

'Oh, piss off, Miss High-and-Mighty.' Rachel forces a laugh and skips the chat. 'Fuck,' she hisses in the silent room.

'How come we saw them again?' Cleo bites her lip, staring from the laptop to Rachel and back again.

'I don't know.'

'I thought it was random.'

'So did I.' Rachel's hands shake slightly as she moves the cursor and opens the settings page. 'I think I must have used the same filters as the first time.' It's all she can think of, but still the chances of seeing the same two girls are one in hundreds of thousands. It doesn't make sense.

'This has got too weird. We need to stop,' Cleo says.

'No.' The force of Rachel's voice surprises them both. 'Please, Cleo. This is way too much fun to stop. You've enjoyed it as much as I have.' She hasn't. Not really. To Cleo, their games have been a distraction from the day-to-day of their lives; for Rachel, the distraction is so much bigger. It's all that's keeping her alive right now. The thought surprises her. Is that true? It feels like it. Playing is the only thing she has in her life. She can't stop.

'But—'

'I'll be more careful with the filters, OK?'

'And giving out addresses?'

'I'll stop. I promise.'

Cleo pulls a face but Rachel can see she's wavering.

They look at each other and something passes unspoken between them. The tension in the air disappears and they laugh, nervous, relieved.

Chapter 17

Cleo

Now

The hallway is cold as I let myself back into the house, but my anger is a fiery heat scorching through my veins.

I'm so pissed at you for disappearing and pissed at myself for being sucked into this lunacy.

'*I never want to see you again.*'

The memory of your voice slices through me.

I've let my guilt and the horrors of what we went through cloud the simplest explanation – the truth. You booked time off work. You told your sister you were planning to get away and that's what you've done. I can't believe I've missed the first week on the *Enchantress* for this. I feel so stupid.

I head straight to Simon's door, knocking so hard my knuckles sting. I hear footsteps and a moment later Simon is standing in front of me in jeans and a red polo shirt, a cup of tea in one hand, his phone in the other.

'Hey, Cleo. You OK?'

'Yeah.' I fight to control the anger in my voice. 'I just wanted to say goodbye and let you know I'm leaving. Thanks for letting me stay last night.' With that, I spin on my heels and stride to the stairs to pack my things and get back to my life.

'Hang on,' he says, following two paces behind me. 'Has something happened? Have you found Rachel?'

I turn to face him, arms folding tight across my body. 'I just came from the police station. Why didn't you tell me Rachel had booked time off?'

Surprise registers on his face. 'I thought you knew. You told me you'd spoken to Beth, so I assumed she'd told you about the holiday booking.'

'Well, she didn't,' I say. 'Rachel is on holiday. That's what the police think. It's what makes the most sense.'

He sighs, defeated, exhausted, and something about it softens the anger squeezing my chest. I drop my arms to my sides and wait for him to talk.

'I can see that,' he says. 'But, for what it's worth, Rachel arranging that time off doesn't change the fact that no one knows where she is, and it doesn't explain why she left the house last Friday with only a tiny handbag. Plus, all her stuff is in her room. She's taken nothing with her.'

'How do you know that?'

'Because I checked, of course. I used my spare keys to open her room and make sure she wasn't in there. I was worried she might be ill or something. And anyway, if she's on holiday, then why isn't she answering her phone? You know she's glued to it.'

'I don't know that. I don't know anything about Rachel any more, just like she doesn't know anything about me.'

'If everything is fine, if Rachel is on holiday like they say, then who was texting her pretending to be you? Who arranged to meet her last Friday if it wasn't you?' he asks, as though I have the answers.

Doubt nibbles at the edges of my certainty. 'I don't know, but it's got nothing to do with me any more. The police have evidence that Rachel is on holiday. They're the experts.'

'So you're going to leave this to the police, because they did such a fantastic job last time?' Sarcasm drips from his voice and his words hit hard. The police never found him, Rach. They never came close.

'It wasn't their fault,' I say, my voice quiet now. 'It was ours.' It was mine.

'I don't think—'

'Who lives in the loft room?' I ask suddenly, desperate to change the subject before the shame of my secret crawls across my face.

'Charlie. Why?'

'Where is he?'

'How would I know? He's cabin crew for one of the airlines. He comes and goes.'

'His door is open.'

Simon shrugs again, his eyebrows rising into a 'so what?' look.

'Did you know he knows Rachel? Faye saw them arguing.'

'Faye?' he asks, and then, as if remembering, 'Oh yeah, one of the girls. Rachel keeps an eye on the place for me while I'm away, so she knows the other tenants. He was probably complaining to her about something,' Simon adds with a wry smile.

'Right.' I close my eyes for a moment, trying to regroup, to find that anger I felt leaving the police station, that energy that was going to propel me out of here and all the way to the airport. I open my eyes and look at Simon. 'I'm going to go. I don't know what else I can do.'

'But you said you didn't have to leave until next weekend. I'm going to Jersey. I've got to be there for the office move and it's Liz's birthday.' His voice is pleading. 'I hate leaving while we don't know where Rachel is. There must be somewhere you can think to look?'

'There isn't.'

'OK.' He nods. 'I'm sorry you've been dragged into this. I know it must be hard for you being back here. Rachel was just so happy you were talking again. I guess I thought you were the best person to figure out what's going on, especially with . . . the game stuff, but if you weren't actually talking . . .' His voice trails off. 'But look, if you need to go right now, then go. The room is yours for as long as you want it. Put your stuff back in the cupboard if you want, or throw it away. Whatever you like. I can call you with updates.'

'Thanks.'

'Take care of yourself, Cleo.' Simon moves up the stairs and we hug. It's warm and awkward, but his body is firm, his arms tight around me, and I sink into his embrace before turning away and heading to my room for the final time.

Tears stream down my face as I throw my clothes into my rucksack. I turn and survey the mess of my old life still scattered across the carpet. This stuff – it isn't mine any more. It's junk. I'm never coming back here again; I'm never going to need any of this.

I drag the boxes closer and begin scooping up the

debris. I'll leave them by the black bin in the garden. Someone will put them out for the bin lorry at some point, or they'll rot outside for another five years. Either way, I don't care.

I hope you're OK, Rach. I really do. But there is no one left to talk to. Simon is wrong. Beth is wrong. We might have known each other inside and out five years ago, but so much has changed. I've changed.

Beth, Simon – they want me to help. They think I'm strong, but I'm not, Rach. I'm not you, and nothing I do here is going to change what happened between us.

I grab at a lump of tangled necklaces. Some of the silvery chains have turned a mottled grey, and I remember how we would wander through Brick Lane Market on Saturdays, feeling so pleased if we treated ourselves to a cheap bit of tat.

It's on the second handful of necklaces that I feel the weight of a different object in my hands. I shake out the beads and that's when I see it – a key. It's attached to a black pompom key ring and I recognize it instantly. It's your key, the spare one you gave me after the weekend you went home to visit your mum and I'd left my purse in your room and had to borrow some money from Simon so I could eat until you came back.

I sit on the floor for a long time, staring at the key.

My phone vibrates with a message. It's Beth.

I'm sorry I didn't tell you about Rachel planning a holiday, but I promise you she only mentioned it half-heartedly at Christmas. She didn't tell me she'd booked anything!! She wouldn't go on holiday without telling me! I'm trying to find

someone to help with Mum so I can come to
London and help. Please, Cleo!!! Don't give up! xx

I don't reply. What can I say other than that it's too late? I've already given up and I'm leaving.

Downstairs, the front door crashes shut and then there's music and the clatter of pots from the kitchen. I catch the sound of female laughter and picture Faye and Lexy cooking dinner for themselves.

My eyes draw to the window. It's early evening, the sky pitch-black. Drizzly rain pitter-patters on the glass. Another memory pushes forwards. The rhythmic whine of windscreen wipers. The smell of pine air freshener. That sound of rain on glass. The whir of orange street lights passing too fast. And that feeling, that knowledge, that absolute certainty we were going to die.

And I know I can't leave now. It's dark outside, dangerous. There are too many shadows, too many places to hide. I have to wait until the morning to leave.

I stare at the key again. The guilt from Beth's message swims through me.

One look. That's all. Then, tomorrow morning, I'm gone.

I'm on my feet and tiptoeing back down the stairs before I can talk myself out of it. Faye and Lexy are still in the kitchen and I take comfort in the hum of their voices.

I slip the key into the lock, push open the door and flick on the light. I know it's stupid, but a part of me still thinks I'll see you sitting on the bed, smiling at me, wine glass in one hand, make-up brush in the other.

103

Ready to play?

But as my eyes blink in your room, an icy cold burns through my body.

Oh, Rach. No. This isn't right.

Chapter 18

Cleo

Now

The déjà vu smacks me across the face – a stinging slap. Something drops in the pit of my stomach. I step into the room and shut the door, hoping my memories are clouding my mind, hoping if I stare at the walls for long enough, I will see I'm wrong.

But I'm not.

Your room is exactly as it was the last time I saw it. Exactly.

Five years. Five whole years and you've not changed a single thing in here. The photos on the wall draw me forwards. They are all of us. Selfies with our faces pushed together, grinning wildly. There is another of us posing with our certificates outside the black-brick building of The London School of Make-up. I run my hands over our faces. We look so young. So happy.

So naive, you mean.

There is a second photo beside it which is almost identical. It's from the following year after we trained in our specialisms: TV, special effects, stage. We really thought we'd make it, didn't we?

I thought you would. People never liked me, remember?

That's not true.

My hands drift across your dresser and the little heart-shaped terracotta dish where you keep your car key. I sniff at the perfume bottle you love so much and I'm hit again – a thousand tiny memories of our friendship, of laughter and silliness, and kindness and support. We had each other's backs.

Tears form in my eyes and I turn my gaze to your make-up case on the floor. It's the same black glittery case with the two levels and fold-out shelves that Beth gave you for your twenty-first birthday. You loved it. It was the only thing you ever kept organized. Your clothes could be all over the floor, clean mixed with dirty; you could have a cup of week-old, half-drunk tea on the side, but every single piece of your make-up would always be in its place. I used to joke that there could be an earthquake, a bomb explosion, an alien invasion, and the first thing you'd do is grab that case.

The lid lifts easily and I take in the tiny strips of black elastic stitched to the inside, holding your mascaras and lipsticks in place. Only one space is empty. It sits at the end of a row of lipsticks and I can just imagine you slipping one into a bag on your way out the door.

I turn around and study your room again. The bedding your mum bought you for Christmas one year – pale blue with a spray of pink petals across the bottom. It doesn't even look faded. There are clothes on the back of a chair. Black trousers and a yellow silk blouse. There's a beige smudge of foundation on the sink and a toothbrush in the stand.

Realization trickles through me, slow at first; then, like a dam breaking, I see it. What this all means. Make-up, toothbrush, clothes. Simon is right. This is not the room of someone who has gone on holiday. A million things might have changed in the last five years, but one thing I'm absolutely certain of is that you wouldn't go anywhere, even for a single night, without your make-up.

Another memory flashes in my mind. Us in this room before I left and didn't come back. You were in a baggy tracksuit of Beth's and you still had the hospital identity bracelet on your wrist. There were tears rolling down your face as you stepped to the wall of photos.

'My life is over,' you said.

'It's not,' I cried. 'I promise it's not.'

'Easy for you to say,' you replied, before snatching at the photos and ripping them one by one into tiny pieces. And all I did was stand and cry. We were both so broken. Being back in London, I feel that same fragility – a snapped bone that never quite heals.

The memories hurt, but the thought of you getting the photos reprinted and placing them back on the wall, just how they used to be, hurts more.

It was just after that moment that I had my first panic attack. I'd left you to sleep and gone to get us dinner. I was walking towards the big Sainsbury's in Bow when someone ran by, nudging my shoulder. Something about the suddenness of it – the force – brought everything back, and I knew as I collapsed on to the pavement, fighting to breathe, that Ingrid was right. I couldn't help us both.

That's when I started thinking about the girl we worked with in Selfridges. Patricia, wasn't it? Do you remember she started after a summer working on a cruise?

She hated it.

I know. But it was why she hated it that stuck like treacle to my thoughts. She said it was like a prison. Trapped on board and working twelve-hour shifts. Always the same people, the same faces.

I knew then, before I'd even found a company hiring, that I would go. Her prison was my safety.

You said it was only for three months.

I lied. Again.

I move to your bed and spot the corner of your laptop nudging out from under the pillow.

Come on, Cleo. Let's play. Your voice rings so loud in my head, it's like you're standing right behind me.

If you're not on holiday, then where are you? That question again. And who did you meet last Friday night? Who was pretending to be me?

My heart thuds in my chest, a bass drum in my ears. I don't breathe as I pull your laptop towards me and open the lid. I remember the password – Cloudydaze21. It's etched in my mind, right beside my childhood telephone number and the pin for my bank card.

I type it in and the screen unlocks, showing the same background photo you've always had. Us, grinning at the camera, looking just on the right side of drunk. But it's not the photo that makes me gasp, that makes my skin crawl; it's the web page that's open. It's that swirly, neon-blue writing that I used to think was so inviting.

Have fun. Make friends. Fall in love. The safe place to meet new people!

I slam the laptop shut and slide to the floor, hugging

my knees to my body as wave after wave of fear crushes against me.

Simon was right. You were playing again.

Why, Rach?

I close my eyes and try to find the answer. I try to remember what it felt like at first, the lure it held. But all I feel is dread.

We were so wrong about CamChat. It wasn't safe. It was a dark, dangerous place, but by the time we realized that, we were in too deep.

My stomach turns, empty and yet still threatening to heave. I rush to the sink and cup cold water into my hands, throwing it at my face and slurping it back.

Panic scratches through my veins like the claws of a hundred scurrying rats. There is not a single part of me that wants to open the laptop again, but I know I have to. Because that's the other thing we didn't know back then – CamChat isn't random.

It isn't millions of people around the world in a big pot, all with the same chance of being paired together. Sure, those bloody filters we used narrowed down the pool of possible people we would speak to, but there's a glitch in the algorithm too. A horrifying, stupid glitch that almost got us killed. The longer you talk to someone for, the more likely it is that you'll be matched to their chat again.

So if I want to know what game you were playing, if I want to know who you were playing with, I have to play too.

Chapter 19

Rachel

Five years earlier

The woman ahead of them in the supermarket is walking at a snail's pace, her eyes roaming every single item on every frickin' shelf. And she's right in the middle of the bloody aisle too, so they can't scooch by. Moron!

'She doesn't even have a list,' Rachel hisses from the corner of her mouth.

'What?' Cleo looks up from her phone. 'Who?'

'Never mind.' She grits her teeth and tries to let it go. It's not like they have anything to rush home to. 'What are you looking at?' Rachel leans over and catches a glimpse of a job site. Her insides sink. She turned off the alerts last week, couldn't bear the ping of hope from her mobile any more; the zing of possibility that sound shoots through her that maybe, just maybe, things will be different, better, amazing even. And the heavy weight of disappointment when it's another advert for a make-up counter role or some pyramid scheme selling beauty products that promises to make her a millionaire.

Rachel knows Cleo will coax her into turning the alerts on again at some point, but right now she needs a break from the roller coaster.

'Have you seen today's alert?' Cleo asks.

'Don't tell me, it's another fantastic opportunity to work at the forefront of customer care at one of the nation's leading department stores. Seriously, Cleo, scrolling job sites is no way to spend a Monday night. Come on, let's grab what we need and go.'

Cleo touches Rachel's arm and when she looks at her there's something flashing in Cleo's eyes. Hope. That bastard hope again!

'What's going on?' Rachel half sing-songs the question. 'I've not seen you look this excited since we won those tickets on eBay for Cirque du Soleil.'

'This is better than that. Just read this.' She hands the phone to Rachel and they weave the trolley over to the side and stop. A man with a basket tuts before reaching over Rachel's shoulder for a bag of pasta, wafting his stinky armpit in her face.

'If this is another sandwich-making role, then I'm giving up. Seriously,' Rachel huffs, but at the same time her eyes are scanning the words on the screen and she's trying to take them in and wondering if this is some kind of joke. Cleo's right: this is better than theatre tickets. It isn't making sandwiches or selling make-up, it's ... the dream. 'Junior make-up artist for *EastEnders*,' she half squeals. 'Oh my God. *EastEnders*!'

It's her shot. It's everything she's ever wanted.

A weird, shaky relief threads through Rachel's body. She laughs, a puffing exhalation.

At last!

Cleo leans in and they hug each other, laughing, giddy and stupid. Anyone looking at them would think they'd won the lottery; they'd think they were nuts for being this excited over one job advert. But this isn't any job, it's Rachel's dream job, and it's the first one that's come up in so long.

'You have to get this job.' Cleo squeezes Rachel tight before letting go again and jumping up and down. 'It's perfect for you.'

Rachel grins so hard her face aches. Cleo is right. 'What about you? Aren't you going to apply?' She doesn't even realize she's holding her breath until Cleo shakes her head and Rachel almost laughs again with relief.

'You know I want special effects,' Cleo says. 'This is your dream job, not mine. We'd be competing with each other.'

Yes is the first word that leaps into Rachel's thoughts, and yet she can still see the look on Cleo's face when she was reading the advert, that excitement. Rachel knows she can't hold her friend back. She won't. She is not that person. 'But it could still be a stepping stone for you. It's TV. How often do jobs like this come up? It's what we've both been waiting for. You can't not apply.'

Cleo shrugs and makes a show of not caring. 'Seriously, this is your job. I can help you with your portfolio and application.'

A physical ache stretches across Rachel's chest. She loves that Cleo is this gallant, kind human being who would offer to step aside from her own dreams so Rachel can chase hers. She throws an arm around Cleo's shoulder and drags her in for another tight hug.

'Don't be an idiot,' Rachel tells her. 'We both have to apply. If I don't get it, then I want it to be you who does.'

A part of Rachel hopes Cleo will say no again, but the moment the smile stretches across her face, Rachel knows she's done the right thing. Rachel just has to make sure it's her who gets the job, not Cleo. She won't let anything stand in her way.

'OK, then,' Cleo grins, stepping across the aisle to the pasta sauces. 'We'll both apply. Now, which one?' she asks, holding up two jars.

Rachel's gaze moves from one to the other. She feels slightly queasy at the thought of another night of pasta.

She shrugs. 'Either.'

Cleo throws one in the trolley and places the other on the shelf.

'Anyway, where were you yesterday?' Rachel asks, pushing the trolley to the next aisle. 'I got back from work and you were out.'

'I was . . . just catching up with Lisa and Katie. They say hi.'

A part of Rachel wants to ask why Cleo hadn't even bothered asking if she wanted to come, but she keeps it in because the truth is, Rachel wouldn't have gone. It's been nice having some time alone. She's been able to spend more time on CamChat.

'Mandy was off sick today,' Rachel says then, keeping her voice neutral, but she watches Cleo's mouth form an O.

'You don't think anything happened to her on Friday night after you gave her address out to that man, do you?'

'Nah. She's probably got a cold or something.' They

keep walking, but there's a weird feeling hanging between them. Rachel wonders if Cleo is thinking how Mandy never takes a sick day.

It's not until the bread aisle that Cleo mentions the make-up job again. 'Are you sure you don't mind me applying?' she asks, dropping a loaf of crappy white bread into the trolley.

'Cleo, if you don't apply for this job, then I'm going to tell Mandy that you're interested in a fast-track to store management.'

'You wouldn't,' she cries, reaching out to swipe Rachel's arm.

'I absolutely would. Just think of all those extra meetings she'll want you to have. She'll make you her little bitch.'

'All right, all right. I'll apply too.'

'Oh my God,' Rachel says suddenly, remembering the thing she needed to tell Cleo. Her hand grips Cleo's arm. 'I totally forgot to tell you – Simon has a girlfriend.'

'What?' Cleo's eyes grow wide and Rachel grins.

'I heard him with someone the other night. I wonder who it is? I guess that's why he's not shown any interest in us lately.' Rachel laughs but it feels hollow. Right from the start they said Simon was off-limits, but that was before Rachel realized how much she liked him. Properly liked him. And now he's met someone and it's too late. Fuck!

'Probably,' Cleo says, turning to grab a pack of crumpets from the shelf. 'Let's work on our portfolios for the applications after work this week.'

'What about CamChat?'

Cleo frowns. 'This is more important. It's real life. I've enjoyed CamChat as much as you have, but . . . don't you think it's taking over a bit?'

'What do you mean?' Rachel swallows, wishing she didn't have to hear the answer. She knows what Cleo is going to say and she's wrong. It's not taking over. And if she really enjoyed it as much as Rachel did, she wouldn't be suggesting they stop.

'Like . . . the other week. You didn't come to Lisa and Katie's housewarming party—'

'I had a headache. Besides, they were always your friends more than mine. I found them a bit annoying most of the time, and they were only nice to me when you were around. Anyway, you seemed to have a good time without me. I didn't even hear you come home.' Rachel's tone is petty and she hates herself for it.

'It's not just that it's taking over, it's . . . what we did to those boys, and then seeing Alex and Denise again really freaked me out. They were really mad at us. We made out that we were being beaten up, Rach,' she says, her voice barely a whisper. 'Then giving out Mandy's address. We crossed a line. These are normal people we're messing with, nice people, and we . . . we're trolls,' Cleo hisses, grabbing a box of washing powder.

'Trolls?' Rachel laughs. 'That's a bit strong, don't you think?'

'And I'm getting a bit fed up with all the penises.'

'We'll skip quicker. Please, just one more go. If we don't both have fun this Friday, then we'll stop.' *And go back to our empty lives*, Rachel adds in her head. The disappointment leaves a bitter taste in her mouth. There's no way she's going to stop. There's time to work on the job application *and* play on CamChat. Rachel is sure of it.

'Fine. But we'll work on our applications and port-folios too.'

'Relax. The deadline isn't for two weeks.'

'Two weeks when we've both got weekend shifts and that charity catwalk show every evening next week.'

'Ergh!' Rachel groans, her good mood deflating. 'I wish I hadn't said yes to that. It's not even paid.'

'It's good experience, though. We need to show we're still putting ourselves out there.'

'I know.' Her reply is snappish, tainted with something sour that hangs between them for a second. Rachel feels Cleo's eyes on her, trying to understand why she's suddenly grumpy. Rachel can't tell her that every time she talks about their future, she feels this weight dragging her down. Every time Cleo gets excited about a wedding or a photo shoot or that corporate video they did last month in that stuffy office, it reminds Rachel that she doesn't feel that enthusiasm any more. If she doesn't get this job, Rachel doesn't know what she'll do.

'Are you—' Cleo starts.

'Yeah, fine. My feet are killing me. Let's get what we need and go.'

'Shall we get those shitty own-brand pizzas for dinner? I'm not sure I can face pasta tonight.'

'The ones that taste like cardboard?' Rachel smiles.

'You mean the ones that remind us of childhood parties,' Cleo retorts, and they laugh.

'Have we got enough for a bottle of wine?' Rachel turns to her, eyes pleading. It's Rachel's money too. If she wants to buy a bottle of wine she can, but they've always split everything down the middle and Cleo is so much better at managing money than Rachel is. Probably because Cleo is so much better at resisting the ASOS sale.

'Go on, then. Anything to beat the Monday blues. But it has to be under a fiver.'

Rachel slides her arm through Cleo's and weaves them towards the wine aisle.

Chapter 20

Cleo

Now

A coldness sweeps through me as the CamChat window opens.

Those blue words dance across the screen. *Have fun. Make friends. Fall in love. The safe place to meet new people!*

Safe? How did we ever believe that?

Let's play. I hear that cackling, raucous laugh of yours in my head and wish I could stop it. I wish I could rewind these last days, months, years, and stop you.

There are no tabs, no drop-down menus, nowhere asking for login details. It's just the neon-blue writing, the black screen and that one button beckoning me into a dark world. *Chat.*

My hand shakes as I click and a moment later a screen pops up – my own face, my own hollow eyes staring back at me. I push the laptop away, snatch a photo of you and me from the wall and move to sit on the bed.

An instant later my image shrinks into the corner, and a woman appears on the screen. She's wearing a black silk dressing gown, one shoulder bare, and it's obvious why she's on CamChat. I expect her to skip forwards, but instead she gives me a seductive smile.

'Hey, I'm Dolly.'

I almost laugh at her absurd choice of fake name and scramble for one myself, but I don't have it in me to lie any more. 'Cleo,' I reply. 'Do you recognize this person? She's on CamChat a lot, I think.' I hold up the photo. It's a selfie of us together in the park by the tube station. Faces smiling, sunglasses pushed on to the tops of our heads.

'Sorry. This is my first time on here.'

Yeah, right.

The chat disappears and I realize Dolly has ditched me. The next chat that appears is a couple having noisy sex.

Skip.

Then a man masturbating. Then another man naked on a bed.

Bloody hell. Was it always like this?

The next chat is a man in a wheelchair with bright-ginger hair. His head is leaning slightly to one side and there's a strap across his forehead.

'Hi, I'm Cleo.'

The man's face doesn't move, but a moment later an electronic voice says, 'Hi, I'm Bob. Nice to meet you, Cleo. Where are you from?'

'London. You?'

'Toronto. So, what brings you to CamChat, Cleo?'

'My friend is missing. She used CamChat and I'm on her laptop. I thought I might be able to find someone who'd spoken to her.'

119

'You know it's not random, then?'

I nod.

'They updated the website a year ago. They're saying it's completely random now but I still see the same faces a lot. Obviously, the filters narrow it down even further. Which ones was she using?'

I glance at the sidebar. 'Friendship, Fun, and Games.' The last one causes a lump to cut into my throat. Why would you put that?

'I've got Friendship and Fun too. Not Games, though. That's a strange one. Have you got a photo of your friend?'

I hold it up. 'It's an old photo.'

'Roxy. I know her. She's got a scar on her face.'

'Yes,' I half shout. The relief of finding someone who knows you is almost enough to squash the pummelling guilt at the mention of your scar. Almost.

'We spoke a few weeks ago.'

I lean closer to the screen. 'What did you talk about?'

There's a pause, and I will him to hurry up.

'She was asking me about other people I've talked to on CamChat. She seemed scared. She said she thought—'

Something changes on the screen. Bob's image disappears and my own returns along with a turning roulette wheel.

What the hell? I check the Wi-Fi signal and click and click again on 'chat', but Bob is gone.

Nothing happens for a minute. Then two. Finally, a new chat loads, showing an almost empty room. There's only one piece of furniture – a single dining-room chair with a woman sitting on it. Her head is bent low, dark hair covering her face.

My heart freezes. A scream lodges in my throat.

There's a black rope binding the woman's ankles to the chair legs. Her arms are secured behind her back. I cry out and she lifts her head, showing her face – *your* face.

Your eyes are saucer-wide and wet with tears. Your face is dirty with smudged eye make-up, but I still see the red line of the scar leading down to a strip of silver duct tape covering your mouth.

No, no, no. This can't be happening.

'Rach?' Your name is strangled. The fear rises up and up, half choking me.

My hands grip the screen as though I can claw my way in, as though I can grab you and pull you away.

You make a noise and I think you're trying to tell me something, but it's muffled, incoherent.

'Where are you?'

You shift forward in the chair, jogging yourself up and down, inching closer to the camera. I lean in too, the tears falling down my cheeks in time with yours.

'Who's doing this?' I sob. 'Where are you?'

Then you stop dead. Your eyes leave mine and fix on something out of shot. Terror contorts your features and even though I can't see behind the camera, I know someone is there. I hold my breath and wait for them to come into view.

Chapter 21

Rachel

Now

'Cleo.' Tears brim in Rachel's eyes and she blinks as fast as she can, pushing them away, letting them fall so she can stare at Cleo's face on the screen. Rachel can't believe it's her. Cleo looks so different – a shrunken, skeletal version of herself, and that hair – but Rachel would know her anywhere. She can't believe she's come back after all the stupid things Rachel said to her in the end.

'Cleo,' Rachel says again and again, but every time it comes out 'Um-mm,' beneath the tape.

Rachel has so much she wants to say. She's freaking out. Despite the chair, the ropes, this room, everything that's happening right now, a giddiness skips through her. She wants so badly to hug Cleo. She wants to tell her how sorry she is for how they left things.

'Where are you?' Cleo's face fills the screen, eyes wide and hollow, voice urgent.

Rachel rocks in the chair, trying to get closer. The

122

legs bang against the floor, the sound echoing in the emptiness. It's pointless. Cleo won't be able to understand her better, but Rachel wants her to see she's trying.

And then the door opens and he's there. Rachel's skin crawls at the sight of him – tiny electrical needles running up and down and up her body. He closes the lid of the laptop and turns towards her.

'How was it – seeing her?' he asks, as though Rachel can reply.

He bends down to untie her feet and she catches the scent of him. It turns her stomach and makes her wonder what will happen next. She hates the bathroom but right now she'd give anything for him to take her back to it. Anything to avoid that mattress.

He clears his throat and his eyes fix on her like he's trying to read her. 'This is what you wanted, remember?' he says, smiling again.

There's a roaring sensation in Rachel's ears and she has an overwhelming desire to throw her head down and crack his skull. She doesn't. She'd probably do more damage to herself than to him.

'You started this,' he continues, his tone almost apologetic as he unties her arms and pulls her up.

He keeps talking, droning on about Cleo and her and him like they're all in some kind of messed-up relationship. Rachel lets him talk. She even nods when he looks at her. She thinks he likes her better with the tape on her mouth.

All the while, Rachel is thinking of Cleo. She's in London. A part of Rachel can't process it. Memories rush from every direction. Bittersweet in a way that pulls at her chest. It all seemed so messy and complicated when Cleo left. It's taken a long time for Rachel to realize it wasn't complicated at all. She dragged them into a whole heap of shit. Then she pushed Cleo away and Cleo left.

What does Cleo think is happening right now? Does she think she's fighting back, trying to escape? Rachel wishes she could tell Cleo that she can't fight. There's an ingrained crippling memory that keeps her in check. She no longer has the fight-or-flight instinct. Just the thought of either, and the back of her head starts to hurt – sharp, digging pains. Rachel remembers that yank of her hair so vividly. She barely runs a brush through it now. Even the smallest tangle, the tiniest tug, and it takes her back.

He leads Rachel from the room and up a staircase. She's shaking her head because she knows what's coming. Tears threaten, but Rachel doesn't want him to see her cry. She wants him to know she's strong, that whatever happens, she is a survivor.

He guides her back to the bathroom and Rachel finds herself alone again, shivering with emotions. She peels the tape away from her mouth and lets the tears fall.

She can't believe Cleo is in London.

Then the reality sinks in, lying heavy on her chest. Cleo is in London. She's part of this now.

Chapter 22

Cleo

Now

Your eyes flick back to mine and for a moment it's like you're trying to tell me something, but then the chat disappears, replaced once more with the loading roulette wheel.

The reality of what I've seen rings in my ears as loud as my attack alarm and I fumble in my pocket for my phone and dial 999.

The operator takes an age to understand. I don't blame her. My words are garbled, a slew of panic and urgency.

She tries to tell me it's a hoax and that she'll report it to the cybercrime unit. Only when I slow down and try again; when I explain that it's not a hoax, not some random woman playing a game, but you; when I say that you're a missing person and I'm your best friend and what I saw was live, does her response change.

'And you're sure it was Rachel Winslow, reported missing on Monday the eleventh of January?'

'Yes.' Your face flashes in my head. The guilt is sharp – the point of a knife slicing through me. How can it be anyone else?

'I'm sending officers to your address to take a statement. It may take some time. It's a busy night. Please don't leave the house.'

I hang up and turn back to the screen to find three girls, eleven or twelve in age, staring back at me. They're wearing pyjamas and giggling behind their hands. I can see a bed and an inflated mattress in the background.

'Who were you talking to?' one of them asks after a nudge from her friend.

'The police. CamChat is really dangerous. You shouldn't be on here.'

'We're old enough to know what we're doing,' another one says, but I see the hesitation lurking in their eyes.

'Please shut this down and go to bed. Tell each other scary stories or play Truth or Dare or something, but don't be on here.'

They roll their eyes before their screen disappears. I sit back, dropping my head into my hands, replaying the last ten minutes over and over. And then I'm crying, big heaving sobs.

I'm so scared, Rach. For you, for me, for what will happen.

My throat constricts. A tremor starts and suddenly I'm stuck, paralysed with an unstoppable terror. Images of you on the screen mix with the memories of the past – that night. The room spins and spins around me, and then everything goes black.

*

The shuddering bang of the front door jolts me awake. My eyelids are sticky, glued shut by the layers of mascara I've not removed.

I look around the room and take in the photos, the sink, the floral pattern on the bedspread. There's a moment that drags on from one second to the next when I'm twenty-four and you've just popped to the toilet or to grab us another bottle of wine. Any moment now you're going to burst into the room.

The thought is shattered by the voices of men in the hall. Loud and authoritative, sending a bolt of something through my body. Not fear, but alertness – a sense I have to act.

My eyes fall to your laptop open beside me on the bed and that's when I see the face staring back at me. I scream, more fox yip than human, as a man with long, greasy grey hair looks out. His lips stretch apart into a wide grimace and I see a tooth missing at the front.

'Hello—'

I slam down the laptop lid. The reality hits me like a shove. I saw you on CamChat. Gagged. Terrified. Tied to a fucking chair. I had a panic attack. I must have passed out. I shake my head, wishing I could think straight.

Something niggles at the edges of my mind. Something about that man just now, but my Humpty Dumpty thoughts won't make sense.

From outside your door, the stairs creak. Someone is knocking on a door above me.

'She's not there,' I hear Simon call out.

It's the police, I realize.

I look at the clock and see it's midnight. Hours have

passed since I saw you and dialled 999. Are you even still alive?

A slow, pulsing throb hits my temples as I step across the room and open your door. Three faces turn to stare. Simon, wearing blue tartan pyjama bottoms and a loose T-shirt, and two male officers in stiff black uniforms and heavy-duty vests.

'Cleo Thomas?' the first officer asks. He has a shaved head and a Harry Potter-like scar on his forehead.

I nod.

'I'm PC Franklin and this is PC York,' he says, motioning to the man beside him. The second officer is short but is trying to hold himself tall, shoulders back, chin tilted up. He has a ready-for-anything glint to his eye, like he'd rather be breaking up a bar brawl than standing here with me.

'Is there somewhere we could sit down?' PC Franklin asks, peering past me and into your bedroom.

I stare between the faces, willing the layer of groggy fuzz to lift from my mind. They're waiting for me to say something, but I can't form the words.

'We can use my living room,' Simon says, and then we're moving, Simon leading the way, me following at the back, exhausted, numb.

There's something surreal about stepping over the threshold to Simon's part of the house after all this time. It's nicer than I remember. Even in my current state I can see it's not like the rest of the house. The walls are freshly painted and the dingy beige carpet has been replaced with dark-wood floors. It's small – only three rooms. A kitchen-living area, a bedroom and a bathroom.

Simon motions us towards two plump brown

leather sofas before heading to the kitchen. He returns a moment later, pressing a glass of water into my hands. I gulp it back greedily, but still I don't speak.

'Miss Thomas,' PC Franklin begins. 'Can you talk us through what happened this evening, please?'

'I . . . saw my friend on CamChat. It's this website where people go to talk to strangers. It's supposed to be random, but it's not. There's a glitch where you get matched to the same people you've talked to before. She's a missing person – my friend, I mean. Rachel. And I saw her tied . . . to a chair . . . scared. She was scared, I mean.' My words stick in my mouth. I'm shaking again, not making sense.

'Take your time,' the second officer says. I've forgotten his name already.

I start again and try to explain. I talk for ages, jumping from one thing to another, backtracking, trailing off.

'So,' PC Franklin says when I lose my train of thought for the fifth time. 'You went into your friend's room and opened this website . . . CamChat, and saw Miss Winslow?'

'Yes.'

'And what time was it that you saw your friend?'

'Err.' I rub at my forehead, wishing my head would stop pounding. 'About nine thirty. It was just before I called you.' I unlock my phone and see the last call I made was at eight thirty-seven p.m. 'Oh. More like eight thirty.'

PC Franklin sits forward in his seat. 'Miss Thomas, I'm sorry if this is an uncomfortable question, but have you taken any substances tonight?'

'Substances?' I ask, before my thoughts catch up and I realize what he's asking.

'Any alcohol or drugs?' the second officer clarifies when I'm already shaking my head.

'I have panic attacks. I had one before you arrived. It's shaken me.'

'I see,' PC Franklin says, although I'm quite sure he doesn't. 'And I understand you visited the police station earlier today?'

I nod.

'And you were informed Miss Winslow's case is low risk, I believe.'

'Yes.'

'Would it be fair to say that this information troubled you? That you've been worried about your friend?'

'Yes. What are you getting at?'

'When you were informed that Miss Winslow's case is low risk, you told my colleague that you'd find some evidence to prove she is missing so that her case would be taken more seriously.'

'I didn't mean . . .'

'I just want to make absolutely sure that you are certain about what you saw and to remind you that lying to the police is a criminal offence.'

'Is it possible,' Simon cuts in, 'that in your panicked state you might have imagined it or dreamt it?' I can see he's trying to give me a way to backtrack.

They don't believe me. The realization sucks away the last dregs of hope. 'No.' I shake my head. The movement causes pain to shoot across my temples. 'Absolutely not. I know what I saw.'

We go through it all again from start to finish. Then I show them your room and the laptop. They even click on CamChat and wait for a chat to load. It's another naked man, and PC Franklin closes the laptop quickly before leading us all back to Simon's living room, where I sink on to the sofa, wishing more than anything that I was back on the *Enchantress*.

'Thank you for your time, Miss Thomas,' PC Franklin says. 'We'll log your statement and pass the information on to our superiors.'

They're halfway across the room before I catch on to what is happening. They're leaving.

'That's it? That's all you can do?'

I expect a warning look but what I get is worse. Pity.

'We will be investigating. You can contact me at the station if you think of anything else from tonight.'

Simon shows them out and as I hear the mumbles of their voices in the hall and the thud of the door shutting, I lean my head back against the sofa cushions and let the tears fall.

'Cleo?' Simon's voice is close. I open my eyes and find him standing over me. 'You OK?'

'No. They didn't believe me, did they?'

'Can you blame them? You're a mess.'

'Thanks.' I snap my reply.

'Did you really tell a police officer earlier that you'd find some evidence to show them Rachel is missing?'

'I didn't mean that I was going to make it up.'

He pulls a face. 'I'm not sure what you expect me to say. It sort of sounds like that's exactly what you meant.'

'I expect you to tell me what I should do now. Earlier today you wanted me to stay, didn't you? You wanted me to find Rachel. Well, guess what? I found her. She's tied to a chair and being held somewhere by some sicko. So now what?'

Simon rubs his hands over his face and when he

takes them away I notice again how tired he looks. 'I don't know.'

'Me neither.'

I pull myself up and leave without another word.

The conversation with PC Franklin replays in my head as I slide into bed, the cool of the covers soothing my throbbing temples. The officers didn't believe me. And the worst thing is, when I close my eyes and try to picture what I saw, the memory is dreamlike, fuzzy, and I'm not sure I believe me any more either.

The stupid bitch was going to leave.
After everything I've done to get the game going,
and she was going to jump on a plane and
go back to her pathetic little no-life.

There's no way I'd get her back again. She was
spoiling everything. All my work.

I don't like having my hand forced, but I had
to give her a clue. A little arrow in the maze,
if you like. And what a clue it was.

I can't have her run away now.
She's only just started to play.

Chapter 23

Cleo

Five years earlier

'And you're really make-up artists? That's so crazy. You must meet a ton of famous people.' The guy on the screen is OK-looking. Dark-blond hair, a bit too much gel. A crisp white shirt rolled up at the sleeves. Toned arms. A tan. He's got a nice smile and hasn't tried to show us his dick in the first five minutes of talking to him.

His American accent bounces with an enthusiasm that makes me want to roll my eyes and skip ahead, but Rachel is laughing at everything he says and I know we're not skipping. We're not even playing the game we planned – two backpackers with a crazy story about hiding from a weirdo in Sydney. But from the moment CamChat threw the first chat at us and this guy appeared, Rachel has been transfixed.

'Who's the most famous person you've met?' he asks.

Rach laughs. 'Unless you've heard of Shane Richie,

then I think you're going to be disappointed. But Cleo has done Tom Hardy's face twice.'

I stiffen at the use of my name, throwing Rachel a warning look. She raises one eyebrow in a 'what does it matter?' reply.

'Really? What's he like?'

It takes a moment to realize the question is directed at me. 'Focused,' I reply. 'He didn't say a word the whole time.'

'Now that's cool. I once bumped into Tom Hanks's wife in a juice bar in LA, but that's my only claim to fame.'

'What's your name, cowboy?' Rachel asks.

He laughs. 'Cowboy?'

'Your accent. You sound like you belong in an old western.'

'I like that. Now I feel like I should have a name like Clint, but I'm Luke. Luke Richards.'

'Rachel,' she grins back. 'And this is Cleo.'

He leans forwards, adjusting the camera angle, and I spot a hotel room in the background. Lavish and expensive and a million miles from the Travelodge-style places I've stayed in.

'Well, hi there, Cleo and Rachel.' He drags out Rachel's name for longer than he needs to.

'Hi,' Rach simpers back.

'Good to meet you. Really good. To be honest, it's nice to see some actual faces. The last two chats have been of some pretty weird genitalia.'

We laugh at that before I ask, 'What brings you to CamChat?'

'The same as most people, I guess. Loneliness. I'm a pretty chatty kind of guy, as you can probably tell already, but I'm away on business most of the time.

135

Stuck in these godawful hotel rooms.' He pronounces God 'Gaawwd', making Rachel laugh again. I watch her from the corner of my eye. It's the first time I've seen her so happy in ages. Her smile is easy and her eyes are dancing. 'It's hard to make friends and I miss human interaction. A pal of mine suggested I try Cam-Chat, and so here I am. To be honest, if you ladies hadn't come along when you did, I'd probably have given up already.'

'We know the feeling,' Rach says. 'And for the record, that hotel room looks far from awful.'

'Try living in it day after day, moving cities every week. You wouldn't believe how many hotels can't even make a decent cup of coffee.'

'What do you do?' I ask.

'I work in oil. It's pretty boring, but it pays the bills and I get to travel a lot. Sometimes I like it, but a lot of the time I'd prefer to be home. My sister has just had another baby and I wish I could be there more. Fun Uncle Luke.'

'Where is home?' Rach runs a hand through her hair, tugging down her top a little.

'San Francisco. I'm in Montana right now.'

'What time is it there?' I don't mean for the question to sound abrasive, but it's only as I ask that I start to wonder if he's telling us the truth. That's the problem with our game. I can't tell who's being honest any more.

'Two p.m.,' Luke replies without missing a beat. 'I'm waiting for my next meeting.'

'What's the weather like?' I press.

'Pretty damn cold.'

Rach jabs an elbow into my side and I stop my

questions. Not everyone is a liar, I guess. Not everyone is like us.

We talk a while more. Luke tells us about the weird things he's found in hotel rooms – a blow-up sex doll in the wardrobe, a can of kidney beans under the bed. He has this way of waving his hands in the air, exaggerating everything, voice booming, in a way that I find annoying but seems to crack Rachel up.

'We should go,' I jump in when Luke finishes telling us about a guy he met in New York who carried a stuffed dog everywhere he went. 'We said we'd do that project.' Rach gives me a blank stare then scowls as though she's just remembered.

'The deadline is a week away. There's not exactly much to update. I doubt they'll care about our wedding photos and some poor-quality shots we've taken of each other.' All this is delivered in a hissed whisper from the side of her mouth.

'Hey, no worries,' Luke calls out. 'I gotta go too. I'm going to be late for my meeting.' Luke leans forwards and I get the feeling he's looking straight at Rachel. 'It's been divine meeting you. Until next time.'

'Goodbye, cowboy,' Rachel says, and just like that, he's gone.

I watch Rachel's expression change from happy to something close to crushed as Luke's face disappears and she shuts the laptop.

'What was that all about?' I ask.

'What?'

'Giving him our real names, for a start, and what happened to our backpacking story?'

'I couldn't be bothered with it tonight. Luke seemed like a normal guy. Is that a big deal?'

'No,' I reply, although it feels like it is. 'But next time, let me know.'

'You're right. Sorry. He was great, though, wasn't he?'

'Who?' I ask.

'Luke.'

'Oh.' I shrug. 'He seemed OK. What does it matter, anyway? It's not like we'll see him again. Come on, let's do our portfolios.'

She sighs. 'You make a start. I think I'm going to get an early night.'

'Really?'

'Yeah. I'll do some tomorrow morning.'

'OK.' I slide from the bed, taking my wine glass with me. At the door, I hesitate. 'Are you all right?' It's the question I ask every day now, and the answer is always the same, so why do I keep asking? 'You seem . . . off tonight?'

She gives a huff of a laugh. 'Thanks,' she says, throwing a pillow at me. I dodge it and close the door, feeling bad for leaving Rachel. She's right, we do have a week to submit our applications for the make-up artist position, but I want to do it now before Simon gets home from his trip to Jersey so I can spend time with him.

I don't know what's going on between us. I keep telling myself it's nothing, but then my stomach somersaults when he texts and I long to see him when he's away.

I'm desperate to tell Rachel, but something keeps stopping me. It's not just that I've broken our pact; it's how down she seems right now. Tonight was the first time I've seen her happy in ages. If she's still in a good mood tomorrow, then I'll tell her, I promise myself.

It's much later, when I'm creeping silently down to Simon's room, that I pass Rachel's door and hear her talking to someone. It's CamChat. I can tell by her voice. The realization that Rach is on there again causes an unease to prickle my skin, but then Simon opens his door, looking rumpled from travelling and sexy as hell, and I push the thought to the back of my mind.

Chapter 24

Cleo

Now

It's late morning before hunger drives me from sleep. I feel hollow, broken, a right mess. Remember those last weeks before I left London, Rach? When you came out of hospital and didn't stop crying. You were devastated and angry, but you weren't terrified like I was. You didn't see monsters around every corner.

We were living through the same storm, but we were on different boats. I couldn't reach you.

Yeah, your boat sailed all the way to the Caribbean.

I had to leave. You must see that. I couldn't face what had happened, what I'd done.

It wasn't your fault.

I close my eyes and cling to the insistence in your voice, the voice I've created for you in my head. What happened to us wasn't my fault, but everything afterwards . . . I can't even think about it.

Do you remember when DS Anik Saha visited us both? You'd been home from the hospital about a week by then and you were only leaving your room to use the bathroom.

We sat together on the edge of your bed, my hand gripped in yours.

He told us he was giving up.

He told us there was no more evidence to pursue. Too many inconsistencies.

Same thing.

Oh, come on, Rach. What was he supposed to do? No way to trace anyone on CamChat, no CCTV, no match on DNA. We couldn't even agree on the colour of his car, let alone tell him the make or model. Even the sketches they produced from our descriptions of him looked different.

'Predators like this do not just stop. He will strike again, and when he does, he'll make a mistake and we'll catch him.' Anik's words were supposed to offer comfort, I think, but all you felt was angry, screaming at him to get out. All I felt was numbing despair. There was nothing the police could do but wait for this sicko to attack again, and it was my fault.

The memory fades like the weak strips of daylight pushing in through the gaps in my curtains.

I can imagine you talking to me all I want. I can imagine you in your ground-floor flat with your little garden. I can even imagine you lying on a beach somewhere, happy. But that's the version of you in my head. The real you is out there somewhere, petrified and alone.

There's an inch of water left in my glass on the nightstand and I drink it back. It sloshes in my empty stomach, leaving me nauseous. I need to eat.

But an idea is taking hold and it's not breakfast I want to think about now, it's Anik Saha.

He will help. He will listen. I know he will.

I sit up in bed and grab my phone. There's a missed call from Beth and then a message asking me what's going on. I reply quickly, a hurried

Nothing to update. I'll call you later.

I know I should tell Beth that I've seen you. She has a right to know, and yet how can I? How can I put that worry and fear on her when I have so little else to go on? How can I expect her to believe me when the police don't? She's already so worried about you, on top of caring for your mum. I need to wait until I have more answers. For now, it's better Beth stays in the dark.

Anik's number is right there, nestled between an Alison I don't remember and Beth. My fingers hover over the call button, my gaze pulling towards my packed bag.

I press 'call' and hold the phone to my ear. Anik answers on the first ring.

'Hello?' The one word is a groggy croak.

'DS Saha?'

'It's DI now, but yes.'

'It's Cleo Thomas. You might not remember me, but—'

'Of course I remember,' he says, sounding more awake. 'What's going on? Are you OK?'

An image flashes in my head. You. That chair. That terror. That shadow behind the camera. Tears prick at my eyes. 'It's Rachel. It's happened again.' The words are a whisper as the emotion strangles my throat.

'Tell me everything.'

And so I do.

'Are you at the house in Bethnal Green now?' he asks when I'm done.

'Yes.'

'And you called the police last night?'

'Yes. They didn't exactly believe me. I . . . I was a bit of a state. They didn't understand the history and I don't know what to do now. I need help.'

'I can help you,' he replies without a second of hesitation.

The relief is like a deep breath of air after being underwater for that moment too long.

'Thank you.'

'And you're sure it was Rachel you saw?'

That question again. Why do people keep asking me that? 'One hundred per cent.' I close my eyes and your face is there again. Those haunting dark eyes. That fear. 'I saw her face.'

'Right. Of course,' he says and I know he's thinking of your scar.

'What do I do now?'

He makes a noise, blowing air through his lips. It's not quite a whistle, but close. 'Are you free today?'

'Yes.' The one word rings with desperation.

'Let's meet this afternoon. One p.m. outside Bethnal Green tube? We can talk more then.'

'OK. Thank you.'

We say goodbye and then I lie in bed for a moment, thinking about seeing Anik after all this time. Will I still feel that buzz between us? Was it even there to start with? I wasn't exactly in the best place when we met.

A burst of energy unleashes from somewhere inside me. I climb out of bed and head to the bathroom to get ready.

Last night I couldn't see how I could find you, but now it's right here in front of me. Anik Saha.

Anik will help. I might owe you, Rach, but he owes both of us.

Chapter 25

Cleo

Now

Weak winter sun hits my face as I stride to the tube station. The sky over my head is the brightest of blues and if I tilt my head up, if I ignore the hum of stop-start traffic, the beep of the pedestrian crossing, and the man shouting into his phone, the smell of rotting vegetables from the nearby bins; if I just look up at that blue stretch above me, then I can believe it's early morning and I'm standing on the deck of the *Enchantress*, before the passengers stir, when it's just me and the cleaning crew.

Anik will help.

The thought continues to dance through my mind and when I turn on to Roman Road and spot DI Saha leaning against the black metal railings of the park, I feel almost giddy with relief.

It's been five years since I last saw him, but he's aged a decade at least. That fresh-faced detective who you never liked is now haggard, trodden in. It suits him.

144

There's grey at the edges of his hairline and the goatee is now a full beard. There's more edge to him too. The skin beneath his eyes is dark and his shoulders sag as he looks up and down the road. When his eyes reach mine, he raises a questioning eyebrow.

I lift my hand in a quick wave, a 'yes, it's me; yes, I know I look completely different' gesture, and he pushes off from the railings and steps towards me, that same walk that seems to start with his shoulders, then his body, and finally his legs.

Cocky.

I'd go for focused. All in.

'Hey,' we say at the same moment and there's an awkward shuffle where I'm not sure if I should shake his hand or if we should hug. In the end he reaches a hand out and squeezes my arm, and even though it's just a friendly touch, I feel that same something fluttering between us that I felt five years ago.

'It's so good to see you again, Cleo,' Anik says, his eyes on mine.

I nod, holding his gaze, and then, out of nowhere, it isn't the energy between us that I feel, it's the punch of everything in that afterwards time. The memories, the sudden clawing emotions break free inside me, burning and fierce. The pavement moves beneath my feet. I feel myself sway and Anik steadying me.

'Christ, Cleo, are you all right?'

I nod, the world tipping with the movement. 'Skipped breakfast.'

'And the rest,' he says, staring at me in a way that leaves me exposed.

'Come on. Let's get you some food.' Anik guides me down a cobbled side road to a gastropub – a skinny brick corner building with stained-glass windows and a chalkboard outside crammed with specials written in tiny white writing.

Inside, there's an open fireplace, charred orange logs burning in the grate. Beside it is a group of six men and women squeezed in on a sofa, playing a battered board game of some kind. Every few minutes there's an 'Ooooh', followed by raucous laughter.

The warmth of the fire, the welcoming murmur of people, of life, and the smell of roasting meats draw me in and I fall gratefully into a chair by the window. As Anik disappears to the bar, I realize I've been here before. A Rolodex of memories turns in my head until I find the one I'm looking for.

We were on our way to the big Sainsbury's in Bow to buy our weekly food essentials, remember? It was a Saturday lunchtime and we caught the smell of burgers and fried onions, pies and beer-battered fish and chips. Our feet slowed as we looked from the pub to each other.

I can't remember who suggested it.

Definitely me.

Sounds about right.

And the next thing, we were at a table with a bottle of wine and two huge burgers.

'I won't be able to eat for a week after this,' you said with one of the widest smiles I'd ever seen on you.

'Good,' I laughed. 'Because we don't have much left for food.'

We drank our wine and for those short hours we pretended we were those girls – Cassie and Roxy – with a bank balance topped up by Daddy every month, and it was perfect.

Remembering makes me miss you so much. That's the thing about the *Enchantress* – when I'm on board there is nothing else. I don't have to think about how much I miss you or how badly I messed everything up.

Anik appears at the table, drawing me back to the present as he slides a bottle of Coke towards me and sits opposite with a pint of bitter in his hand. There's a wooden spoon tucked under his arm with the number five snaking across the middle.

'I hope you're not a vegetarian,' he says.

I shake my head and sip at my drink, feeling the instant sugar high.

'Rachel's in trouble and I don't know what to do,' I start to say, but my words trail off when Anik shakes his head.

'I'm not going to talk about Rachel until you've eaten, OK? You practically fainted back there.'

He's exaggerating, but I let him make small talk as we wait for the food. Anik tells me about a failed engagement and his promotion that came with a move to the Metropolitan Police and Kentish Town Police Station. I tell him about life on the *Enchantress*.

Twenty minutes later, two mountainous plates of burger and chips are slid in front of us. My mouth waters and I take bite after bite. It's salty and delicious and exactly what I need.

'Thank you,' I say when my plate is empty, and I sit back in the chair, feeling more relaxed than I've felt in days.

'Glad it helped,' Anik smiles. 'You look better for it. Now, tell me everything you told me on the phone again. Don't leave anything out.'

I start in Southampton with the text from Beth. I tell him about someone texting you, pretending to be me. I tell him about you seeing Luke Richards on your way home, and about the police and how little they're doing, and end with the question that's been burning inside me for hours now: 'What kind of sicko would put her on CamChat like that?'

'A bad one,' Anik replies. 'Was last night the first time you've been on CamChat recently?'

'Yes, but it's exactly the same. I used the filters Rachel had up, and straight away I spoke to this guy who remembers her. It's supposed to be completely random; anyone paired with anyone, but we saw the same people a few times when we used to play, and after what happened, I Googled CamChat and it turns out there's this massive glitch with it and the more you speak to someone, the more chance there is of you seeing them again. It's why Rachel saw Luke more than once.'

'So me seeing Rachel tied up wasn't random, it was because whatever computer was being used to film her is one that she's spoken to before.'

'And you think it's Luke?' Anik asks.

'Who else would do this? Besides, Rachel told Beth she'd seen "the cowboy" following her, and she only ever used that name for Luke.'

We fall silent and I watch Anik's face. He frowns, lost in thought. I'd forgotten how easy he is to talk to, how being with him makes me feel safe.

He finishes his pint and looks as though he's going to say something, before he shakes his head.

'What?' I ask.

'Nothing. I was just thinking.'

'And?'

'CamChat is a dead end. The force tried to get them to release an IP address that could track Luke Richards. It took weeks just to get a reply out of them last time, which was useless anyway because CamChat doesn't store any records of its users. It's the perfect place to target vulnerable people.'

I open my mouth to say something but the pain is too great. Isn't that what we loved about CamChat? The anonymity? We didn't think we were vulnerable; we thought we were invincible.

'So what do I do?' I ask. 'It has to be Luke doing this. Who else would text Rachel pretending to be me? So if we know who it is, there must be something we can do.'

He reaches a hand across the table and places it over mine. 'You mustn't do anything.' His touch is warm and as his fingers brush mine, something stirs inside me – a feeling of being wanted, of wanting. It's been years since I've felt it, but it's there all the same. 'I'm here now. Let me help you.'

The memories of the past surface again, curdling in my thoughts. I bite the inside of my lip and fix my gaze on a pigeon outside the window pecking at a discarded bread roll, until the tears stop threatening to fall. 'But if I go back on CamChat, I might see Rachel again and I might be able to help her.'

'It'll be playing into the hands of whoever is behind this. They're playing a game and I don't want you to be part of it. I'm just glad you called me. I'll do some digging and we can meet up again in a day or two. Come on, let me walk you back.'

I'm about to protest, but then I notice the darkening sky and think of all the corners, the doorways, the nooks where the street lights don't shine, and I nod. With Anik beside me, my eyes don't dart around me, my hand doesn't clutch my alarm. I'm safe.

Only when I'm back in my room, in this damn house with its damp smells and crappy furniture, do I realize Anik is right – going on CamChat again is playing Luke's sick game. But what if playing the game is the only way to find you?

Chapter 26

Rachel

Five years earlier

On the screen in front of her, Luke is smiling his 'I see you' smile, hitting Rachel dead centre in the chest – a lightning bolt. The last hour has flown by and she's desperate for it not to end.

'Childhood teddy?' he asks.

Rachel smiles. 'A scruffy toy dog called Cloudy Daze that my sister threw in the paddling pool one day. It never recovered.'

'Favourite film?' he asks.

'Anything scary, but not too scary. I love *Jaws*.'

'A classic. Did you ever watch *Jaws 2*?'

'Dreadful.'

'Completely,' Luke laughs. 'Favourite drink?'

'Champagne, of course.' Rachel doesn't know if that's true but she likes the sound of it. She likes the light tone to her voice, the happiness dancing through her.

'Me too. Although I don't drink it much. There

hasn't been much to celebrate in the last few years. Well, not until now, anyway.' He looks up at her and it's like the screen between them disappears and it's just the two of them. 'You're truly something, Rachel. I've never met anyone like you. It's fate, right? For us to keep meeting like this?'

'It has to be,' she agrees with a wide smile that makes her cheeks ache. Fate and hours skipping hundreds of videos to find him. It's the third time they've spoken, the second time just the two of them, no Cleo, and the more time she spends with Luke, the more time she wants to.

'You wouldn't think I was so special if we met in person.' Rachel's tone is light, but the moment the words are out she regrets them. She feels her mood plummeting back to the darkness so fast it's like a light switching off.

'Hey, why do you put yourself down like that?'

'I don't know.' She fidgets on the bed, face flushing. 'I just do. I'm rubbish. Honestly, if it wasn't for Cleo I'd probably never get out of bed in the morning.'

She realizes Luke is waiting for her to go on and there's something about the earnest look in his eyes that makes her want to tell the truth. 'I don't exactly have much luck in relationships,' she starts. 'Men use me. I'm always a pint-in-a-pub date, never a restaurant. My calls and texts are ignored for days, and when they get what they want, it's over. It's not nice. That and how my life is right now – it's made me pretty down. It's why I wanted to try CamChat, I think.' Rachel doesn't try to laugh the bitter edge from her voice. It's the truth, and it's the most honest she's been with anyone about how she feels.

Luke's eyes blaze with intensity. 'I know what you

mean about feeling down. Some days I just don't know what the point is. I don't know who I am any more. Sometimes I get this feeling like I have to do something totally crazy to shake things up a bit.'

'Exactly,' Rachel smiles, the connection between them swimming through her.

'And, Rachel?' he continues.

'Yeah?'

'I will never treat you like that.'

'I know.' She smiles, fighting a weird desire to cry. It's like he's telling her they're at the start of something new and completely theirs. It's on the tip of her tongue to confess the stupid white lie she told him on their first chat about being a make-up artist instead of just a wannabe. Rachel is desperate to tell him how much she hates Mandy. It's almost a shame that weirdo on CamChat she gave Mandy's address to was a no-show. Mandy was just off sick, and worse still, it's because she's pregnant, so now they're being subjected to constant talks about pregnancy and babies, as if Rachel cares about that.

She opens her mouth to tell him, but Luke speaks before she gets the chance.

'You know . . .' He pauses, rubbing the side of his face. 'I don't want to overstep the mark here, but sometimes it seems like the way you talk about Cleo, the men in your life aren't the only ones who put you down.'

'What do you mean?' Rachel sits back, surprised at Luke's words. He's got it wrong. 'Cleo's not like that. She's my best friend.'

'I know, and maybe I have the wrong end of the stick, but the way you talk about her, like how she helps you with stuff, it's like she doesn't think you're capable of doing it on your own, when you are, Rachel. You're amazing.'

Rachel starts to reply but she doesn't know what to say. There's a grain of truth to Luke's words that sits heavy on her thoughts.

'Oh shoot, I gotta go.' Luke grins. 'It's too easy talking to your beautiful face. One of these days I'm going to miss my flight. I got another trip to Chicago now. Can we talk tomorrow night your time?'

'Of course. Do you want to Skype or something?'

He grins. 'Let me give you my cell phone number. It might be fate that we keep meeting on here but I don't want to risk losing you now I've found you.'

'Goodbye, cowboy.'

Luke blows her a kiss and disappears from the screen. Rachel shuts down CamChat and all she can think is how gorgeous he is, how everything. But God, she wishes more than anything he lived in London, or even on this continent. They'll meet one day, she just knows it. Rachel sends a quick text telling him she can't wait to talk again. His reply is instant.

Me too. You're really something, Rachel xx

Rachel's door flies open then and Cleo falls into the room, damp hair tied into a messy ponytail. 'Forgot my sodding umbrella, didn't I?' she says, dropping her coat to the floor and kicking off her shoes before crawling on to the bed beside Rachel. 'I'm so tired. Tell me we have something tasty for dinner tonight?'

'By tasty I guess you don't mean leftover mac and cheese.'

Cleo throws her hands over her face and groans. A worm of guilt wriggles inside Rachel. It should be her feeling this way. It was Rachel's seven-hour Sunday shift that Cleo has just finished, volunteering to do it for Rachel so she could work on her portfolio and complete the application for the *EastEnders* job. The deadline is tomorrow morning, Rachel reminds herself with a flutter of nerves. And she hasn't done a thing yet. Instead, the day has totally disappeared in two loads of washing, and chatting to Beth, then her mum and then Luke. Plus the time spent on CamChat trying to find Luke.

'Have you finished?' Cleo asks, her voice muffled behind her hands.

'Yeah, I just sent it.' The lie feels weird and Rachel is glad Cleo isn't watching her.

'You've sent it?' Cleo sounds surprised. Her hands drop from her face and she looks at Rachel.

'Ten minutes ago.' Another lie.

'I thought you wanted my help with it tonight? I changed my plans so I could help.'

'What plans? You should've said.'

'It doesn't matter. I was . . .' Her voice trails off.

'I didn't help you with yours,' Rachel says, her mood souring.

'I know, but—'

'But what?' she asks, feeling suddenly annoyed. Rachel thought Luke's comment about Cleo was off-base, but maybe he has a point. There's something about talking to Luke that has given Rachel a new lease of confidence. Like she can actually be Roxy, not just pretend. 'You always do this.'

'Do what?' Cleo looks at her, all bemused and 'WTF?', in the way she does when she doesn't get something. It's not usually directed at Rachel, though.

'Act like you've got all your shit together and that I haven't, and you have to help me.' Rachel is being unfair, sort of, but the irritation is itching under her skin. It's mostly at herself for leaving her application to the last minute. Cleo would've been royally pissed off if Rachel had told her she'd wasted the day, but she would still have helped her tonight. And Rachel knows she's being shitty, but she really wishes Cleo hadn't applied for the job too. It is a stepping stone for Cleo, but it's *her* dream.

'That's not true,' Cleo says.

'It sometimes is.'

'I just . . .' Cleo trails off, her eyes moving from Rachel to the laptop. 'What's that?' She points at the screen before Rachel has a chance to close the lid. 'Are you looking at flights?'

Rachel shrugs, wishing Cleo hadn't seen the web browser she'd left open.

'Where to?'

'San Francisco.'

Cleo laughs – a snort of surprise. 'Why are you going to San Francisco?'

'Luke,' Rachel says breezily. 'I thought I could go out there for a weekend.'

'Who?'

'Luke. The blond, good-looking one we spoke to last week. You know – the cowboy?'

'You've spoken to him again? When?'

'The other night. And today.'

'You're going on CamChat a lot, Rach.' A frown pinches Cleo's brow.

Rachel shrugs. 'You've not been around much to play. Are you seeing someone?' She means it as a joke. No way would Cleo start seeing someone and not tell her, but her sheepish expression, the pink glow to her cheeks, says it all.

Cleo fidgets, running a hand through her damp hair.

'You are, aren't you? Did you meet someone at the house party?'

Cleo gives a reluctant nod. 'It's not serious or anything. That's why I didn't mention it.'

'You could still have told me,' Rachel says with a light huff. It hurts to know Cleo has been keeping something from her. 'I tell you when a guy so much as looks at me.'

Cleo gives a weak smile. 'Things have been hectic, that's all, and I'm not sure I'm ready to talk about it. It really isn't anything.'

Rachel doesn't believe her, but she lets it go, knowing Cleo will tell her after a few glasses of wine.

'But what about you? Are you really going to fly halfway around the world for someone you barely know?' Cleo is incredulous and Rachel hates that it feels like they're bickering. They never argue. But Rachel can't stop herself. Cleo just doesn't get it.

'We've talked for hours. I know him better than any man I've ever dated. We've even swapped numbers.'

'Oh, you're dating now.' Cleo makes a face. 'So you know when his birthday is, right?'

Damn. Trust Cleo to ask the one thing Rachel doesn't know.

'You realize he's probably married?'

'He isn't.'

'And how are you going to pay for the flights? Magic beans?'

'It's actually not that expensive. If I wait for a last-minute deal, I can get there and back for three hundred pounds and I won't need a hotel room or anything because I can stay with Luke.' Rachel grits her teeth.

She doesn't even know why she's saying all this. She was only daydreaming about going to San Francisco. She wasn't seriously looking, but Cleo's total lack of support is pushing all of Rachel's buttons.

'Right, because three hundred pounds isn't much?'

'I can save,' she huffs, hating that Cleo is right again, but unable to backtrack.

'How? We barely have enough to get by, and our lives, in case you haven't noticed, are pretty miserable. Don't make it worse for yourself by trying to save this money. If Luke is who he says he is—'

'He *is*.'

'Then it's nothing for him to fly to London and meet you here, is it?'

Rachel sighs, furious that Cleo has the answer to everything. She stands up, wanting to be out of this room, out of this nothing fight. 'Fine. You're right, OK? You're always right.'

'I'm not. That's not what I'm saying. I just . . . I want you to be careful.'

'I am.'

Cleo nods then. 'I'm sorry. I'm tired and grumpy.'

'Me too.' And just like that, the tension evaporates. 'Thank you so much for doing my shift today. It was a massive help. Why don't I pop out to Mr Hakimi's and get us a bottle of wine?'

'And some chocolate,' Cleo says, her voice softening.

'Obviously. And I'll get us a pizza to share.'

'And garlic bread.'

'You bet,' Rachel grins, glad things feel normal again between them.

'All right, then, but hurry up because I'm starving and *Strictly* is on soon.'

Rachel nods. The guilt from earlier morphs into

worry. She's going to be up all night finishing her application.

Bollocks to it, Rachel thinks as she steps out into the rain, not caring that her hair is going to be stuck to her head in a matter of seconds. She'll send her portfolio as it is. The producers don't care about wedding make-up and the crappy photos they've taken of each other. Everyone knows that it's the practical part of the interview that matters and Rachel knows she can nail that.

Her mind turns back to Luke. He's all she thinks about now. Cleo is right about going to San Francisco. It's not just the money, it's how desperate it looks. But that's the thing about Luke: he doesn't make Rachel feel like the desperate loser that every other man has made her into.

Chapter 27

Cleo

Now

It's eight p.m. and I'm restless. Too early for sleep, but nowhere to go. Downstairs, I can hear the clatter of plates in the kitchen, the beat of pop music. I open my door an inch and catch the spiced scent of curry wafting through the house.

Your housemates are more domesticated than we ever were.

That's not exactly hard.

True.

Hearing their laughter hammers home how alone I am. How much we lost that night.

On the landing, I stop and listen, my eyes on the stairs that lead to the loft room. I think of the empty room I saw yesterday. That locked wardrobe. Where does your housemate Charlie fit into all this?

I shiver and move to the stairs. I need to talk to Simon. I want to tell him that Anik is helping now, but when I reach his door I find a yellow Post-it note stuck to the wood.

Gone to Jersey.
Back Monday night.
(Cleo – call me with updates!)

I feel a flicker of annoyance at Simon for leaving me alone here, but then he did feel bad about going and it's not like there's anything he can do either. I think about his girlfriend, Liz, and the life they have mapped out together. Marriage, a new house, and kids someday too, I bet. It feels a world away from my life.

I move to your door, slip the key into the lock and step inside. Guilt swims through my body as I close the door. It's not the same as the guilt in the pit of my stomach. That guilt is old and weathered. This feeling is a new pair of shoes, pinching and uncomfortable. Once upon a time we had no secrets. Once upon a time I wouldn't have thought twice about throwing open your drawers without asking, borrowing a top or a bag. We're not those girls any more and what I'm about to do feels invasive, wrong, but if I want to know more about you, if I want to know about your life now, then I'm going to have to dig deeper.

I start with the chest of drawers below the mirror where you keep most of your clothes. Then the wardrobe and the boxes you keep beneath the bed.

I'm meticulous and slow, looking at every piece of paper I find, searching every corner, under the bed, the top of the wardrobe.

After forty-five minutes, here is what I've discovered:
One: You work as a Senior Account Manager for a

public relations agency called Harley & Plum PR. I've no idea what that is, but it sounds like more than answering phones and making coffee.

Two: You have money. Your clothes are nicer, for one thing; so are your shoes. All those Converse trainers you love so much. And then there's the Michael Kors shoulder bag in your wardrobe. I laughed when I saw it, remembering how badly you lusted over that label when we saw it in the shops.

Here's what I don't know:

One: Where you are.

Two: Who took you, or why.

Three: Who you were meeting the night you disappeared.

Four: Why you continued to live in this cesspit of memories and nightmares when I think you could've afforded something better. You haven't even upgraded your car, Rach!

Five: Everything else.

I slump on to the bed and breathe in the lavender fabric softener and the faint scent of your perfume. I'm tired again. Deflated. What have I really learnt?

Nothing.

I close my eyes and listen to your housemates move through the house. They're talking softly and when they reach your door they stop.

Silence.

The hair on the back of my neck prickles.

I'm sure I catch the tiniest hiss of a whisper before it's gone and the stairs are creaking and their voices are normal again.

I sit back on your bed and open the lid of the laptop before clicking through every single document you have saved. It's mostly work files – press releases on pharmaceutical drugs I've never heard of, and Excel spreadsheets with numbers that make no sense to me.

I find the old photos we took after practising our make-up on each other, smiling at the familiarity of them. There are so many photos of me, and I laugh at the one you did with the blue glitter that spreads from my eyelids across to my hairline.

You were so good, Rach.

You were better.

You didn't have to give it up.

The sadness hits me with the force of a punch and with it comes a desperate need to do something, anything. Anik's warning to stay away from CamChat swirls in my thoughts, but he doesn't understand. He doesn't see that this is all I have of you.

The website loads before I can change my mind. A face appears – a woman in her fifties with coppery permed hair. She smiles but I skip ahead. I don't want to talk today. I just want to find you.

My mind rakes through yesterday's image of you. I was so focused on your face, on your eyes, that I didn't take in the background. It was an empty room. Wood floor. Dirty. The only sound your muffled yelps.

If this was one of those cheesy episodes of *CSI: Miami* we used to watch on your old TV on a Sunday night, then I'd remember the noise of a train or bus and I'd track you down to a road and a building. I'd rescue you. But there is nothing else.

With each click, each skip, my mood sinks. Then the next chat loads. It's the man from last night. The one who was watching me when I woke up. The strands of his grey hair are lying flat against his head. His nose is bulbous, his cheeks flushed red.

162

Something nudges at the edges of my thoughts. The police were outside your door, my head was all over the place, but I remember now – that feeling, the way he said hello. It was like he knew me.

The man smiles, teeth crooked and yellow. 'There you are,' he says, and there's something in his tone that sends a bolt of fear straight through me.

'I'm looking for someone,' I say.

'You've found them.' He spreads his hands out in a 'here I am' gesture and sits back in his chair, allowing me a better view of a room – dirty-white walls, an old carpet, no other furniture.

'It's nice to finally meet you, Cleo,' he says, and the use of my name is ice to my veins. How? I want to ask, but panic snatches the words from my mouth. Every muscle in my body tenses.

He laughs, a bellowing noise, his mouth so wide I see the glinting silver of his fillings.

'How do you know my name?' I force the question out.

'Oh, Cleo, I know a lot more than that. Are you ready to play?'

I shut down CamChat as the scream catches in my throat. I push myself off the bed, eyes fixed on your laptop as though this is a horror movie and any second now the screen is going to light up and a hand shoot out.

Who was that man, Rach? How does he know about the game? How does he know my name? How is he connected to Luke Richards?

The world tilts. I can't be in this room any more. I rush at the door, grabbing the handle. It's turning in my hands when the lights go out and I'm plunged into darkness.

Chapter 28

Cleo

Now

I freeze, blinking in the silent black nothingness, fighting so hard to breathe. My eyes adjust and the faint glow from the street lights outside casts your room in shadows.

It's just a power cut, I tell myself. Another thing that hasn't changed.

It's not connected to what I just saw – that man – but the timing: fuck!

I'm shaking as I grip my alarm in my hand and open your door. The hallway is a black hole, but it's no longer silent at least. I can hear Faye and Lexy laughing upstairs. And something else too – the creak of floorboards above me, of someone else.

Charlie – your other housemate. It must be. I think of my door handle moving that night. That padlocked wardrobe. That empty room.

Another creak. Another footfall. This one closer.

'Hello?' I say, my voice stronger than I feel.

No reply.

He's on the stairs. There's movement – the rustle of clothing, breathing.

I swallow hard and press the torch app on my phone. The white light illuminates the hallway and for a split second I see him – a tall, lanky figure moving on the stairs, pressed close to the wall. He's wearing a jacket, hood up, face in shadow. In the next moment, he launches himself at the front door and, with a rush of cold air, he's gone, the door slamming shut behind him with such force that the window in your room rattles in its frame.

The anger comes from nowhere and I don't think as I give chase. I yank open the door and I'm shouting, 'Hey!' as I leap down the steps and into the drizzling rain.

'Stop!' My voice bounces off the empty road.

I turn in a slow circle, not daring to breathe as I listen. He's hiding. He has to be. There's no way he could've made it all the way down the road.

A gust of wind blows a spatter of icy droplets into my face and I shiver, cold and something else. The feeling of being watched. Eyes on me.

I peer gingerly between two cars, and it's then, as I'm leaning sideways, phone light stretched out, that I'm shoved from behind. It's a full-on shoulder barge, and there's nothing I can do to stop myself flying through the air and hitting the road.

I let a moment pass, then another, as I collect my thoughts, scooping them up with my phone and the alarm I didn't have time to use. From somewhere far away I can hear the smack of feet running on wet pavement. Whoever just pushed me is long gone.

I pull myself up and feel the dark street and the shadows closing in around me.

There's another movement behind me and I spin around, fumbling for my alarm, but it's Faye and Lexy, standing at the open front door with identical questioning frowns printed on their faces.

'Cleo?' Faye says, as though it might be someone else.

'Someone pushed me,' I gasp. 'Did you see anyone?'

Faye glances around her, but it's Lexy I'm looking at. I swear her lips are twitching with amusement. Our eyes meet and she is all concern again as she asks if I'm OK.

I nod and wonder if it's true.

'The power's out,' Faye adds, holding up the torch on her phone.

'It used to happen all the time,' I say, my words still quick, panicked.

'We just knocked on Simon's door but he's away and we don't even know where the fuse box is.'

'It's pretty scary in the dark,' Faye adds with a giggle that makes Lexy tut.

I step forwards, legs wobbling beneath me. 'Something probably tripped the electrics. The fuse box is in the cupboard under the stairs. It used to happen if someone tried to use an electric heater, but Rachel's hairdryer set it off sometimes too.'

I hold out my torch and lead the way to the cupboard. The hall along to the kitchen is pitch-black and as I gaze into the darkness my skin prickles.

'You OK, Cleo?'

I start at Lexy's voice and realize I've stopped walking. 'Yeah. I thought I just saw something.' Someone.

'Oh God, don't.' Faye gives a little yelp. 'I've already got the heebie-jeebies.'

I can tell instantly that Faye is someone who has

166

never known real fear. The 'I'm going to die' fear. She's the type to go to those Halloween fright nights where she'll scream her head off, swearing she'll never go again, but always will. And yet her mock fear settles something inside me and I'm glad they're here. I'm glad I'm not alone.

My eyes stare into the darkness for another moment before I find the handle to the cupboard. It opens with a creak of old hinges and wood and before I can take a step, there's a crash of noise, something falling, followed by a sharp pain as it hits my foot.

'Ow,' I hiss, shining my phone down to the floor to find the hoover has toppled over. As I lift my torch light back to the cupboard, I realize it's a mess of boxes and carrier bags bulging with clothes, a sleeping bag and a stack of dirty pillows. I'm clearly not the only one who has left stuff in this house over the years.

I scooch down and step over a chunky orange torch and a mop and bucket before I reach the fuse box. All the smaller switches are up. Nothing seems to have tripped it. I turn the main fuse back on and a second later there's a beep from somewhere and the lights jump to life.

'Amazing,' Faye says with a relieved sigh. 'Thanks, Cleo.'

'Yeah, thanks,' Lexy adds, and as I look up our eyes meet and it's like she's trying to work something out about me, a quizzical scowl. I take a step, tripping over something on the floor.

'You OK?' Faye asks as I scramble to my feet and nod.

The girls disappear upstairs and only then do I feel around on the floor for whatever tripped me. My fingers brush against soft leather. It's a bag. A beautiful white leather Michael Kors clutch. It looks brand new. It looks like the kind of bag you love. But why is it hiding in here?

Simon's words leap into my thoughts. *'It doesn't explain why she left the house last Friday with only a tiny handbag.'*

I scoop the bag into my hands and head back to my own room. I get ready for bed quickly, shivering as though a coldness has settled deep down inside me. I double-check the door is locked before sliding into bed and picking up the clutch.

The top is folded like an envelope and fastened with a gold clasp that clicks as I press it. I flip open the top to reveal two silk-lined compartments. The first is empty and I feel a stab of disappointment, but the second, the smaller one, has one thing in it – a lipstick.

The colour is a deep red and I already know that if I were to pad downstairs and open up your make-up case, this lipstick would match the other brands exactly. It would slot perfectly into that one empty space.

I search the bag again, tip it upside down and shake it out, but there's nothing else. No money, no bank card, no phone.

If this is the bag you had with you that Friday when you left the house, then how is it back here, hiding in the back of a cupboard? How did it make it home when you didn't?

The really great thing about paranoid people is that it doesn't take much to rattle them.

A creak of a floorboard.

The lights going out.

A little nudge when their back is turned. Now, that I couldn't resist!

She hasn't figured out yet that she's being watched.

It's too easy, really.

Still, the best is yet to come.

Chapter 29

Cleo

Five years earlier

Selfridges is warm today. The heating whacked on to full blast, making the stream of shoppers sweat in their winter coats. My eyelids are heavy and it's an effort to concentrate. I can tell by the dishevelled state of the couple who've just walked in that it's raining outside, and all I want to do is get through the next hour of my shift, go home, take a shower and get ready for my date with Simon.

An actual date that isn't in his flat. The thought hums through me.

I try to catch Rachel's eye from across the shop, but she's talking to a customer – a woman with a neat blonde bob and an expensive beige coat. There's something off about their body language, like they're arguing. I step around my counter just as Rachel's voice carries across the space between us.

'If you take that rod out from up your arse for two minutes, you'll see that I'm right.' Rachel half smiles and tilts her head in a way I've only ever seen her do when we're stringing someone along on CamChat.

'How dare you.' The woman's voice is high, angry, and Mandy appears beside Rachel before I can reach her.

I step back to my counter and watch a hushed conversation before Rachel spins on her heels in the direction of the staffroom. I watch her go, my mouth agape. Mandy bustles to my counter, placating the woman in the beige coat with a free lipstick and a goody bag. Only when she's gone does Mandy's smile drop and she tuts before following after Rachel.

I can't believe what just happened. I can't believe Rachel could be so rude to a customer, and yet, at the same time, I'm not surprised. There's been something different about Rachel since we started playing on CamChat. I've been trying to ignore it, but after her outburst, it's hard not to see what's staring me in the face. It's not so much a newfound confidence, more a defiance. And on top of that, she hates this place. I really hope she gets the *EastEnders* job. More than I want it for myself, I want it for Rachel. The thought settles along with a gnawing worry.

'Excuse me?' A mother and daughter approach my counter and I lose the last hour of my shift to helping them select wedding make-up.

The minute I escape, I rush into the staffroom, hoping to catch Rachel, but she's gone and there's no sign of Mandy. I grab my things and hurry out, spotting a glimpse of Rachel's coat weaving through the shoppers in the direction of the tube, but by the time I'm on the platform, the eastbound train is already pulling away.

*

Heavy rain clouds cover the sky as I half walk, half run up the steps of Bethnal Green tube. I can see Rachel in the distance, walking fast along Roman Road, head down against the cold.

'Rachel?' My voice is lost to the juddering rattle of a bus pulled up beside the road. A group of schoolgirls in navy blazers and tartan skirts jump off in the direction of the tube.

My feet ache from a day standing in heels but I push on, suddenly desperate to reach Rachel.

After what happened on the shop floor, I don't blame Rachel for leaving Selfridges without me, but the worry is still eating away at me. Rachel has never been rude to a customer before. And to do it in front of Mandy – it's like Rach had a death wish.

'Rach,' I call again as she turns down the side road and this time she stops, spinning to meet me. I expect her to be crying, but she's not. She looks angry. Furious.

'Hey,' I say, breathless from the exertion of my walk. 'Thanks for waiting.' I smile to show I'm joking, but stop when I catch the glare on Rachel's face.

'I needed some air,' she says, her tone harsh. 'Sorry,' she adds, softer this time.

'What happened?'

'Nothing.'

'You told a customer to—'

'I know what I said. She called me a brainless bitch.'

'That's awful. I'm sorry. But Rach, you can't speak to customers like that. What did Mandy say?'

Rachel gives a bitter laugh. 'Oh, she's never been happier. She gave me a total bollocking and a formal warning. Plus, I have to write a letter of apology.'

'She didn't fire you?' I ask, relief washing over me. 'I thought . . .'

'Me too.' The defiance slips and I see tears build in Rachel's eyes. 'I just hate it so much. I have to get this *EastEnders* job.'

'You will. I know it.'

I slide my arm through hers and we walk together towards the house.

'Shall we order takeaway tonight?' Rach asks as we turn on to Lockton Road.

'Actually' – I pull a face – 'I've got plans.'

'With your mystery man, by any chance?'

I shake my head, feeling awful. 'It's nothing.' The lie is a stone in the pit of my stomach. I promised myself I'd tell Rach about Simon if her mood picked up, but it hasn't. I should never have waited so long.

'The "nothing" you've been doing quite a lot of recently. Doesn't matter. I was hoping to chat to Luke later anyway.' Her expression changes, her lips twitching like she's got a secret.

We're almost at the door when Simon walks out. My insides flip at the sight of him.

'Hey,' Rachel says as he approaches. 'You look nice. Going somewhere fancy?' she asks, and I look up, taking in his black trousers and freshly ironed shirt.

'I was supposed to be going somewhere very nice,' he says with a wink to me. 'But I've just been called in to work so I have to cancel. I'm sorry.' His eyes don't leave mine as he speaks and I feel my face flush under his gaze as the realization of his words hits.

Rachel narrows her eyes, her stare piercing. 'No.' She shakes her head. 'Seriously. Simon is who you've been shagging?' She looks between us and the answer is obvious. I've been so stupid to keep it from her.

I open my mouth to speak but close it again. What can I say? Simon brushes my arm as he passes. 'I'm

173

sorry about our plans. But I really do have to work. I'll call you later.'

Anger rises up and I want to tell him not to bother. He's just cancelled our date and, worse than that, he's just told Rachel about us. Even as the anger burns I wonder if I'm being unfair. I always assumed we'd keep our relationship quiet, but we never talked about it, and he can hardly be blamed for not realizing I hadn't told my best friend.

'Rach, I'm sorry,' I say as she spins away from me and storms towards the house.

'Whatever.'

'Please talk to me. I never meant for it to happen. We got drunk at Lisa and Katie's party. It's nothing, honestly.'

'That party was weeks ago. You've been sleeping together all this time and you call that nothing? Come off it. I can't believe you didn't tell me.' She shoves open the front door before turning back to me. 'What about our pact?'

My head hangs. 'I'm sorry,' I say again, the words not enough. 'I wanted to tell you, but you've been so down about work lately and I knew you'd be upset. I didn't mean for it to happen.'

'Oh really? How many times didn't you mean for it to happen, exactly? I can't believe you've been keeping this from me.'

Guilt swills in my gut. 'I'm—'

'Sorry, yeah, I get it,' Rachel snaps. 'You know what – I don't care. I don't care about the shitty job at Selfridges. I don't care about you and Simon. I don't care about anything.' She opens her bedroom door, steps inside and slams it shut.

I move to follow her but stop when she shouts out,

'Don't,' and instead I go to my room and flop on the bed, angry at Simon and Rach and me. Mostly me. I should never have got involved with Simon. I knew it was wrong, and worse than that, I knew it would hurt Rach.

But on top of it all, the worry continues to eat away at me. I've allowed myself to be distracted by Simon. I've ignored how often Rachel has been on CamChat. It can't be good for her. What happened today is evidence of that. She's speaking to Luke all the time too, calling in sick one day last week because they'd arranged to talk. She never wants to go out any more, and now she's in trouble at work.

I stare at the ceiling and promise myself I'll be a better friend. If she'll let me.

Chapter 30

Cleo

Now

Sleep comes in snatches. I doze off only to jolt awake from a nightmare – or, worse, my own thoughts – and the faces floating behind my eyes.

Luke Richards.

The man with the grey hair on CamChat.

Charlie, your housemate, running out the front door. Pushing me to the ground.

And always it comes back to you tied to that chair.

I watch the grey daylight seep into the dawn, my mind buzzing too much to sleep. I'm certain it's Luke who has you, Rach. But if that's true, then how do the other faces fit into my theory?

I need to think logically, I tell myself over and over. What do I actually know?

Someone kidnapped you ten days ago and has you tied to a chair.

That's it. That's all I know for sure.

The reality of it spins in my head like those god-awful revolving dance floors.

I love those dance floors!

How could I forget? You dragged me on to enough of them.

I shift in bed and listen to the house waking around me. Faye and Lexy hurry in and out of the bathroom. No time for chatting on Mondays, it seems.

I grab my phone, itching to call Anik and ask him what he's found, but it's still early. I only saw him yesterday. He won't even be at his desk yet. I need to wait.

A text arrives as I'm still staring at my phone. It's Donovan from the *Enchantress*.

How's your mum? We're all missing you here!

I type ten different versions of a reply before giving up. The *Enchantress* will be cutting through the vast open water of the Atlantic Ocean right now. Eight days straight out at sea. It's the spa's busiest time. I hope Gemma is coping with the restless passengers, the ones who've yet to find their holiday pace and want to try everything the cruise has to offer with a desperate ferocity.

The longing is acute. I miss it so much. I miss the smell of the spa, that mix of eucalyptus and expensive oils. I miss the balmy warmth, the tranquillity we offer.

I know you're rolling your eyes, Rach, and I would have done too, once upon a time, but it's peaceful there. I know it's not make-up, but come on, that dream of ours died the night we almost did.

You mean the night I almost did.

We were both there, Rach.

The front door opens, the wood sticking in the frame like it always does and freeing itself with a shudder. It takes Faye and Lexy two attempts to bang it shut, the noise bouncing against the walls.

The silence of the house tucks itself around me. It's the itchy wool of a blanket on bare skin; it's someone standing too close, invading my personal space. And as I stare again at the ceiling I feel stuck, glued down, chasing shadows and going nowhere fast.

I throw off the covers and force myself up. Lying in bed isn't going to help find you. It isn't going to get me back to the *Enchantress*, either.

When I'm showered and dressed, I creep upstairs to the loft room again. Every step makes my pulse judder in my ears but I have to see.

The door is open again, the room just as it was the last time I looked. I can't figure it out. Does someone live here or not? And what the hell is in that locked wardrobe?

The Post-it is still on Simon's door. I think about calling him but I've hardly got much to tell him. I'll wait until tonight to ask about the bag I've found and tell him about Anik.

The smell of mould clogs my nose, the stillness continues to rub, and so I grab my backpack, tuck my alarm into my pocket and hurry out the door.

I need more facts and I'm not going to find them inside this house.

Chapter 31

Rachel

Five years earlier

There's a knock on Rachel's door and her insides squirm. The very fact that Cleo is knocking instead of bursting in shows that things are still weird between them. She hates that they can't seem to go five minutes without bickering. It's like there's a distance separating them. Cleo thinks Rachel is mad about her and Simon, but she's not. She's got Luke now. She just wishes Cleo had told her at the start. Luke thinks it's because Cleo doesn't trust her. She's starting to wonder if he has a point.

The door opens and Cleo pokes her face into the room with a soft 'Hey.'

'Hey,' Rachel replies, waving her in and forcing a smile.

'Who were you talking to?'

'Luke.'

Cleo makes a face and it's obvious what's coming – another lecture.

'What?' Rachel sighs.

'I'm just worried about you. How do you know he's not married?' she says.

'Oh my God,' Rachel huffs. 'How many times do we need to go over this? He's *not* married. Can you stop treating me like I'm an idiot, please?' She sits up, hot and bothered, and tugs off her jumper. 'You know what? Luke was right. You're jealous of us. This whole thing is about you trying to come between us.'

'Jealous? You think I'm jealous? What a surprise Luke was the one to think that up.'

'What a surprise, another dig at Luke. You can't stand that I'm happy, can you? I'm happy for you and Simon. Why can't you be happy for me and Luke?'

'There is no me and Simon.'

'Whatever.'

They fall silent and Rachel doesn't have to look at Cleo's face to know she's sorry she said anything. Good!

The truth is – and Rachel really can't tell Cleo this because she'll hit the roof – Rachel is starting to think Cleo might be right. When Rachel asks Luke about his life, he's vague sometimes. She doesn't think he's lying to her, just omitting certain details, and even though it's wrong and screwing over the sisterhood, she actually doesn't care if he's married. Rachel has finally met a man who likes her for who she is, who doesn't just want to shag her.

And Rachel might not be naive enough to think that they'll have a fairy-tale ending, he'll move to London and marry her instead, but it does happen.

'OK. I'm sorry. So, how is Luke?' Cleo asks, her voice a touch too casual, like it's suddenly a massive effort just to talk to Rachel.

'Good. Really good. In fact, he says his company have a big meeting happening in London. He doesn't normally travel to the UK, but he's put his name down for it. He's going to be here next week. He's taking me out next Friday night.'

'That's great.' Cleo's voice is deadpan.

Rachel's excitement fades again. She's so tired of having to defend herself and her decisions while Cleo sucks the joy out of her. 'Don't sound so happy about it, will you?' Rachel's voice drips with sarcasm.

'I am happy for you. I just want you to be careful. I think I should come with you. A bit of backup, just in case.'

'In case what?'

'In case he turns out to be a weirdo, Rachel. You don't know anything about him.'

'That's total bollocks. I know him better than any man I've ever met.'

'Well, I'm coming with you.' Cleo folds her arms across her chest like a mother scolding her child.

'Whatever.'

'Rachel, please. I just want to look out for you. I'm glad you've met someone. I'm happy for you. Honestly, I am.'

Her words hang between them and Rachel really wishes she could believe her.

'Fine. Come, then,' she shrugs. If Cleo coming on their date is the only way to convince her that Luke is a decent guy, then so be it.

'Do you want to watch something?' Rachel asks, because she feels like she should, because it's what they normally do.

'Er, yeah, sure,' Cleo says, cautiously now, and Rachel wonders if she'd rather be somewhere else too.

Cleo's phone vibrates on the bed and as she picks it up Rachel watches her whole face change. Surprise, disbelief, excitement.

'What is it?' Rachel asks.

'I got an interview for *EastEnders*! Check your phone.'

Rachel reaches around and grabs her phone from the nightstand, making a show of checking it even though it's been silent all day. Disappointment twists in her gut. She missed the application deadline by five minutes because of a sodding power cut. Would they have even looked at it?

'Well?' Cleo asks.

'Nothing.'

'Maybe yours will come through tomorrow.' Cleo's false hope is grating, but Rachel pastes on a smile anyway.

'Yeah, maybe. Anyway, that's really great news for you. When is the interview?'

'Next week. I'll need to swap a shift.'

'I can help.'

'Thanks. Can we watch something another night? I should probably get started on some interview prep.'

'Of course.' Rachel runs her hands through her hair and smiles, wondering if Cleo will see how fake it is, but she's already skipping out the door, her mind on the job that Rachel wanted so badly.

Rachel wishes again that she'd never told Cleo to apply. She wishes she could ask Cleo to call them up and tell them she's not interested, but she can't. This is Cleo's shot too. And Rachel is happy for her. At least, she will be when the disappointment stops feeling so caustic. Rachel should've tried harder. It's her own stupid fault.

An emptiness sweeps through her, loud and echoing, and for a moment it feels like she's losing everything – her dreams, Cleo, their friendship. Rachel reaches for her laptop and opens CamChat, feeling instantly better as the familiar logo swoops across the screen. That make-up job will be all hours and it's not like the pay will be any better than what she earns now. Plus, travelling to the arse end of London every day isn't exactly her idea of fun.

If Rachel got that job, there'd be no time for Cam-Chat or Luke. The thought soothes something inside her and she settles against the pillow and smiles her Roxy smile as the first chat loads.

Chapter 32

Cleo

Now

My eyes flit between the gaps in the houses, the spaces between the cars, as I walk the length of Lockton Road. Where did Charlie disappear to last night?

Mushy cold sleet falls from clouds the colour of dirty snow and when I reach the market on Roman Road, I pull up my hood and keep walking, taking the same journey you should be making right now.

Central line to Oxford Circus, then six stops on the Bakerloo line.

The office of Harley & Plum PR isn't an office at all. It's a house on a side road south of the river, near Elephant & Castle tube. One of those Victorian mini-mansions that's been converted into offices. There's a gold plaque outside the door with a buzzer for each business. A solicitor's office on the top, an accountant's in the middle and the PR agency on the ground floor.

It's just gone nine a.m. and I'm about to press the

bell when a girl hurries up the steps, keys jangling in her hands.

'Sorry,' she says, cheeks red, brown hair damp from the sleet. 'I overslept, then my umbrella broke. I was like, come on, Darcey, run for it and they'll never know you were late. Mondays, eh?' She gives me a wink and a wicked grin, reminding me so much of Gemma. It's the way her thoughts spill out of her mouth, laying her life open for all to see.

'No problem,' I smile, noticing a folder under her arm and a swirling purple letterhead that reads 'Harley & Plum PR'. 'I think it's you I'm looking for, actually.'

Darcey pauses, her expression changing from conspiratorial to horrified. 'I'm so sorry. Do you have an appointment? Have you been waiting long?'

'Don't worry. My name's Cleo. I'm here because I'm a . . . a friend of Rachel Winslow.' The word 'friend' seems stilted in my mouth and I hate that I trip over it. We were so much more to each other than that, weren't we? And yet I don't know what we are to each other any more.

'Phew,' Darcey replies before opening the front door into a white hallway with black and white chessboard-style floor tiles. She unwraps her scarf to reveal a beautiful yellow turtleneck. 'I thought I was going to be in big trouble then. Rachel's on holiday at the moment, lucky cow. Have you got her number?'

'She's been reported as a missing person—'

'Oh, I know,' Darcey cuts in, the pitch of her voice rising a notch as though the gossip is going to burst right out of her. 'Her landlord called us last Monday and the police stopped by on Tuesday, but it's all a big mistake. She's on holiday.'

'How can you be so sure?'

'Well, for one thing,' Darcey says, pulling her phone out from her bag, 'she sent all of us this email last week.' She taps on her screen before showing me.

Wish you were here! x

Darcey opens the attachment and a photograph of a beach appears. The sand is pale yellow, the sea and the sky an aqua blue. There's an empty wooden sun lounger sitting below a leafy palm tree with a cocktail beside it. It looks like the Caribbean.

'It was all so last minute,' Darcey says, tucking her phone away.

'What was?'

'The holiday. That's why we think her landlord and sister reported her missing. She must have been in such a rush she forgot to tell them. We were all expecting her in last Monday like normal, but then Stella – that's our boss – comes in and tells us Rachel emailed her late on Friday about a great deal she'd found on a last-minute holiday and asked for two weeks off, and since we're quiet at the moment and Rachel is owed loads of holiday, Stella said it was fine.'

'She only arranged it on Friday night?' I ask.

Darcey nods. 'Weird, right? But then she emailed this photo on Monday evening so I guess she just really fancied a holiday.'

'And you showed that photo to the police?'

'Of course. We're all just glad she's OK. Bet she'll be so embarrassed when she gets back and realizes what a fuss she's caused. Stella emailed her on Tuesday to tell her the police had been here, but Rachel's out-of-office was on so we're not sure if she's seen it. No way I'd be checking my emails while I was on holiday.'

My mind is see-sawing, one thought then another. The first fills me with a dizzy lightness. You're on holiday, just like the police said. Here is the proof. The second thought is a heavy stone dragging me down as I remember your face on CamChat. That fear. This wasn't a pre-arranged holiday. You only sent the first email on Friday night. And that photo – on the surface it's proof, sure, but you're not actually in it, are you? It's like one of a hundred stock photos we use on board the *Enchantress* to advertise our port stops.

Anyone could have found that photo online. Anyone could have sent those emails as a way to throw the police off when they made their stupid risk assessment. Luke's face looms in my thoughts. That slow, knowing smile that haunts my sleep.

'And it was just emails? Rachel didn't call?'

Darcey gives me a quizzical look. 'Just emails,' she confirms, shifting her bag on her shoulder and glancing towards the office.

'Has Rachel been acting differently at all recently?' I ask.

Darcey thinks for a moment. 'Er . . . no. She's always been quiet. Keeps to herself, but she works super hard, and everyone likes her,' she's quick to add. 'Obviously, I don't need to tell you that because you're her friend, but in a small office like this, getting on with everyone is really important.'

'And Rachel does?'

'Of course.'

'Has she talked about a boyfriend at all? Someone she's been seeing, or a housemate?'

'To be honest, no. It's funny, she has this way of,

like, dodging questions. When I ask her something, she'll come right back with a question about me and then that's what we're talking about. The only time she ever mentioned anything was when she was laughing at something at her desk and when I asked, she mentioned you, actually. Some meme you sent her about Monday mornings.'

Darcey glances down the hall again. She's already late and I'm holding her up, but I'm not ready to leave yet.

Desperation, urgency – they snag at my insides. I open my mouth, about to ask another question about you, about what kind of person you are now, when something in Darcey's face changes.

'What is it?' I ask.

'I've just remembered. It's probably nothing, but we went out to grab sandwiches together a few weeks before Christmas. Rachel thought someone was following her and it really freaked her out.'

'Did she say who it was? Did you see him? What did he look like?'

'That's the thing – I didn't see anyone. She dragged me into a cafe and we hid at the back for ages. She was pretty shaken up about it. She kept saying, "It's happening again." But when I asked her about it the next day, she sort of laughed it off. It was weird. I can't believe I forgot about it, but honestly, Rachel was fine afterwards and I just thought she'd spooked herself.'

'Did you mention it to the police?'

Darcey shakes her head. 'It was Stella who spoke to them. They were only here a few minutes. It doesn't matter anyway, does it? She's clearly on holiday. This is all just a big mix-up. She'll be back at the weekend with a gorgeous winter tan that's going to make me want to hate her,' Darcey adds with a smile.

A phone rings from somewhere in the building. 'I'd better go,' she says, already hurrying down the hall.

I turn away and walk back down the road. I've nowhere to go but my pace is fast, even for me. I can't escape this feeling that I'm running out of time. How much longer will you be tied to that chair, Rach?

I pull out my phone and call Anik. I want to tell him about the man on CamChat, your housemate's strange behaviour, the bag, the last-minute holiday booked by email, and how twice in the weeks before you disappeared you saw someone following you – once with Darcey and once while on the phone to Beth. There is something here. Some clue, some thread that Anik can use to find you in a way I can't.

Anik answers with a groggy 'Hello?'

'Anik, it's Cleo. Did I wake you?' I glance at the time. It's nine thirty. Surely he's at work by now.

'No.' He clears his throat and there's a rustle of papers from somewhere. 'I just haven't had a coffee yet this morning. Is everything OK?' he asks.

'Yes. I mean, I don't know. Stuff has happened since yesterday. Can we meet?'

'I was just about to call you.'

'Have you found something about Rachel?' My heartbeat quickens.

'No. It's about Luke Richards.'

My mouth dries. I lick my lips and taste that bitter dirt.

'Look, it's my day off today,' Anik continues. 'If I go into the station, I'll get dragged into a million other things. Can you meet me outside Tottenham Court Road tube station at eleven thirty?'

'Yes, sure.' My words come quick and I have to bite back the desire to ask Anik to meet me right now, this very second.

We say our goodbyes and I start to walk again.

I've got plenty of time to get across London. Too much time.

The sleet has stopped and even though the cold feels like pinpricks on my cheeks I decide to walk. It's only a few miles and it'll be nice to walk along the river. Nicer than the tube, at least. All those faces I can't keep track of.

We loved the South Bank in the summer.

I smile at the memories. Remember that drama festival at the Southbank Centre we accidentally joined?

The one we thought was a cocktail-making class where we'd get some free drinks, but we'd got the day wrong.

No one else turned up and they were so happy to see us that we couldn't admit we'd made a mistake.

You ended up dating one of the actors for a few weeks.

Don't remind me. He kept borrowing my make-up and spent hours in front of the mirror.

The blast of a horn pulls me back to the road and the ugly cement-block architecture. Elephant & Castle roundabout is just ahead of me and there's a frenzied feeling to the traffic, like commuters on the Central line at rush hour. A delivery van swerves around a bin lorry. A bus ploughs on to the roundabout without slowing. A cyclist veers across three lanes.

My phone buzzes in my pocket and I pull it out to see three text messages from an unknown number.

Let's play a game . . .
Warmer or colder?
Right now you're getting warmer, Cleo!

A tremor takes hold of my body and I instinctively look around me.

There's a cyclist with long brown hair tied in a ponytail. He's leaning his bike against the wall a few metres ahead of me and looking for something in his backpack. In the other direction is a woman with a pushchair but no child inside it. And there's a man in white overalls carrying a bucket into the building next to me.

My eyes draw back to the messages and I stare at the words, trying to comprehend what I'm reading.

I tap out a reply.

Who are you?

An answer appears a second later.

That would be spoiling the game!

A sound escapes my mouth and I tap out three more messages.

What game?
Where's Rachel?
I don't want to play!

The noise of the traffic seems suddenly too loud, too intrusive, as I hurry to the underpass that leads beneath the roundabout. But, three steps down, an unease washes over me. I peer into the gloom below, the smell of urine wafting back at me. Is someone down there waiting for me?

Goosebumps rage across my skin and I turn away

and chance the road instead, climbing the railings and sprinting between four lanes of traffic, dodging a motorbike and barely making it across before a bus roars by.

The whole point of a game is that it has to be fun.

Otherwise, why play?

*And we can't have poor little Cleo
getting bored now.*

Chapter 33

Cleo

Now

My heart is hammering in my chest as I half walk, half run the length of Tottenham Court Road – the shitty end with the gyms and the nondescript office blocks before the high-street shops begin to take over.

The tube station has had a revamp since I was last here. It's no longer a hole in the wall with the original creamy-beige tiles. It's all rising glass and shiny grey facade.

People are everywhere. Shoppers, students, tourists with backpacks staring at Google Maps on their phones, couples, cyclists. As I near the tube, an electric scooter mounts the pavement and shoots by, narrowly missing an elderly couple who jump out of the way.

'Total death traps,' someone says from beside me.

I turn to the voice and find Anik. Our eyes connect and he smiles in a way that makes me want to collapse into him.

'Paris has hundreds of them,' he continues, stuffing his hands into the pockets of his jacket. 'They're becoming popular here too. It's getting to be a real problem for the Met. You all right? You look like you've seen a ghost.'

I take a shuddering breath and shake my head. The texts have left a jittery disquiet humming around me, like the engines of the never-ending traffic.

But with it comes another feeling. The urgency is back. Amplified. Cranked up to max.

I pull out my phone and show Anik the texts. I watch him frown for a moment before reaching for his own phone and taking down the number.

'Screenshot and forward me these messages and any more that come through. It's probably an unregistered pay-as-you-go, but I'll check with the station later.'

Hearing Anik's quiet authority has settled my nerves. I don't feel scared any more. I feel emboldened, desperate for answers. I tap the number with my thumb and wait for the call to connect.

'What are you doing?' Anik snatches my phone so fast it almost falls to the pavement. He holds it away, cancelling the call and looking at me – eyes intense, angry.

'I was going to call the number and . . .' My voice trails off. And what? I don't know. Something, though.

'Cleo, we don't know who we're dealing with here. Let me take over.'

He hands me back my phone and I slip it into my pocket, feeling admonished but frustrated too. Anik's reaction seemed over the top. He's playing it safe. Warning me not to reply to the texts, telling me to stay away from CamChat. But safe means slow, and you don't have time for that.

'Come on,' Anik says, pointing to the pub beside us.

'The Flying Horse?' I frown. The black paintwork and pink flower boxes look squished in beside the flashing adverts of a Carphone Warehouse on one side and a McDonald's on the other.

'It'll be quieter in there than anywhere else at this time of day.'

He's right. Inside, it's all shiny wood, leather chairs and mirrors. It's also empty. The air is stale and smells of toilets and cleaning products.

I sit at a table in the corner as Anik waits at the bar to order, returning a few minutes later with a coffee for me and a pint of bitter. 'It's my day off,' he says defensively, as though I've questioned the alcohol. He raises the glass to his lips and takes a long sip. He's wearing the same jeans-and-jumper combo he wore yesterday and something about his clothes and the drink causes another pulse of frustration to throb inside me. Is he taking this seriously?

'So, tell me, what else has been happening?' he says, dabbing the froth of beer away from his beard.

'You first. Please,' I reply, sipping at my too-hot coffee.

He waits a beat, his eyes on me, as though he's trying to decide something. 'So, I have something I think you'll want to hear.'

'About Luke Richards?' I lean forward, wrapping my hands around my coffee cup, trying to absorb the warmth.

'Yes. There's a case from four years ago. It should've linked to your case in the system originally, but the detective on the other case chose some' – he frowns – 'odd keywords, shall we say, and no connection was ever made.'

'He did it again?' A tumbling sickness coils around me.

'I think so.'

I draw in a shallow breath. 'Tell me.'

'Nine months after your abduction—'

'Attempted murder,' I correct.

He raises his eyebrows in a 'what does it matter now?' look and I want to tell him it matters, that there's a difference between knowing someone is going to hurt you and knowing someone is going to kill you, but I keep it in. 'There was a case in North Essex of a man who met a woman on a dating website, and after taking her for dinner he abducted her and drove her to a nearby woodland.'

An anguished sob leaves my mouth. I try to swallow but I can't. 'What happened?'

'Some teenagers were having a party in the woods and saw him. They called the police and the man ran. There was a car chase and he crashed. He died on impact. The detective in charge flagged the abduction but not the woodland location, which is why I wasn't alerted originally. It was only through combing the police database that I found it at all.'

'And you think it's the same man?'

He nods. 'It's definitely a possibility. The timing fits and the man's name was Richard Gilders. Coincidences happen all the time, and Richard is a common name, but the two things together feel like more than a coincidence.'

Anik reaches across the table and places his hand on top of mine. His touch is warm and charged with a current that passes between us. After a pause he speaks again. 'I think he's dead, Cleo. When I'm back in the office I'll print a photo from the file of Richard Gilders and you can see if he's the same man as Luke Richards. I know you had trouble remembering anything after the abduction, but it might jog your memory.'

Guilt is a festering hot swamp. I push it down and focus on the present. The man who ruined our lives, destroyed our friendship, who drove me out of London. The man who I've looked for, the man I've seen in every face, every dark corner, every nightmare for five years, could be dead.

Tears form a wall in my eyes before falling in two lines down my face, and all I want to do right now is pick up the phone and call you and tell you we're safe, tell you it's over.

But it's not over, is it?

You're not safe. Luke Richards can't be dead because he has you. You told Beth you saw him. This is his game we're still playing.

'But Rachel,' I say, when I can speak again. 'Who?' The word is a croak.

Anik shakes his head. 'I don't know. I'm sorry.'

'There was a man on CamChat last night. He knew my name and he . . . he asked me if I wanted to play. It's like the texts.' I clench my jaw in an effort to stop myself crying. Tension throbs in my temples.

'You went back on CamChat?' Anik's tone is disbelieving but his gaze is hard.

'I had to. I have to find Rachel. She needs my help.' I ignore Anik's frown and carry on talking. I tell him about the power cut, your housemate running, the shove in the road, your bag in the cupboard.

'And you're sure the bag belongs to Rachel?'

'Her lipstick is inside and I know she loves that brand. I'm going to ask her landlord when I get back.

He saw her leave that night. But if her bag is back in the house, then maybe Rachel came home that night too.'

'Playing devil's advocate for a moment, that assumption adds more weight to the argument that she could have left early for a holiday the next day.'

'But she only sent an email about a holiday to her boss late Friday night. Then another one on Monday with a photo of a beach.'

'How do you know that?' He sounds surprised and his hand has tightened around mine.

'I spoke to someone she works with this morning. But she wasn't in the photo. Anyone could have sent those emails from her phone or forced her to do it, couldn't they? It's enough, right?'

'Enough for what?'

'For you to upgrade Rachel's case. You'll take it more seriously now, right?'

'I'm already taking this seriously.'

'Are you?' My eyes fall to his empty pint glass. 'You just suggested she's on holiday, but I saw her on Cam-Chat, remember?'

'I'm not forgetting, Cleo. I'm just thinking through all the scenarios. But you're right: if that is Rachel's bag, then it changes the timeline and location of a possible abduction.'

'Your team are taking it seriously,' I say, as much to myself as to Anik.

'Sorry?'

'You said a minute ago, "I'm already taking this seriously," but you mean your team are, right? It's not just you.'

He swallows, his Adam's apple bobbing up then

199

down. 'Of course. I think we should talk about what happened in the woods. See if you remember anything. I always hoped you'd get in touch when the shock cleared. We always thought you'd be able to help the investigation, but you never called.'

My cup rattles in the saucer as I lift it to my mouth, taking a long sip, washing back the taste of the dirt.

'But you just said Luke Richards is dead. How can it help to go over it?'

'I just think it might.' His gaze is unwavering and intense as he waits for me to respond. For a horrible moment I think he knows my secret.

'I'd rather not, if that's OK?' I force a cheeriness into my voice and slide my hand out from under his. 'I'd better go, actually.'

'That's OK,' he's quick to say. 'Tell me about Rachel's housemates instead.'

'There's nothing else to tell you.' I stand and shuffle out from behind the table, feeling hot, trapped. Anik rises too and we face each other for a moment. 'I need to process what you've told me,' I say. 'I'll call you.'

'Cleo, wait.' Anik's voice is urgent and I stop. 'We need to keep working on this.'

'I know. Just . . . call me when you find something.'

'Of course I will. Be careful. No more replying to texts, or CamChat. And, Cleo?'

'Yeah?'

Anik moves close enough for me to smell the scent of his aftershave. That feeling passes between us again, a slow, burning desire to reach out and touch him. 'I know your head isn't in the right place for this, and I should wait, but I tried that last time and then you left before I had the chance to tell you.' He swallows. 'I just want to tell you how good it is to see you. I think

200

about you a lot and I always felt like there was something unfinished between us. I always hoped you'd call, not just about the case.'

My stomach flips. Anik is right. There is something here – a chemistry that fizzes between us – but how can there ever be anything more between us when every time he looks at me, it's like he sees right through my lies?

'I . . .'

'It's OK,' he continues. 'You don't have to say anything. Our timing is terrible, isn't it?' He laughs and I smile. 'I get why you left London. I know you needed time to process what happened, but I hope you'll stick around.'

I step back, knocking against the wall.

'I should go.' I push through the heavy pub door and out into the cold before Anik can say any more. He thinks I left because of that night. You think I left because of that night, because I was too scared, too anxious to stay. I let everyone believe that, but it's not true, and that fact makes me want to run away all over again.

Chapter 34

Rachel

Now

There's too much time to think in here. Every thought seems to drag her into a twisted maze of weirder thoughts, questions she can't answer. Too many memories. Rachel is a live-in-the-moment person. She has to be. She can't look back, for obvious reasons, but she can't exactly live in the moment right now either. This room, the relentless dripping tap, is her moment.

Day after day, drip after sodding drip, in and out of that room, the material of the mattress so cold it feels damp against her skin and she has to close her eyes so she doesn't see the dirt, the grime, and wonder how many other women have lived these moments and what happened to them.

Looking forwards is hard too. Sometimes she lets herself jump ahead to a time when the surgery on her scar is done and she won't have to see it every day, won't have to have her head and body filled with memories and crippling fear and his taunting, evil voice.

All that money. She doesn't care. She'd pay double, triple, ten times over to have her face again. She doesn't even care if it's her face. Any face that won't make her remember what happened over and over.

Rachel keeps thinking about the time in hospital when she wished she was dead. The frustration a throbbing, angry beast. No one was listening to her.

'Beth,' Rachel sighed, pleading over and over with her sister. 'I want to see.'

'But why? Just wait. Leave it a few days. Everything will look better then. There's no need to upset yourself.'

Beth was trying to protect Rachel, but her sister had always been a terrible liar.

'I want to see. You must have a mirror,' Rachel pleaded.

'I don't.'

'Where's Mum, then?' Rachel asked, eyes on the doors. The ward was busy with visitors. People talking softly, holding hands, reading to loved ones. And all she wanted to do was scream.

She didn't. But to hell with keeping her voice low. What did she care about making a scene? They were all staring at her anyway, just as curious as she was about how fucked up her face was under the white gauze covering one side of her head.

Well, good, Rachel thought, wanting more than anything for the nurses to move her to a private room.

She was practically a mummy with all the bandages. All they'd let her see was a deep purple bruise blotching up from the cast on her leg; broken in three places. They were operating the following day, worried the bones weren't healing right. They were worried about her leg, the long-term implications of a limp, as if she cared about that. She didn't even remember breaking the damn thing.

Rachel just wanted to see her face and the cut that was tight and itching like crawling insects beneath her skin.

Then Cleo appeared, looking as bad as Rachel felt. A hot mess of greasy hair, skin white and papery. Rachel was so glad to see her. So glad they were both still alive. Cleo had saved her. Rachel would be dead if it wasn't for Cleo.

Cleo reached the side of the bed and Rachel sat up, trying to hug her, but stopped when the pain ripped through her cuts. All of them just deep enough to need a few stitches, deep enough to sear with pain, but not deep enough to kill her.

Beth's dagger eyes were on Cleo then. The fury crackling in the air. Beth thought it was all Cleo's fault and Rachel didn't have the heart or the energy to tell her it was hers. Rachel regrets that now. It made Cleo think Rachel blamed her.

'Can you give us a few minutes?' Rachel asked, turning to her sister.

Beth's lips pursed but she nodded. 'Two minutes.'

Only when she'd walked away did Rachel squeeze Cleo's hand. 'Give me your mirror.'

'What?' Alarm sparked in Cleo's eyes. That look said it all, but Rachel had to know for herself.

'Your compact. It's always in the front pocket of your bag. Give it to me, quick. No one will show me my cuts, but I have to see.'

'Rach, I—'

'Please!'

It took another minute of pleading before Cleo caved and handed over the circular silver compact

Rachel had bought her last Christmas. She flipped it open and angled it to see her face.

She was a mess. Her hair was flat and dull, and her nose and right eye were swollen, the colour of plums. No wonder the other patients were staring so much. But it was the clean white gauze taped over one side of Rachel's face that she was interested in. Rachel swallowed hard and peeled it away.

'Rach, I'm not sure you . . .' Cleo started to say before giving up.

Rachel remembers how her skin tugged painfully from the tape, just like that awful duct tape, but she kept going and then it was hanging down and her whole face was visible. Rachel cried out. She couldn't help it. A guttural sob shook her body. The cut was a jagged line snaking from the edge of her eyelid all the way down to her jawbone. There were stitches along the cut, and a point in the middle where the skin seemed to bunch up. It was so much worse than she'd imagined.

'*You stupid bitch.*' She heard Luke's voice growl in her thoughts and jumped.

Tears formed in Rachel's eyes. She slammed the mirror shut and threw it across the room. It landed with a thud and a clatter and someone yelped in surprise.

She couldn't stop the tears rolling down her face. Rachel knew her life had changed forever. She'd never work in make-up again. It wasn't just how everyone would stare at her; it was the mirrors, the bright lights, how she'd have to see herself.

She was right on both counts. It never got easier to look at herself. Every time, the memories flooded back, and with them the heart-pounding, breath-taking fear.

Rachel found a job in PR. Entry level at first, but she worked hard, she gave it her all, putting in double the work, not even caring when she was held back from client meetings and all those boozy events.

It's no wonder she found solace in CamChat again, dimming her light and angling the camera.

But it's not the moment she saw her face for the first time that Rachel is thinking of now. It's Cleo standing by her bedside. Her trembling body, her pale face and skittish movements. Rachel was so wrapped up in herself that day and the weeks that followed. She couldn't look past what had happened to her to see that Cleo had been through so much too. It was so much easier to accept the blame Cleo gave herself than for Rachel to admit the truth, because there really was only one person to blame for the mess they found themselves in, and that was her.

Cleo has always been there for her. All those times when the darkness threatened, it was Cleo who dragged Rachel away. Cleo never realized how much Rachel needed her, and she wonders now how different their lives would have been if she'd told Cleo how she'd felt, instead of clinging to Cleo's optimism, her unwavering belief that they'd make it, pretending she felt the same.

And now Cleo is back and Rachel is dragging her into trouble all over again. The hurt in her chest is so raw she gasps.

This is all her fault.

Chapter 35

Rachel

Five years earlier

The tube jolts to a stop at Holborn and finally they're here. This is it! At last. Date night with Luke. She seriously does not know how she's survived the waiting. Time has slowed, the days blending into one boring shift after another – Mandy a constant shadow, waiting for Rachel to step out of line again so she can fire her.

They emerge from the tube into the dry night air. It's cold, but not that biting chill kind of cold, and Rachel is glad she's been able to wear her leather jacket instead of her bulky winter coat.

'Where is this place? I thought it was in Covent Garden?' Cleo asks from beside her and Rachel has to fight back the niggling annoyance that Cleo is here. She's twenty-four. She does not need a sodding chaperone.

'I said it's *near* Covent Garden,' Rachel replies, glancing at Cleo in her tight black jeans and the green silk top that matches her eyes and makes her hair look like it's glowing. 'I don't know why you've come. I don't need a babysitter. You could be spending the evening with Simon.'

Cleo turns her face to look at Rachel as though trying to work out if she's pissed or not. She is. 'You're meeting a stranger from the internet. No way are you going alone.'

They're quiet for a moment. The only sound the tap of their heels on the pavement and the rush of traffic from the road.

'I'm not seeing Simon any more,' Cleo says after a while.

'Why?'

'Because it was stupid to get involved with our landlord and because he's a workaholic, and mainly because I hate that it feels like it was getting between us.'

Rachel lets this news sink in. She doesn't know how to feel about Cleo breaking up with Simon. She doesn't like Simon like that any more, and she wants Cleo to be happy, doesn't she? Still, she's glad.

'How did he take it? Are we going to be having cold showers for the rest of our lives?' Rachel's joke lands flat and the smile drops from her face.

'Probably,' Cleo replies. 'I'm telling him tomorrow.'

'Good luck.'

'I'm sorry,' Cleo blurts out. 'I've been a massive dick.'

Rachel smiles. 'It's OK.' And it really is. Something eases in Rachel's chest – a tightness, an anger at Cleo. Rachel is about to meet her cowboy for the first time. That's all that matters. And even though it's really corny, she thinks this is the start of the rest of her life.

'Stop a sec,' Cleo says then. 'My phone is ringing.'

Rachel doesn't want to stop, but Cleo is already fishing in her bag and they're early anyway.

'Hello,' she says. There's a pause and then, 'No, it's fine. Now is a good time,' which makes Rachel roll her eyes because now is not a good time. For a moment she wonders if Cleo is about to make other plans for the evening and the thought washes over her with a mix of annoyance and relief. When Rachel told Luke that Cleo was joining them, he said he was fine with it, making a quip about needing to make sure he's not a serial killer, but Rachel could tell he was disappointed. She's disappointed.

'That's amazing,' Cleo squeaks, her face lighting up. 'Thank you . . . Yes . . . Yes, I will. Bye.' She pulls the phone from her ear and as she stares at it with disbelief, a stone drops inside Rachel for what is coming.

'I got the job.' Cleo looks at Rachel then, pure joy on her face, and Rachel ignores the crushing disappointment and rushes to hug her friend.

'That's amazing. Congratulations.' Rachel's voice wobbles but Cleo doesn't notice as she jabbers on for a minute about how she can't believe it. Rachel cracks a joke about Mandy crying like a baby when she hears the news, and all the while she feels empty and sad and foolish too. Why has she been clinging to a dream that will never happen for her?

'The second I'm there, I'm going to start telling them all about you,' Cleo says, giving Rachel's arm a squeeze.

'You'd better.' She plasters on a grin as they start to walk again, forcing her mind back to Luke. She won't let anything spoil her night.

*

Rachel can tell before they turn into the road that the restaurant isn't what they're expecting. It's no Bond Street eatery, no riverside view.

Her eyes fall to her brand-new little black dress with the killer neckline, which she really couldn't afford. They're dressed for The Ivy, and instead they're tottering down some backstreet with black rubbish bags on the pavements. All Rachel's fantasies of delicious, decadent food and celeb-spotting in the toilets drain away as she catches sight of the red-and-white awnings of the only restaurant on the road – a cheap-looking Italian with a poster in the window advertising a two-for-one meal deal.

The disappointment stings but Rachel keeps smiling. Who cares where they eat, anyway? Her stomach dips then soars. She's desperate to tell Cleo how nervous she is, how excited, but she can't bear another lecture on taking it slow and being sensible.

A figure turns down the road from the opposite end and Rachel can tell before he steps into the light that it's Luke. She's never seen him walk. Never seen him from the waist down, and yet it's as if she knows him so well that her head can fill in the rest, like those long legs and that confident stride.

Questions dart into her thoughts. What if he doesn't like her in person? What if their chemistry is only on the screen? But then he smiles, wide and open, and all her nerves disappear and she quickens her pace, her heels tap-tapping to reach him.

'Hey, beautiful,' he says, staring straight into Rachel's eyes as he reaches to kiss her cheek. She catches the citrus of his aftershave and her insides burn with longing. 'Hi, Cleo.' He gives a wave but makes no move to kiss her cheek as well, and Rachel is glad.

He leans in, his mouth right next to Rachel's ear, his breath hot. 'You look stunning,' he whispers.

Luke pulls his eyes away from her and looks up at the restaurant. 'I'm going to kill my boss,' he laughs. 'He said this was the best Italian in London.'

'It doesn't look like it,' Cleo says, and even though her tone is light and teasing, Rachel bristles anyway. Can't she see Luke is trying? It's not his fault his boss gave him bad advice.

Luke's face falls. His gaze moves from Cleo to Rachel. He looks like a lost little boy and Rachel instinctively slips her hand into his, like it's the most natural thing in the world, like they've known each other forever. 'Shall we try somewhere else?' he asks, entwining their fingers.

Rachel bites her lip, hesitant. This is not the restaurant she imagined in any of her million fantasies, but she doesn't want to upset Luke.

'I'm sure this place is fine,' she sing-songs. 'Maybe it will be a hidden gem.'

Luke's face lights up and Rachel knows she's made the right decision. 'All right, then, let's give it a go.' He pulls her gently towards him, wrapping an arm around her. She feels the warmth of his body, the muscles of his arms, and together they walk into the restaurant, Cleo trailing behind.

Chapter 36

Cleo

Now

My eyes blur as I stare at your laptop screen. The moment the chat loads and it's not you, I'm gone.

Skip. Skip. Skip.

My thoughts flip-flop over Anik's words earlier. His pushing me to talk about what happened, his confession about his feelings. One then the other.

Skip. Skip. Skip.

My phone rings. It's Beth. I stare at her name for a moment before shutting down CamChat. I don't want to speak to her. I don't know what to say, but she's so worried about you, it's not fair to ignore her.

It's been two days since I've seen you and I've still not told Beth. I've not told her about Anik being involved or the bag I found, either, or the weird man on CamChat, the texts I've received. I've been a coward for not calling her myself.

'Hi, Beth,' I say.

'Hi. Have you found anything?' she asks, her voice

fast and breathless. Panicked, I think with a wave of sickening guilt, because the answer is yes. I've found so much and yet how can I tell her that I've found you, that you're trapped somewhere, in danger, suffering?

'I . . .'

'Cleo, what? What is it?'

'Stuff has been happening.'

'What kind of stuff?'

I take a long breath, picking out the pieces of truth for her. 'I think you're right. I think something has happened to Rach. I've been getting text messages. I think someone was messing with her and now they're trying to mess with me.'

'Oh my God,' Beth cries. 'I knew it. I could feel something was wrong. I called the police again this morning but they still won't do anything until Rachel doesn't come back from this stupid holiday they're convinced she's on. What are we going to do?'

'I don't know.'

'Are you safe?' she asks.

'I'm not sure.' Safer than you are, Rach, is all I can think.

A silence draws out between us. Beth sniffs and exhales loudly. 'I'm going to come up to London. I can't keep sitting around down here. I'm still trying to find someone to help with Mum. There's a neighbour who might be able to do it. I'll come up at the week-end, OK? Hopefully Sunday,' she says in a way that makes it seem as though she's thinking out loud rather than talking to me.

I think of the days between now and Sunday. Five whole days of this. I'll find you before then, though, won't I? I have to. My flight to Bermuda is booked for Sunday.

'I know it's days away,' Beth says, as though reading my mind, 'but it's all I can do right now. I'll call you if I figure something out before then.'

'OK,' I say. 'Thanks.'

'I've got to go,' Beth says. 'Call me if you find anything.'

She hangs up and I'm about to start CamChat again when the front door opens then slams, and Simon calls my name.

I throw my phone on to the bed and hurry across the room. If he's surprised to see me in your doorway, he doesn't show it. His black suit is crumpled and his tie is loose. He looks exhausted.

'Hey,' he says.

'Hi.'

'I'm sorry I had to go to Jersey. Are you OK?'

I shrug. There is only one answer to that question and I'm sure it's written all over my face.

'Come talk to me while I dump this stuff and get something to eat. I'm starving.'

Simon steps towards his door, wheeling a small carry-on suitcase behind him. It still has the white-and-orange airline tags on the handle.

'This is for you, by the way,' he says as he reaches his door. He holds out a duty-free bag and I take it, finding a huge bar of Toblerone inside.

'Thanks,' I smile. 'My favourite.'

'I remember.'

As he finds the right key, I pretend the air between us isn't suddenly charged with awkwardness, pretend I'm not thinking about the last time Simon bought me Toblerone and we ate it in his bed, fooling around, laughing.

It was another lifetime, and even though it was

214

never serious, it was nice. I'd give anything to undo it now, though – that first drunken kiss at the house party you skipped and everything that followed. It's not just the betrayal of our 'off-limits' promise we made to each other; it's the time I spent with Simon instead of you, the time you were growing close to a psychopath on CamChat.

I follow Simon inside and as he steps into the kitchen and opens the fridge, I let the words tumble out. The power cut, your bag, visiting your office, the weirdo on CamChat, the texts. I tell him everything I couldn't tell Beth. My words come too fast and I can tell from the way Simon is frowning that he's worried. Whether about me or what's going on, I don't know.

'And Darcey – that's the girl I spoke to who Rachel works with – showed me this photo Rachel sent her.'

'A photo? What photo?'

'It was of a beach, but she wasn't in it. Anyone could have found that photo online.'

'So anyone could have sent those emails.' He gives a slow nod and I realize how good it feels to be believed. When Anik questioned what I'd told him, he said he was thinking through all the possibilities, but I know it was more than just devil's advocate.

Simon places a large Tupperware pot of leftovers in the microwave and I can't help myself. 'You cook now?' I ask, remembering the six slices of buttered white toast Simon used to eat and call dinner. He was the only one who made our cookery skills seem advanced.

He gives a sheepish smile. 'I took classes a few years ago. It was about time.'

'Lucky Liz.'

Simon looks thoughtful for a moment before he

replies. 'No. I'm the lucky one. I was having a really bad time of it at work. She really saved me.'

'That's great,' I say, and I mean it.

'Have you spoken to the police again and told them what's happened?'

'Sort of. I've been speaking to the detective who worked on the case five years ago – DI Anik Saha. His team are working on it.'

Simon's eyebrows shoot up. 'Really? Wow, that's really good news. So you're staying, then?' He looks at me, eyes pleading.

'I can't exactly leave knowing Rachel is in trouble, can I? Whether I like it or not, I'm involved in this somehow.'

Simon lets out a sigh like he's been holding his breath. 'Thank goodness. I'm back to Jersey this week, but knowing you're here makes all the difference.'

The microwave pings and Simon takes a moment to slide the plastic tub out, nudging the lid off with his fingers and unleashing a plume of steam. The smell of spices and sauce fills the room. Simon spoons some of the food on to a plate before turning back to me, fork mid-air. My stomach rumbles, a hollow sound, reminding me how little I've eaten today.

'I just can't work out how Rachel's bag made it back to the house and Rachel didn't.'

Simon tilts his head to one side as he eats. 'Are you sure it's her bag? Loads of people leave stuff behind when they move out. Whatever I don't bin goes in the cupboard.'

'It's a brand-new two-hundred-pound Michael Kors clutch with Rachel's favourite brand of lipstick in it. Who else could it belong to?'

'Good point,' he says with a mouth full of food.

'And there's no way she could've come home that Friday night?'

Simon puts his plate on to the counter and rubs his hands over his face. 'Pretty sure. Like, ninety per cent. I was working until really late and then I couldn't sleep. I'm sure I would have heard her come in.'

We fall silent. Exhaustion sweeps over me. It's more than just a 'twelve-hour shift on my feet' kind of tiredness. It's an emotional emptiness that leaves me hollow.

Simon picks up the Tupperware box and hands it to me. 'You look like you need this.'

I grip the pot in my hands and breathe in the fragrance until my mouth is watering and I'm shaking with hunger. 'Thanks.'

'I've got a meeting in the London office tomorrow morning and then I'm back in Jersey,' he says. 'Will you be all right?'

I shrug. 'I have no idea. I don't know what else I can do.' My voice is small, defeated.

Simon steps forwards, wrapping me into a hug. His body is firm and warm but does nothing to stop me feeling completely alone in this.

'You'll think of something. Now, eat that food. It's good,' he says as he sees me out.

I head to the main kitchen, not even bothering to turn on the light, and use the glow from the hallway to find a fork. Standing at the counter, I eat the lot, barely chewing, barely swallowing one mouthful before the next is in. It's hot, the meat succulent, the sauce tangy and full of spice.

And it's then, as I'm scraping the last forkful from the pot, that I hear something – a noise outside the window. Someone or something is in the garden. I drop down, crouching on the floor. My pulse races, hammering in my ears. I crawl towards the window and slowly, silently, I lift myself up and stare out.

The garden is one dark shadow, but something clatters, like a pebble being kicked, and I gasp as the shape of a figure emerges.

I spin around, stumbling over my feet, before sprinting through the hall and back to Simon's door, my knocking loud and urgent.

He appears a moment later, his face frowning with concern. 'Cleo, what's wrong?'

'There's someone in the garden,' I hiss.

'Wait here,' he says, pushing past me and running towards the kitchen. A moment later I hear the back door open and then there's nothing but silence. Minutes pass and I hug my arms to my chest, panic swimming through my veins.

Then I hear the back door shutting and Simon appears in the hallway. 'I didn't see anyone.' I wait for him to ask me if I'm sure of what I saw, but he doesn't and I'm grateful.

'Maybe it was an animal?' I say, although I don't think either of us believes it.

I head to my room and lock the door. The air rattles in my throat. My head spins and I collapse on to the bed. The front door crashes open to the sound of your housemates as I fumble for my phone and, with shaking hands, I call the one person I never thought I'd speak to again.

Chapter 37

Cleo

Now

It was my mum who found Ingrid. A week after it happened, when you were still in hospital and Mum came to stay with me, holding me close while I cried and cried. She spoke to Anik and they both thought talking to a professional would help, but I knew what they wanted – they wanted me to remember everything that happened to us that night so I could help with the investigation, and I couldn't do that.

Mum did it in the same way she's always looked after me, like the extra meals she used to make for us – cottage pies and casseroles in foil containers – packing them in a bag for life after every visit home. Unobtrusive, a rock of support. She knew we'd need professional help and she found it for us, booking one appointment for me and one for you.

I remember telling you about the appointment with Ingrid, standing in the doorway of your room. Curtains drawn. Lights off. Me feeling like an intruder.

But you listened. I remember you leaving the house, a thick scarf wrapped around your neck, hood pulled up, head down. I assumed you went. You seemed stronger afterwards.

Ingrid did try to help me, and her breathing techniques to calm myself down when I'm anxious have been useful, but it was the talking I didn't like. Those gentle questions, the encouraging nods. The more she asked, the more I shut down. It was a relief on our final session when I told her I was leaving London.

And yet, I'm here again, being buzzed into a nondescript apartment building on the riverside in Canada Water, the rising skyline of Canary Wharf towering up on the other side of the river.

The lift takes me to the sixth floor and when the doors open, Ingrid is standing in her doorway just as she was on that first, second and third visit. Does she think I'll get lost in the ten paces between the lift and her door?

She looks just as I remember her, right down to that sharp, ice-blonde bob that is sitting so perfectly, so exactly the same as it did five years ago, that I wonder if it's a wig.

She's wearing loose-fitting black trousers, a cream diamond-patterned blouse and a warm smile.

'Cleo, how lovely to see you again,' she says with the same strong Swedish accent I remember as she beckons me into her flat. It's a white-walled, new-build type, with wood floors and spotlights in the ceilings. Every door is closed and I wonder, as she leads me to her office, what the rest of the apartment is like. Is it a mess? A riot of colour? Is all this calm and tranquillity an act? Does she have pink spiky hair hidden under that wig?

'Thank you for seeing me on short notice,' I say.

'Of course. I was hoping you'd come back to finish our sessions one day. Although I didn't expect it to be five years later.'

'Oh, I . . .' She thinks I'm here for me. Last night, after talking to Simon, after being so sure that there was someone in the garden looking in, I was lost, rattled. I called Ingrid on a whim, planning to ask her if she'd seen you recently, if you'd ever made it to that first appointment. But I couldn't get the right words out and the next thing I knew, Ingrid had coaxed me into an appointment for the next day.

'Sorry,' I end up saying as she motions me in – another portal back in time. The same desk, same chairs, same stripy rug on the floor and fake plant in the corner.

'Please take a seat,' she says, before settling behind her desk and making a show of opening her notebook, picking up her pen and tilting her head in her 'I'm listening' pose.

'Now, if I remember correctly,' she begins, pronouncing each word carefully and slowly, 'the last time we spoke you were going to spend three months working on a cruise.'

I nod. 'I was – I mean, I am.' I'd forgotten how nervous it makes me to sit in this chair. I think of the things I should say – the long-buried truth of that night. My face feels hot under Ingrid's gaze. 'I still work on a cruise ship,' I say at last. 'I'm Spa Manager now.'

'You must enjoy it very much.'

'I do. Being on board the ship – it makes me feel safe.'

She jots something on her pad. 'And when you're not on the cruise ship, how do you feel then?'

Jumpy. Paranoid. 'OK.'

'But not safe?'

I shake my head.

'You used to have nightmares about your attack. Are they still occurring?'

Every night. 'Sometimes.'

'How frequently, would you say?'

'It's under control. I know you think it was running away when I left, but it really helped.'

'I'm glad,' she says with a soft smile. 'We are all different, Cleo. We all face things in our own time.'

I nod.

Now would be the time to confess. To explain that I didn't run away because of what happened to us. It wasn't fear or panic or worry that Luke Richards would jump out at me from every corner that made me take my first cruise job and my second, my tenth. It was what I did that night and afterwards – the secret I've carried, the guilt that made it so hard to look at you for fear you'd see the truth in my eyes.

I tried to tell Anik once. It was in the aftermath of the attack, in the muggy warmth of the hospital cafeteria when the dirt was still under my nails, all over my skin, and I was in shock, not thinking straight. I half confessed before I realized what I'd done and then I snatched back the words, told him I was muddled, that I couldn't remember anything.

'I can see you're still finding this hard,' Ingrid continues. 'I want to talk about some exciting developments in EMDR – rapid eye movement therapy – that I think would really help you. It allows your mind to process negative events in a different way to more traditional talking therapies. I think it could be very useful in your case.'

'Um . . . thanks. I'll think about it.'

There's a pause. Ingrid is waiting for me to say more, but I have nothing.

'Cleo, may I ask what made you call me last night? You seemed very distressed on the phone.'

'Rachel is missing. She's in trouble and I'm trying to find her. I wanted to ask you if you've seen her recently? I know you can't talk about your other clients or tell me anything confidential, but can you just . . . I don't know . . . nod your head if you've seen or spoken to her in the last couple of weeks or months?'

'Cleo, Rachel has never been a client of mine. I've never met her, so there is no confidentiality breach.'

'Oh.' I sink into my chair. You never went to that first appointment, then. It's another dead end.

'Right now I'm worried about *you*,' Ingrid continues. 'Can you see the similarities to the last time you were in this office? You were so concerned with your friend and what she was going through that you refused to acknowledge your own pain. Five years ago, for instance, you told me that you were struggling to eat anything. Is this still a problem you face?'

Ingrid's comment burns. I only mentioned once that I'd lost my appetite, and how much better I felt when my body shook with emptiness. It wasn't a big deal. It isn't a big deal. I've been careful, always going to the staff restaurant on my break, making sure I have my three meals a day. I know I'm thinner now, but that's because I'm eating salads instead of pizzas all the time.

'It's OK.' That word again.

'It's very normal to develop disorders around control after a traumatic experience. It can make a person feel stronger to know that even though they can't control their emotions, they can control certain elements of their life, such as food intake.'

223

I've heard this speech before. The truth is, I don't mean to skip meals; I'm not purposefully starving myself. The last few days have been hectic, that's all.

'What about your family?' Ingrid continues. 'Have you reached out to them for support? Having a strong support system in place would be a great help, Cleo.'

Another silence. I don't know what to say.

A single creased pinch forms between Ingrid's eyes.

My phone vibrates in my pocket and I feel sick as I dig it out, as though I know before I see the screen who it will be. The unknown number again, the taunting words.

Getting hot now, Cleo.
Ready for more?

Ingrid clears her throat. 'Is everything all right?'

My muscles tighten. The air in here is unbreathable.

I jump to my feet, desperate to leave. 'Thank you. I should go now.'

'Cleo, my door is always open. When you're ready, I really think I can help you. Please call me, anytime.'

Outside, the cold rain soothes the heat burning through my body. I stare at the messages again before taking a screenshot and sending it to Anik. He and his team can deal with them.

I'm getting closer to you. Is it seeing Ingrid? But how? You never came here.

I walk away, head pounding in time with my feet hitting the pavement. I walk fast, stopping at Mr Hakimi's shop, stocking up on food. Filling the basket with all the stuff we used to eat, as though proving something to Ingrid and myself.

I want Ingrid to be wrong about me. I'm not

avoiding my life. I'm not pushing my family away, and yet even I can see that there is some truth in her words. I've not spoken to Mum since Christmas Day. Me from a port in St Lucia, and her at home with my brother and his kids. The noise and shouts of the children in the background made me feel better about not being there. I could almost convince myself I wasn't missed, wasn't missing something. My mum doesn't even know I'm in London.

I pull out my mobile and text my mum. I pretend I've found some signal on the ship. I send an old photo of a sunset skyline over the ocean, and before I can stop myself or think about what I'm saying, I tell her I'll be coming home when the cruise is finished.

I read the words back and realize I mean it. I'll go home. For a visit, for something longer, I'm not sure, but being back here, listening to Ingrid, I think . . . I think I've been avoiding so much. However desperate I am to get back to the *Enchantress*, I'm also starting to see that it's not good for me.

As I walk home, I wonder how different things would have been if I'd told you the truth about that night.

The fear rises up suddenly, and with it a torrent of panic and shame, and I squash the thought away.

The grand finale is getting closer.

It's time for my next move.

*I know how desperate Cleo is to see
her very best friend and I would just hate
to keep her waiting too long.*

Chapter 38

Cleo

Now

Just after seven p.m. I open CamChat on your browser and press 'chat' before I can change my mind.

The first chat loads and it's the same woman in her fifties with short copper hair who I skipped last time. 'Hello, love,' she says, raising a glass of wine to the screen.

'Hi,' I say.

'Nice to see a pretty face on here for a change.' She laughs, a cackle of a noise that reminds me a little of yours.

Gee, thanks.

Sorry.

'Bet you get all the dicks out on here, don't ya?'

That makes me smile. I'm sure I've seen more genitalia in the last three days than I have in my whole life, and I wax a lot of places in the spa.

Your photo is sitting beside me, crinkled now from how many times I've held it to the screen, but I don't

227

pick it up yet. After being skipped so often, I've realized that aside from the perverts and those wanting to practise their language skills, what draws people to CamChat is loneliness, and if I want to find out more about you, then I need to tread a little softer.

'I'm Cleo,' I say.

'Jan.'

'What brings you to CamChat, Jan?' I ask.

'Ha, well, that's my late husband's fault. The silly old sod went and died of cancer a few months ago, and knowing my love of a little glass of something, he made me promise on his deathbed not to drink alone.' She gives an exasperated sigh but there's moisture glistening in her eyes. 'I mean, of all the bloody things he could've made me promise – travel the world, treat yourself, find love again – he comes up with this. But I'm not ready to get out yet and so here I am, sharing my drink with you.'

She raises her glass again and smiles. 'Clink.'

'Cheers.' I lift my glass of water to the screen too.

'I'm going to pretend that's a very strong gin and tonic and I'd appreciate it if you didn't tell me otherwise.'

'I won't,' I reply, adding a wince as I take another sip.

She laughs. 'You're a good 'un. So, why are you here?'

'I'm looking for my friend,' I say, lifting your photo to the camera. 'Her name is Rachel but she calls herself—'

'Roxy.' Jan nods.

'You know her?' Hope sparks.

'Oh yes, I know Roxy. We've spoken a few times.'

'Do you—'

'Oh my God.' Jan cuts me off. 'I've just made the connection. You're Cleo. I'll be damned. She talked about you non-stop.'

'She did?'

'I feel like I know you.' She gives a tinkling laugh. 'You don't look like you're on a cruise ship right now.'

I shake my head and find myself telling her everything. I mention Luke, describing his appearance but not what happened to us. Instead, I tell Jan he's an ex-boyfriend. Then I tell her about your disappearance. When I'm done, Jan stares at me open-mouthed. 'And the police aren't interested?'

'There's a detective helping me. He's the same detective who was involved last time, but I don't think he's taking this seriously. Did Rachel seem OK to you? Was she worried about anything?'

Jan places her glass on the table beside her and pushes it away before shaking her head. 'The last time we spoke, she said you'd been texting a lot and had plans to meet you. She really missed you, you know? She didn't go into detail but I could tell she was sorry about how things were left between you.'

I nod; sudden tears sting my eyes. I still can't wrap my head around the idea that you thought we were talking and how happy that made you.

Fuck! I'm sorry, Rach. I'm so sorry for the radio silence, for leaving you. For everything.

'Just go, then. Fuck off.'

'Rachel, let's not leave it like this.'

'GET OUT OF MY LIFE!'

'It sounds like things were going well with her boyfriend,' Jan continues, pulling me away from the memories.

'Boyfriend?' I sit up. This is the first mention that

you were seeing someone. Whoever it was, you kept it from Simon and your sister. 'Did she tell you a name?'

I hold my breath and stare at Jan as she hesitates for a moment. 'If she did, then it's gone. I'm sorry.'

'That's OK.' A name would've been better, but it's something to go on. 'You haven't seen a weird guy on here, have you? Longish grey hair—'

'Bad teeth?' Jan gives a vigorous nod. 'Oh yeah.'

'Who is he?'

'I don't know. He never tells anyone his name. There's a few of us who talk about him. To be honest, after the first time, I got such a bad vibe that I just skip him. At least with the naked guys you know what they're after. He was different.'

'Did Rach – I mean Roxy – talk to him?'

'I don't know how much she talked to him but she definitely spoke to him. She even thought she saw him in real life once. It freaked her out.'

'When was this?'

'Sometime in December. It happened during her lunch break. I spoke to her a few days later.'

I chat to Jan for a while more. I let her talk about her dead husband, her loneliness, her plans to travel, and when we say goodbye, I close the lid of your laptop, too drained to talk any more.

I try to make sense of what I know. Anik thinks Luke Richards is Richard Gilders, a man who died four years ago. But you told Beth you saw Luke. And then there's the weirdo on CamChat who knows my name, who talked to me about playing a game. A man you told Jan you think you saw once.

So who has you?

Both?

Neither?

The text churns in my thoughts.

Getting hot now, Cleo.

To what? To finding you, or being dragged so far into something that I'll never get free?

It's been three days since I saw you tied to that chair, Rach. Are you still alive? Tears blur my vision and I cover my face with my hands and cry and cry. Whatever this is, whatever is happening, I'm not sure I'm strong enough to do this.

A pain throbs around my head.

I lie back on your bed, breathing in the covers that smell of you and a thousand memories of being here.

I'm no longer in your room, I'm outside. The air is cold and sharp, the ground beneath my feet hard.

The urge to run beats through me as the woods stretch out in every direction. I spin around and around, twigs, leaves, brambles digging into my feet, scratching at my legs.

I'm lost.

Someone is chasing me.

There's something on my hands. It's sticky and warm. Blood.

I start to run, stumbling through thick foliage, shivering all over. Cold. Fear.

Everywhere I look it's black. Thick, impassable trees appear from nowhere, blocking my path. I run one way and then the other, crashing through bushes. I'm crying, great big heaving sobs. Tears roll down my face and all I want to do is sink to the ground and cry, but I know I must keep going or he'll get me.

Then the world flips in that way it can only do in dreams and I'm not being chased any more; I'm looking for something. I don't know what it is, but it's nowhere and I have to find it.

A path appears before me. The ground is smoother but it's still so dark. There is no light. No moon. No hope. I keep running, sprinting faster and faster until the ground disappears beneath my feet and I'm falling, down, down, down. There's earth all around me, pouring over me like cement. It's in my mouth and my throat, my nostrils, my eyes. I'm drowning in it.

A strange click sounds from something near by. The earth rustles around me.

And then I'm awake, my eyes flying open, and before my brain can catch up, I'm pushing myself up to sitting, arms flailing, gasping for air, just like I always do.

Except . . . except the dream wasn't finished. Something woke me – a noise.

The realization crawls over me, a thousand tiny spiders.

What was it? My head is still foggy, still two paces behind me, back in that nightmare. And then the truth settles on me and I know – it was your bedroom door shutting. That's the noise I heard in my dream, the sound that woke me.

The thought is an electric shock and I jump away from the bed, throwing myself against the wall. My elbow knocks against the sink. Pain shoots up my arm as your toothbrush clatters into the basin. The nightmare forgotten, only the taste of earth remains.

My heart lurches in my chest and I hold my breath, slowly, very slowly inching my way around the bed to check inside your wardrobe. I feel like I'm in a horror movie, about to have a knife plunged into me, but your room is empty, so either the door woke me when someone was on their way out, or I'm being paranoid and imagined the whole thing.

I listen to the sounds of the house; it's silent in the way it only can be in the middle of the night. No traffic outside, no passers-by. No squeak of floorboards. No rattle of pipes or doors opening. Silence.

I grab for my alarm, stashed under your pillow, but it's gone. My hand pats the empty mattress one way then the other, and then I'm throwing your pillows on the floor, then the duvet, eyes darting in every direction until I eventually find it in the tangle of the duvet at the bottom of the bed. I clasp it in my hands and hold it to my body as though it's my most precious possession.

I open the door and stare into the empty hall. There's no one. I tiptoe to Simon's door, but there's another Post-it.

> *Had to go back to Jersey for*
> *longer than planned. Sorry!*
> *Back Saturday evening.*
> *(Cleo – stay in touch!!!)*

Damn it!

I head upstairs, certain now that I heard something, certain someone was in your room with me. On the first floor, I walk across the hall to the next set of stairs. Every groan of floorboards seems impossibly loud in the silence.

But before I reach the top, a door bangs from somewhere below me. I gasp, a bolt of fear shooting through me as I sprint to my room and lock the door.

In bed I draw in breath after breath. My stomach cramps. The room spins. I huddle beneath the covers as the panic circles in a tornado around me and I wonder if this is what crazy feels like.

My phone buzzes and I'm sure it will be another message from that unknown number, but it's Beth.

Are you awake? I can't sleep! I'm so worried.
Have you found anything?

Nothing yet, I reply.

I'm definitely coming on Sunday x

Beth deserves more, but I don't have it in me to tell her right now. I won't be able to keep it from her on Sunday, though. She'll see right through me, like always.

Sunday. Five days to find you.

What if I can't? Can I really get on the flight to Bermuda with you still missing?

I could email Donovan and ask for more time. He'll suggest skipping the cruise altogether, and the thought of spending the next four months here fills me with dread.

Just hours ago I was questioning whether I should go home to my mum's for a while, but now all I can think about is escape, whether I find you or not.

Chapter 39

Rachel

Five years earlier

The restaurant is busy, the air warm with the rich smell of sauces and garlic. A lot of garlic. The place is packed with chairs set in twos and fours around rickety-looking tables. Faded posters of Italian vineyards cover the walls.

A family dining by the window watch with undisguised interest as the three of them wait to be seated. It's the post-theatre crowd of families and older couples in fleeces and baggy denim and comfortable shoes for their journey home. They're not Londoners. Rachel doesn't even know how she can tell any more. Maybe it's their faces: the curiosity, the weariness. Londoners see every kind of person – goths, City workers, punks, weirdos, students, cleaners – they all cram into the same tube carriage every day. They've seen it all and know better than to stare.

A dark-haired waiter appears – red-faced and

harassed – and leads them to a table at the back of the restaurant. The table is tucked inside an alcove and feels separate from the other diners in a way that makes Rachel relax.

Luke holds out a chair for her and then for Cleo before sitting opposite them. The table wobbles as he pulls his chair in and Rachel spots a cardboard coaster wedged under one of the legs, and a forgotten chip on the floor.

Big plastic menus appear; food on one side, drinks on the other. Cleo tries to catch Rachel's eye from the seat beside her but she makes a point of not looking, of smiling at Luke, who is glancing around the restaurant, looking nervous now, and she reaches for his hand, reassuring him she's happy.

Without a word, the waiter appears, brandishing a bottle of champagne, glistening with condensation. 'Champagne,' he declares in what Rachel is quite sure is a fake Italian accent.

Luke pulls a face and laughs. 'My boss must have set this up,' he says with an amused shrug that makes her laugh too.

'So you've never been here before?' Cleo's tone is edged with an accusation that makes Rachel want to kick her. Hard. She settles for a pleading nudge to the ankle. A 'don't ruin this' look. This is Luke. This is everything.

'No way,' Luke laughs. 'First time in London. Hey, shall we all try the pizza, then?'

When the waiter has taken their orders, Luke raises his champagne flute. 'A toast to us,' he says, his gaze locked on Rachel's. 'I can't believe this is the first time we're meeting. I feel like I've known you forever.'

Cleo barks a laugh of surprise. Rachel flashes her a

warning look and turns back to Luke, smiling so hard her cheeks hurt.

They talk like they do online, finishing each other's sentences, laughing, joking. Rachel is so glad of this alcove, this hidden-away place. It wouldn't be the same if they were in the fancy restaurant she'd imagined, all linen tablecloths and hovering waiters. Here, it is just them. Her and Luke, and Cleo, who they're doing their best to ignore.

The pizzas arrive along with another bottle of champagne and Rachel doesn't even care that they are definitely not the best pizzas in London. She seriously doubts they're the best pizzas in this postcode. But they eat, they talk, they laugh. Every so often Cleo jumps in with a question and it's so obvious she's trying to catch Luke out in some imaginary lies she thinks he's told them. There's a hard edge to Cleo's tone that riles Rachel, but Luke doesn't care one bit. He tears his eyes away from Rachel just long enough to answer.

And then, before she knows what's happening, the evening is drawing to an end and Luke disappears to pay the bill and all she can think is that she's not ready to say goodbye. She doesn't think she'll ever be ready.

'So, this has been fun,' Cleo sighs the minute they're alone. Her voice drips with sarcasm.

'I didn't ask you to come,' Rachel says, unable to stop herself smiling as she pulls out her compact and reapplies a layer of lipstick.

'I wish I hadn't,' she groans.

'At least you know he's normal now,' Rachel says. 'You don't need to worry about me.'

'Is he?' Cleo frowns. 'Don't you think he's a bit creepy?' she says with an exaggerated shiver.

'Er, have you been at the same dinner?'

Luke reappears before Cleo can reply. Rachel doesn't want to hear it any more. Cleo has got her dream job – Rachel's dream job – and she stole Simon from her, even if it is over between them now. Why can't she just let Rachel have this?

Luke is holding a small silver tray with three shot glasses in the centre. 'I don't know what this stuff is, but they were not letting me pay without taking it.'

Rachel laughs. 'It's limoncello. It's an Italian liqueur. Try it, it's nice.'

He hands a glass to her and then one to Cleo. 'When in Rome,' he smiles.

The shot is sickly sweet and strong, hitting Rachel's already fuzzy head. She's totally buzzing in the best possible way.

'Do you want to—' Rachel starts to say, just as Luke speaks too.

'So, I'm not sure about you girls,' he says, pronouncing it 'gals', 'but I'd love the evening to continue. How about another drink? I've got this wicked Airbnb. It's a gorgeous house. You've gotta see it.'

'Where is it?' Cleo asks.

'Oh, what's the place called?' He snaps his fingers. 'St John's Wood. You'll love it. Even has one of those open fires.'

'Sounds amazing.' Rachel is already standing up, wobbling in her heels from a little too much champagne.

Chapter 40

Cleo

Now

It's Thursday already. I've been in London six days now and I'm no closer to finding you. Yesterday I spent all day in the house. I searched the cupboard under the stairs and your room again, and I spent hours skipping through CamChat looking for you.

It's been five days since I saw you and the more time that passes, the less real it all seems.

When I woke up this morning the walls were closing in. I knew I had to get out. I left early and walked towards Liverpool Street and then down to St Paul's, holing up in a Starbucks in Paternoster Square beneath the looming dome of the cathedral. My second large cappuccino is steaming on the table beside me, while the caffeine from the first is rippling through my body. I'm fidgeting, exhausted yet wide awake.

Anik texted me first thing. He has news but can't see me until tonight. Seven p.m. in the Flying Horse again. The desperation to learn what he knows is burning through me alongside the coffee.

I pick at the flakes of a stale croissant and watch the passing City workers. Men and women in sharp suits – focused, professional – hurrying in and out of buildings and sandwich shops. Others huddle over laptops on the steps of the tall grey-stone monument in the middle of the square.

I'm the only one sitting alone. The only one not in a suit, and I like that. It's easy to spot outsiders here, easy to spot someone out of place. I scan every face I see, searching for a man with long grey hair. I search for Luke Richards in every face too. Anik says he's dead, but old habits die hard.

When my second coffee is mingling with my first and I'm so jittery my left leg is bouncing up and down and I feel queasy with it, I pick up my phone and call Beth. I can't put it off any longer. I have to tell your sister what I know, what I saw. Images of you strobe through my mind. It can't wait until I see her.

The phone rings and rings in my ear and I'm about to give up when Beth answers.

'Oh, Cleo. Thank God you've called,' she says before I can say hello. There's a rustle in the background before she speaks again. 'I've been picking up the phone to call you every five minutes,' she adds. 'But I didn't want you to feel pressured when you've already told me you haven't found anything yet. I knew you'd call me if you had news. Have you found Rachel?'

'No. I'm sorry.'

There's a muffled sob.

'I guess you haven't heard anything either?' I regret

my question the minute it's out. The answer is obvious.

'Nothing. I'm so worried about her. I've been keeping it all from Mum as best I can, but I don't know how long I can keep it up. She knows something is wrong and it's confusing her even more. The police at Bethnal Green are being sympathetic, but until Rachel doesn't show up to work on Monday like they think she's planned, they won't do anything.'

'I know.' We fall silent for a moment before I speak again. 'Can I ask you something?'

There's a pause. 'Can it wait until we see each other? It's just I'm about to take Mum shopping.'

'It's just a couple of things,' I push. 'You saw Rachel at Christmas, right?'

'Sure.'

'How was she?'

'Fine. She was totally fine.'

'Simon said he'd heard her moving around late at night. Did she talk about having trouble sleeping?'

'No. Honestly, Cleo, she was good. Better than I'd seen her in a long time, actually. She looked . . . happy. Hopeful, even.'

'Do you know why?'

'No. I asked, though. I thought she might be seeing someone, but she went all coy. You know what she's like.'

Coy? You?

Hey, I could be.

Never with me.

'She didn't mention a boyfriend?'

'No one she told me about. I'm starting to wonder if she might be on holiday after all, you know.'

241

'She's not.' I shrink into my chair, scrunching my eyes shut.

'Oh my God. What do you know?' she asks.

I picture you tied to that chair again. It's the eyes I keep coming back to. Desperate, terrified. But the words to tell your sister aren't there. What purpose will it serve? There's nothing Beth can do. Nothing I can do either, but I'm trying.

'Cleo, what?' Beth says and there is so much emotion in those two words, so much hope, so much fear, so much love, that I know I can't tell her.

'It about Luke Richards,' I say instead. 'The man—'

'I know who he is.'

'He . . .' I still can't believe I'm saying the words. '. . . might be dead. There was another case—'

'I know,' she cuts in.

'What?'

'I know,' Beth repeats. 'I assumed you knew. That detective told Rachel last month.'

A hole opens beneath my feet and I have a feeling of falling. It's hot. Boiling suddenly.

How did Anik tell you that Luke Richards was dead last month when he only found out on Monday morning while scanning old cases?

Chapter 41

Cleo

Now

'Cleo?' Beth's voice rings in my ear. 'Are you still there?'

'Yes. I . . . I bet Rach must have been happy to hear about the death.' It's half question, half statement, and I don't even know why I'm asking. I can't get my head around Anik lying to me. He knew about Luke on our first meeting and didn't tell me.

Another pause. 'Yeah, but she wasn't as convinced as the detective was about it all. I don't know what happened, but I got the impression she was pretty pissed at him about something.'

'What?'

'I don't know. She just said she'd be calling the police herself if he turned up again. I made a joke about how you can't call the police on the police and we had a laugh about it. She was OK, just annoyed.'

You never did like him.

You liked him too much.

My head spins. The milk from my cappuccinos curdles in my stomach.

'What wasn't she sure about?' I ask.

'She said the cases looked similar on the surface but there was no knife and no grave,' Beth continues. 'The guy didn't have a shovel in his car or anything. She said that using a traceable dating app wasn't Luke's style. She thought he was too smart for that. And then Rach asked that detective for a photo of the dead man and he said he didn't have one.'

'Anik said that?' But he told me he was going to print one out for me to look at. It's the only way to be absolutely sure he's dead.

'Yeah. Rachel said she was going to contact the dead guy's brother on Facebook and talk to him.'

'When was this?'

'A few weeks before she went missing.'

'And did she contact him?'

'I don't know. She didn't mention it again. I never like to be the first to talk about it. Sometimes she can get really down.'

I swallow hard, the guilt a sharp rock in my throat. 'Was she OK about what happened to us, Beth?'

'Sometimes, yes,' Beth replies, her tone hard. 'Sometimes she was like the old Rachel and it felt like she was finally moving on. Like I said, she was happy at Christmas. But other times, she was a shadow of herself. Like she was still so lost. I thought it was you leaving as much as what happened.' There it is. That red-hot blame I felt from your sister all those years ago.

'I . . .'

'I'm sorry,' Beth says quickly. 'I didn't mean to make you feel bad. Whatever I felt at the time about you leaving, Rachel understood.'

Tears form in my eyes, blurring the room, my thoughts with it. We talk for another few minutes. Nonsense stuff about your mum and Beth's wedding last year. It's nice, actually. Despite everything, talking to Beth feels like a window to you.

I've missed you so much, Rach. So much. But cruise life is an alternative reality in so many ways. Time loses all meaning. The longer I spent on the ships, the safer I felt, and the more impossible it became to leave.

You could've called me, though.

I know. I should've called or emailed or written you a letter. I should've replied to your texts last month, returned your calls over the years, and I'd give anything right now to go back and do it all differently. But my safe little bubble of a life only existed by ignoring reality, and that meant you.

'Will you keep looking for her?' Beth asks. There's something strange about the question, something hidden beneath the words as if she's asking me something else, but I don't know what.

'I . . . Yes, of course.'

'You don't sound sure?'

'I am. Of course I am. It's just my job on the cruise ship – I'm supposed to be meeting the ship in Bermuda.' I stumble over the words. 'There's a flight on Sunday night.'

'But I'm coming on Sunday!' Beth exclaims. 'It's all arranged. Look, don't make any decisions now. Wait until we see each other. I have to go.'

I open my mouth to say something, but the line goes dead and Beth is gone.

I rub my hands over my face, the tiredness returning in a tidal wave of exhaustion. *I'm doing my best*, I want to tell Beth. Aren't I?

The coffee shop is suddenly busy. A man with an overflowing coffee cup lingers by my table, eyeing the empty chair. I grab my coat and leave before he can ask to share.

One question runs through my mind as I push through the queue and out into the cold air. Why did Anik lie to me?

He's an idiot.

It's more than that. This isn't incompetence; it's deceit. And not just about Luke Richards. He didn't tell me he'd seen you recently, either.

My mind races back over my meetings with Anik. The warmth of his hand on mine, that connection. I shove it aside and focus on the other parts. *'I think we should talk about what happened in the woods.'*

Those words play on my mind. Why did he want to talk about it? What good would it do now?

There are other things I noticed too. The bloodshot eyes I put down to being overworked. The casual clothes, the pint at eleven thirty a.m. on a Monday because it was his day off. Meeting away from the police station.

A slow, persistent alarm beeps in my mind. I reach for my phone again and Google the number I'm looking for. If Anik answers, then I'll ask him outright, but something tells me he won't.

It takes three transfers and a lot of vague explanations about an ongoing case before I find myself speaking to a DCI Heather Greenwood. 'How can I help you?' she asks in a tone of 'how quickly can I get you off the phone?'

'I'm trying to get hold of DI Anik Saha.'

'May I ask what it's regarding?'

'It's about a case he worked on five years ago.'

246

'I'm afraid DI Saha is on personal leave at the moment. If you tell me the case, then perhaps I can help?'

'On leave? How long for?' My stomach knots. I don't want to believe it, but what choice do I have? Anik has been lying to me the entire time.

'I'm afraid I don't have that information at this time.'

'So he's not working?' God, I sound like a dumbass, but I have to be sure.

'That's correct. But I can help you. What case was it?'

'It's a missing persons case. Rachel Winslow. Anik – I mean DI Saha – was helping me.'

'I'm not aware of that case, I'm afraid. Can I take some details and call you back?'

I give my name and answer all the questions I'm asked and DCI Greenwood promises to get back to me.

Fucking hell, Rach. There is no team on this. No whiteboard with your photo in the middle. It's just me and I'm not exactly keeping my shit together right now.

My jaw tightens, the pain throbbing up to the top of my skull. I'm so fucking angry, Rach. What the hell is going on?

Chapter 42

Rachel

Now

He's getting nervous. He's popping in and out. Hovering. Sometimes Rachel hears him moving around and braces herself for the bathroom door to open, but it doesn't.

She hears other things too. Something being dragged on the floor. He's setting something up in that empty room.

It feels like she's been here weeks, months, her whole goddamn life lived within these shitty walls.

She doesn't move when he's in the house. She stays quiet with the light out. Once, he opened the door and looked in on her and she pretended to be asleep and he left her like that. Now it's all she does when she hears him coming. Sometimes it works, sometimes she's left alone, but sometimes he comes in and talks to her. He wants to know how she's doing and Rachel has to bite her bottom lip so hard it bleeds just to stop the screams from escaping.

She winces when he touches her now. He sees it too and he doesn't like it. He's talking more, telling her about Cleo. He's watching Cleo closely, and even though it's horribly wrong and Rachel hates that he's out there with her while she is in here, she longs to hear about Cleo. She'll never forget what Cleo did for her.

Rachel doesn't want to know what will happen after this. She's strong, but even she is starting to wonder how much more she can take. It's this room. It's getting to her. She keeps thinking about the night in the woods and all the ways her life and Cleo's would have been different if they hadn't got into that car, if she hadn't been so hell-bent on playing that game.

Chapter 43

Rachel

Five years earlier

Luke takes Rachel's arm, guiding them through the restaurant.

'I think we should probably go, actually,' Cleo says from over Rachel's shoulder, ever the flipping killjoy.

Luke's smile falters as his eyes move from Cleo to Rachel. 'Of course. If that's what you both want?'

'I'd love to see your house,' Rachel jumps in, her voice louder than she means it to be.

Outside, the temperature has dropped. The icy air should be a sobering smack but it has the opposite effect, sending her spiralling into drunkenness.

'I'm parked around the corner,' Luke says with a grin. 'Wait here, OK?'

He jogs up the road and it's then that Cleo rounds on her.

'You're drunk,' she says.

'No, I'm not.'

'Rach, you're totally hammered. Did you not notice

that he was topping up our glasses more than his own? I hardly drank anything but I'm not feeling great either,' Cleo adds, pressing her fingers to her temples.

'Because he's driving,' Rachel says, her words slurring. 'Look.' Rachel summons the most sober part of herself. God, how is she suddenly so drunk? 'I'm fine,' she says. 'Cleo, I love you and everything, but Luke is into me, not you, and you're being a third wheel.'

'No way am I leaving you with him.'

'Stop being jealous.' Emotion chokes Rachel's voice. That fucking desperation again. 'You can't have Luke. He's mine. You've already taken Simon and my job, you can't have Luke as well.'

Cleo gasps as though she's been slapped. She takes a step back, staggering a little. 'I don't want him,' she says, rubbing at her forehead. 'You can't think I'm interested in him.'

'What's not to be interested in? He's amazing. Gorgeous. Really, really nice to me.'

'Rach, I'm not jealous of you and Luke. I just want to look out for you.'

'Because I can't look after myself, you mean.'

'That's not what I said.'

'It's what you meant. It's what you always mean. Luke picked up on it straight away.'

'Can't you see he's turning you against me?'

Before Rachel can reply, headlights fill the empty road and she stumbles slightly as she moves to the edge of the pavement.

The car that pulls up beside them is not the sleek, expensive hire car she was expecting. Even with the alcohol sloshing through her blood, she's surprised. It's some dark-silver saloon thing. A Ford, maybe, or a Citroën.

Luke jumps out, the engine still running. 'Don't,' he laughs, reading her expression. 'It's not my preferred style of car. It's my boss's UK assistant's car. I went straight to the office from the airport and didn't get time to hire my own. It's a heap of junk, but it goes.'

'That's the main thing,' Rachel smiles, feeling warm and fuzzy and a little bit dizzy now as Luke opens the passenger door for her. A second later, the door behind her opens and Cleo climbs in too.

'I'm not leaving you,' she hisses as Luke walks round to the driver's side. 'Something . . . isn't . . .' Cleo's voice trails off and Rachel isn't sure if it's her who stops listening or Cleo who stops talking.

The world seems to slow down around her. She's aware of Luke opening the door and climbing in. Then the motion of the car as they drive through London, the street lights and the buildings blurring in the window.

'Everything OK?' Luke asks and she thinks he looks at her then, before glancing in the mirror at Cleo. 'I can drive you both home if you've changed your minds.'

Rachel wants to laugh. She wants to shake her head and tell him that she'd be crazy not to go back with him. That it's all she's thought about for days, weeks. Her mind wanders. She pictures them kissing. She wants him so much it hurts.

But it's weird, because Rachel knows what she wants to say, but she's so sleepy. She can't keep her eyes open.

Chapter 44

Cleo

Now

Tottenham Court Road is quiet tonight. The shops are closed, the shoppers long gone, and I guess the cold wind blasting straight down Oxford Street has driven the tourists inside.

The Flying Horse is heaving with people. The smell of stale beer and bleach has been replaced with crisps and body odour. The lighting is low, the heaters blasting, and I already feel too hot, too penned in among the joviality of the Thursday night drinkers. I shuffle between the tables and a group of red-faced men in suits – ties loosened, pints clasped in their hands – step aside to let me pass. I walk quickly, head down, avoiding the eyes on me.

The windows are steamy with condensation. Outside, the night is so black.

I find Anik where I left him three days ago. Same table. Almost the same clothes. By the bloodshot look in his eyes, I could easily believe he hasn't left.

He straightens up when he sees me, and for the first time I notice the effort he puts into holding himself. Every movement planned. I thought it was about precision, thinking everything through, but now I see it for what it is: he's drunk.

'Cleo, hi.' He gives me a lopsided smile and motions to the chair opposite, a glass of white wine already waiting on the table in front of it. I ignore the gesture and stand over him.

'You lied to me.' My tone is sharp.

From somewhere in the bar, a tray of glasses drops to the floor and a cheer erupts. My eyes don't leave Anik.

His smile falters. I recognize the look, the feeling coursing through him – it's guilt. 'What? No, I haven't.'

'How long have you known about the other case – Richard Gilders?'

'Around six weeks, I think.'

'You told me you'd only just found out!'

'What? No, I didn't.'

I stop and think for a moment, trying to replay our last conversation.

'If you've known for six weeks, then why didn't you tell me when we saw each other on Sunday?'

'Because you seemed quite . . . fragile,' he says, choosing his words carefully. 'I didn't want to over-load you or confuse you.'

'I'm not a child.'

'I know that, Cleo. I'm sorry. Maybe I should have told you straight away. Why don't you sit down and I'll get us another drink.'

'I don't want a drink, I want the truth,' I say, but Anik is already on his feet, wallet in hand, and if he hears my protest, he doesn't show it.

It's busy and by the time he returns, my wine glass is empty. The alcohol is a filmy coating over my thoughts, softening the sharp edge of my anger. And even though I know I shouldn't, I take a long sip of the second glass as soon as it's in front of me. It's cold and tangier than the first, reminding me of that awful Frascati from Mr Hakimi's.

'You might not have lied to me, Anik, but you've been liberal with the truth at the very least. You didn't tell me you'd seen Rachel last month. And I know you're on personal leave.'

Utter despair draws across Anik's face. 'The leave is temporary,' he says. 'This job – it gets to you after a while. I can't begin to tell you the evil things I've seen.' He takes a long gulp from his pint and I can feel the memories crowding him the same way they do me. 'You have to have an outlet. And I found the wrong one.' He raises his glass. 'I'm not an alcoholic,' he adds. 'I just need a bit of time off, that's all. I never drank on duty or anything, but . . .' His voice trails off.

'Do you expect me to feel sorry for you? You've lied to me. You made me think your team were working on Rachel's case.'

'I might not have a team at the moment, but I promise you I'm looking into it. Do you think you're the only one who feels guilty about what happened that night? I know I let you both down when I couldn't catch that bastard. I think about it all the time. It haunts me. Every damn day, you and Rachel are in my thoughts. Sometimes I feel like you're all I think about.'

'What happened with Rachel?' I ask, refusing to let his words take root in my mind.

'What do you mean?'

'She didn't believe you, for starters, and she told her sister that she was pissed off with you.'

'I honestly have no idea why she'd be mad at me. She asked to see a photo of Richard Gilders and I said I'd get it for her, but when I called again to arrange a time to meet, she didn't pick up. I left a message and never heard back.'

'Have you got the photo with you?'

'Not on me, no. But I can get it and show you tomorrow.'

It feels like another excuse to meet, to delay.

Thoughts spin around my head. Is Luke dead or isn't he? Do I believe you or Anik? And if I believe you, then does that mean Luke is behind your abduction?

There is something else – another realization, a horror I haven't dared to admit to myself while I've been chasing shadows this week. If Luke Richards is behind this, then it's all my fault. I am the reason he has you. I am the reason he was never caught.

The truth – my secret – rises up from that dark corner I keep it in, growing, spreading, until it's all I see. The moment Beth threw that cowboy comment at me in Southampton, I knew I had to come, I had to help you. I had to make up for what I did last time.

The air disappears from the room. I can't draw breath. My head spins.

'This is all my fault.' I stand suddenly, my legs knocking against the table, sending our glasses crashing to the floor. Another cheer ripples through the pub. I fumble with my coat, walking on legs that don't want to move.

'Cleo?' Anik's eyes are wide with alarm. 'What's wrong?'

The same group of men step aside to let me pass. I trip on something.

'Aye, aye,' one of them calls out. 'Had one too many, love? I'll help you home if you like?' They all laugh.

I throw myself at the door with only one thing on my mind. Escape.

That bitch. That absolute fucking cow.
Does she still think she can get out of this?

Fine, then. I'm changing the rules.

It's my game. I can do whatever the hell I like.

And I say that it's time to stop the game
and play for real.

Chapter 45

Rachel

Five years earlier

There's a noise. A voice. It's Cleo. She sounds distant. Scared. Rachel wants to reach out and tell her it's OK, she's here, but she can't.

Her head is spinning – teacups at the fair. Rachel tries to open her eyes but the world is moving too fast around her. There's a burning in her throat and she thinks she's going to be sick.

Where are they?

Luke's car.

Don't be sick.

Did she fall asleep?

Cleo speaks again. Louder this time. 'Where are we?'

'We're almost there,' Luke says, but there's something not right. It's Luke, but it's not Luke, and Rachel can't work out why.

'Your accent is gone,' Cleo says, getting there before Rachel.

'So?' The one word is cold and hard. Rachel feels herself frowning but still she doesn't open her eyes. A prickle of unease dances across her skin.

'Rach, Rachel?' Cleo's voice is loud in her ears. A hand touches her shoulder. 'Wake up, Rach.'

Rachel tries to tell her she's not asleep, but the words are mumbled, incoherent.

The indicator starts to click, click, click. Tears build in her eyes but she doesn't know why. Nothing is right.

'Luke?' Her voice is a whisper.

'We're almost there,' he says, bright and breezy like a harassed dad, like they're the annoying kids.

'Let us out,' Cleo says.

Rachel tries to laugh at that. What a stupid thing to say. Why would they want to get out when they're almost there?

Except, Cleo is right. Rachel wants to get out too.

She forces her eyes open. The street lights are gone. It's pitch-black outside her window. They're bumping up and down in their seats and when Rachel looks ahead at the windscreen she sees an unmade road and trees lit by the headlights.

They're in woodland. The thought is crazy. Woodland in London?

She fell asleep. For how long? Where are they? Nothing is right.

'Let us out!' Cleo screams. It's piercing and sharp. There's a panic in her voice that shakes Rachel awake. This is all wrong. Luke is wrong. She is wrong. Cleo is right. Always right. The thought lands with a horrible queasiness.

Rachel shifts in her seat. It's an effort to move, but she does. She turns her face to Luke. The first thing she notices is the gloves – black leather. Why is he wearing them? His eyes are on the road ahead but there's a strange look on his face. Desperate. Gleeful. Mad, she thinks.

She twists around to Cleo in the back seat and their eyes meet. Even in the fog of her thoughts, a silent understanding passes between them. They're in trouble. They need to get away. Rachel's head hurts, her mouth is dry, but she swallows and gathers herself. She's about to say something when she catches sight of movement. Something flying at her. It's close – a blurred fist, knuckles. Luke's punch smashes into her right eye. The force throws her back and she slams into the car door.

Cleo is screaming and screaming; shrill, raw panic. Rachel's face throbs. Her hands tremble as she grabs at the door handle, but it's locked. And then Cleo is by her side, clambering between the seats, her hands flying at Luke.

The car veers suddenly to the left, then the right. Cleo loses her balance.

'Rachel.' Cleo's voice is desperate and Rachel knows she needs to move, to act, to shake herself out of this, but her head feels like it's been set on fire. The pain is so sharp it's hard to breathe. Hard to think.

'Shut up, you bitch.' Luke's loud growling voice sends a fear shooting through her body. He throws a hand back at Cleo, trying to grab her, hurt her.

The path ahead of them narrows and they're bumping and jolting as they speed along it. Luke throws another fist in Cleo's direction. Rachel stares, helpless, as his hand connects with Cleo's face. She seems to dodge it at the last moment and it doesn't knock her back like it did Rachel.

What can she do? Rachel feels helpless and lost and

something else. They're in the middle of something utterly terrifying, they're in trouble, and yet there is still the sting of humiliation for how wrong she's been.

Rachel yanks at her door handle again but nothing happens. She glances at Luke's door. If she can reach the controls, then she can unlock all the doors. Luke is driving. He's fighting with Cleo. He can't stop them both. She fumbles to unclip her seatbelt and, just as he reaches a hand out to grab Cleo's leg, Rachel throws herself across the seats, landing hard on Luke. He swerves, and she hears the scratch of branches hitting the car.

Something pounds into her stomach. She's winded, unable to breathe, desperate to curl up into a ball, but her hands are already on the door and she finds buttons. She doesn't know what they are, but she presses them all and screams at Cleo. 'Go,' she shouts. 'The doors are open.'

Luke's hand grabs at Rachel, his fingers squeezing hers, but somehow she reaches the controls and then a cold wind blasts through the car and Rachel realizes a door is open. Luke shouts out, one hand reaching to stop Cleo. Rachel is still sprawled across the seats and she lifts her elbow and jams it hard into his crotch.

She's weak and her elbow doesn't carry the force she wants, but he still cries out in pain, and then he's no longer holding Cleo but grasping Rachel's neck, grabbing, choking her. He pulls her up and throws her back into her seat.

Another fist smacks her right between the eyes and her head explodes in pain.

Chapter 46

Cleo

Now

The cold wind does nothing to shake off the panic tearing through me.

It's my fault.

It's my fault.

I did this to Rachel.

I am a liar.

A coward.

I take an unsteady step and then another and another, and then I'm running.

Escape, escape, escape. The one word rolls around my empty head. My fingers grab at my alarm and I squeeze it in my hand.

I turn into the entrance of the tube, the steps looming below me. I grip the railing, but there's someone coming up – a man with his hood up. I can't see his face, but there's something menacing about him, something dangerous, and I lurch away and keep walking.

The headlights of the passing traffic punch into my head as my eyes flit back, left, right, everywhere. There's a couple walking on the opposite side of the road. I'm not alone, but I feel invisible.

My mind is a spinning top, round and round. Nausea burns in my throat. I lean into an empty side street and gag.

I straighten up and lean against the wall. I'm shaking all over, sweating.

A shadow moves in the corner of my vision. My heart skips a beat and then another. There's someone coming. They're sticking close to the wall. I can't see who it is. I look across the road again but the couple have disappeared. There are no cars passing, no traffic at all. It's just me in this world. Me and this shadow moving closer and closer, picking up speed.

It's nothing, I tell myself. Someone on their way back home from work, a late-night jogger. But my reassurance is a lost whisper compared to the screams of my paranoia.

The figure steps nearer and glances behind them and then it's not my imagination any more, he's right up close. Still a shadow, a balaclava covering his face, hood pulled up, and I know it's Luke. I know he's here for me. I've been waiting for this moment for five years.

I scream, but I don't have enough breath to carry the sound out into the night.

My pulse pounds in my ears, a dance beat, a bass drum. And before I can move, a hand is gripping my arm and I'm being dragged into the side road, the darkness.

'No.' I shake my head, trying to pull myself free, but

I can't. And so I do the only thing I can do: I yank the chain from the alarm, waiting for the wailing screech that will tell me I'm safe.

Two thoughts hit at once. The first is so glaringly obvious I can't believe I've never realized this before. An alarm is only good if there's someone, anyone, to hear it. Alone, it is useless. My eyes drag back to the main road. There's traffic again, but it's passing too fast to notice the man in the shadows of the side road and the woman he is holding.

The second thought is far more urgent, desperate. There is no noise. No wail. Not even a soft beep. The only sound is the panting of my breath and the scuffle of feet.

I want to fight, to run, but I can't. My mind is still fixated on the silent alarm and the danger I'm now facing.

The man shoves me to the ground and I hit the pavement with a hard thump. I screw my eyes shut and shuffle into myself. My bag is snatched from my shoulder and I hear the zip pull open before something drops to the floor. Footsteps smacking the pavement. Silence. I keep my eyes shut.

Seconds pass before I dare to open them.

'Cleo?' Anik races towards me, face red from exertion. 'Are you OK? What happened?'

'I've just been mugged,' I gasp.

Anik is by my side in an instant, pulling me up, both of us unsteady on our feet.

'He came out of nowhere and pushed me over.'

'Did you get a look at his face?'

'He was wearing a balaclava and it was dark.'

'Opportunistic bastard.'

I look at the ground and give a shaky sigh of relief

as I spot my backpack, the contents spilling out on the floor. I scoop everything back in. Keys, mirror, make-up bag, and my purse and phone too. Is anything actually missing?

Yes, I realize. One thing.

I rifle through every compartment before peering around me, running a hand over the damp pavement. It's not here.

'What is it?' Anik asks.

'My passport's been taken.'

'Could you have left it at the house?'

'No. I always keep it with me.' I heave a sob, the shock of the attack hitting me in pounding fists, one after the other.

This is London. People get robbed all the time. An empty road, a woman on her own. And yet this feels connected.

'He didn't take my phone or my purse. Just my passport.' My teeth chatter as I talk.

'It's OK. You can get another one.'

Another sob catches me off guard. I stare down at my hands. The chain in one, plastic in the other. 'My alarm.' I hold it up – my comfort blanket, my safety net. It failed me.

'Let me see?'

I pass the pieces over before hugging my arms to my chest. I glance out into the road. A lone car with its headlights on is parked twenty metres away, engine idling.

'The battery is gone.' Anik shines the torch from his phone on to the alarm. He's taken the back off and I can see an empty circular hole where a battery should be.

'But it worked. Last week. I . . . it worked,' I finish, not wanting to tell him about Selfridges.

'Have you left it out somewhere? On a table in a restaurant? That kind of thing.'

I see where he's going. Someone's tampered with my alarm. Someone didn't want it to go off. 'I keep it with me all the time. No one could—' My words stop short. The other night, the nightmare. Waking up in your room. I thought I heard the door shut, but the house was silent. I thought I'd dreamt it, but then my alarm wasn't under the pillow where I'd left it.

I sense Anik moving closer until I can smell his aftershave, and feel the warmth of his body as he draws me into his arms. 'It's OK. You're OK.'

It's not the first time he's said those words to me. Those exact words. Another hug, another time, and yet it feels like yesterday. There's a heady warmth, a safety, to him that draws me close.

I lift my face up to meet his and then his lips are on mine, soft at first, then urgent. My mouth, my body, responds and then he's stepping back, rubbing a hand over his face. 'Sorry,' he says, voice a hoarse whisper. 'I shouldn't have done that. You're just so beautiful. Shit. I'm so sorry. I need to work on my timing.'

He shakes his head before looking at me. 'What happened in the pub just now?' he asks. 'Why did you leave like that?'

'I . . .' A lump forms in my throat, choking. I can't keep it in any more. 'I'm the reason this has happened again.'

'What?' Anik frowns.

'It's Luke Richards doing this. I know you think he's dead, but he's not. Him being alive, him having Rachel. It's the only thing that makes sense, and it's my fault you didn't catch him five years ago. I . . . I lied. I told you I couldn't remember anything, but it's

267

not true. I remember every second of that night. I just . . . I just couldn't tell you and admit what I'd done.'

'This is about when you were in the woods, isn't it? What you saw?'

I gasp. He remembers. 'Yes.'

'You started talking about it in the hospital cafeteria, but when I tried to get more details, you said you couldn't remember.'

'I know. I'm sorry I lied to you, to everyone. I . . . just couldn't face what I'd done.'

'Cleo.' Anik takes my hand. 'Five years ago, did you know an address for Luke Richards that you didn't tell the police about?'

I shake my head.

'Did you know where he went after he left the woods?'

'No, but—'

'Did you know anything that could've helped us track him down that you didn't tell us?'

'No, but—'

'You might not have told us everything about that night, but there was nothing that could've been used to find him. I promise you that. CamChat was untraceable. He picked a restaurant with no CCTV on the street. The car was stolen, then abandoned and torched. He was meticulous and thorough.

'If I'd thought for a single second that you had information that could've led to Luke Richards's arrest, then I would've continued to question you, and you would eventually have told me, but you didn't and I didn't see any reason to push you. There's nothing you could've done back then and nothing you've done wrong now.'

I nod, crying too hard to speak. I've carried this secret for so long, but confessing to Anik – the one person who already knew – has changed nothing. I wish I could believe Anik's words, but he wasn't there. He doesn't know. I could've changed things that night. Maybe not for Luke, but for you.

Anik starts to guide us back to the pub but I shake my head, and when the glowing light of a black cab comes into view, I wave my hand in the air.

'Cleo, hang on.'

'I need to go.'

The moment the taxi pulls over, I open the door and dive in, my breathing still fast. My gaze fixes on Anik as we drive away, and all I can think is that one minute I was with him, the next I was alone and someone stole my passport. Someone wants me to stay. And the very next minute, that someone is gone and Anik is there, breathless from running.

As if . . .

Could he . . .

I stop my thoughts and push the paranoia away. Am I seriously thinking that Anik has anything to do with what happened just now, with you being missing? It's ludicrous. I know he's struggling with his own demons right now – the pressure of work, an alcohol problem – and I know he'd like us to be more than friends, but not even I can believe he'd go this far. Everything that's happening right now is about you, not me.

Chapter 47

Cleo

Five years earlier

The car door flies open in my hands and I throw myself towards the opening. No hesitation. No thought to the speed of the car or the fall that will come.

'You fucking bitch,' Luke shouts. A second later there's a hand on my ankle, gloved fingers gripping my skin, holding me back. I'm halfway out and for a moment I think I'm going to be stuck hanging out of the car, dragged under the wheels. But then Luke yells in pain and whatever Rachel has done, his fingers slide from my ankle and I'm flying through the air. Suddenly it's not wheels I'm worrying about, it's the landing, the tree I'm sure my head is about to smash into.

The ground comes up to meet me with a thud that rockets through my body, and as my face drags along the track, I taste bitter, grainy dirt in my mouth.

I lie still, sprawled on the ground, the shock of the fall shaking the thoughts right out of me. Then it all comes back, hitting me with the same force as the cold night air. Shivering, terrified, I throw myself into the undergrowth, thinking only of escape.

But even as I'm pushing my way through bushes and brambles, stones cutting into my hands, my knees, branches hitting my face, I hear the engine of Luke's car growing distant. When I peer back towards the path, I see only darkness.

My head is woozy as I pull myself carefully to my feet. The dirt in my mouth scratches at my throat. I long for water, anything to wash the taste away. My teeth chatter. It's hard to think straight. We were drugged. I'm sure of it. Not the champagne. I hardly touched it. How, then?

The limoncello. It was Luke who brought it over, not the waiter. He could easily have slipped something into it.

I take a step and realize I'm barefoot. My heels must have come off in the car. Grazes and cuts sting in the cold air and there's something wrong with my back – the pain a dull ache that makes me feel sick – but I'm OK.

An image flashes through my head. Luke's fist smashing into Rachel's face. Oh God! Rachel! I have to help her.

I stumble back to the path on wobbling legs. Twice I step on something sharp and yelp in pain. *Think!* I will myself. How far into the woods did Luke drive? A mile? Two? Everything is fuzzy. I don't know how long we were in the car for or where the hell we are.

My feet reach the soft mud of the track. It's dark. Almost pitch-black, and as I look one way then the other, I can't remember which way Luke's car went. I cry out, a muffled sob, but I stop myself from crumbling, from allowing the fear to take over. I've got to keep it together. Rachel needs me.

I replay the moment I threw myself out of the car and pushed myself into the undergrowth to hide. I turn and stare into the nothingness. Luke went this way. I turn again. Which makes the exit from the woods this way.

Indecision rips through me. I see myself running after the car, finding a heavy log and creeping up on Luke, smashing him over the head and rescuing Rachel. Except I'm breathing so hard. My movements are jerky, clumsy. How am I going to creep up on him? And what if he gets me too?

But running away from Rachel feels wrong. I'm barefoot in the middle of woodland. How long will it take to find help? Twenty minutes? More? I don't have the answers. All I know is that Rachel doesn't have that long.

Another minute ticks by. I bend down, patting the ground for my bag. If I could just find it, if I could get my phone, then I could call the police. But it's not here. It must have dropped into the footwell of Luke's car during the struggle.

Fuck!

I stare once more in the direction of Luke's car. The fear of what he'll do to me is a noose choking the life out of me. I turn and run in the opposite direction, towards safety, towards help.

Chapter 48

Cleo

Now

Weak sunshine pushes through the dirty kitchen window as I make myself a coffee, heaping two loaded teaspoons from a dried-out pot of instant that's been left on the side for too long.

My face feels puffy from last night's crying, and as I drop the spoon into the sink I see my hands are still shaking.

I was mugged. Someone stole my passport.

Anik called it opportunistic – bad luck – but they didn't take my purse or my phone. Just my passport, the one thing I need to leave. I'm stuck here now, and that thought alone makes me want to run far away.

But more than the mugging, I can't shake Anik's behaviour from my thoughts. I barely slept thinking about his lies. He made it all seem so justifiable – how he didn't tell me what he knew about Luke Richards, or even that he'd seen you just last month, how he's on leave from the Met.

A bolt of anger shoots through me. He made me believe his team were working on your disappearance, he made me believe he'd help me – why? All because he likes me?

I'm staring into the garden, blowing on the hot steam from the mug, when I hear a door opening. My first thought is that Simon is home early. I stride down the hall and knock on his door.

Silence.

There's another sound – a drawer shutting – but it's not from Simon's flat. It's coming from your room. My pulse quickens and when I move again, hot liquid from the mug spills on to my hands. Droplets hit the carpet, disappearing instantly among the rest of the stains.

'Rach?' I say, reaching for your door at the same moment that it opens, and I find Lexy standing before me. Hair wet, white dressing gown wrapped around a pair of red PJs.

She jumps when she sees me, hands clutching her chest. 'Cleo, you scared me.'

'Likewise,' I say, shifting slightly to block Lexy's path. 'What are you doing in Rachel's room?'

'Oh, I was just looking for my hairdryer. Rachel borrowed my old one last month and I need it back.'

'How did you get in here?'

'Rachel gave me a set of keys in case I needed my hairdryer and she wasn't here.' Lexy's face flushes pink and I'm sure she's lying.

'Where is it, then?' I ask.

'I couldn't find it,' she says with a shrug.

'That's not it there, then?' I ask, pointing to a black hairdryer by the mirror.

Lexy lets out a 'ha' noise before nodding. 'That's it. I can't believe I missed it.'

She scoots over to pick up the hairdryer. 'Have you heard anything from Rachel yet?' she asks.

'No.'

'I'm sorry. I hope she's OK.'

'Thanks.'

My brain fires with questions. Was Lexy really in your room for a hairdryer? Would you give a set of keys to her? I don't think so, but there's something else troubling me right now. Remember those girls from CamChat? The two students. Our first game. That story we told them about being domestic abuse victims was so awful.

They fell for it. Hook, line and sinker.

And then we saw them again and they were so mad.

It was only a bit of fun.

For us, maybe.

The thing is, I can't remember what those girls looked like, I can't remember their names or the colour of their hair, but when I look at Lexy, that memory keeps pushing forwards.

Lexy hovers for a moment before moving towards me, and it's then, as she brushes by and I'm stepping out of the way, that something falls from her hand, hitting the worn carpet with a thud. She drops down, scooping it up, but not before I see it – a phone. It's an old style with a tiny screen and a keypad. The exact type of pay-as-you-go phone someone would buy to send anonymous messages on.

A shiver races through my body.

Lexy catches me staring and smiles. 'I dropped my iPhone last week. Got this piece of junk until it's repaired.'

She disappears up the stairs but I stay where I am in your doorway. My gaze moves around your room, looking for anything out of place, but I see nothing.

When I'm back in my own room again, I grab my phone from the bedside table, pulling up the taunting messages.

Getting hot now, Cleo.
Ready for more?

I stare at the words for a long time before I throw on my coat and leave the house.

It's much later, when the darkness is closing in and rain is pouring down in icy sheets, that I venture back to the house. There's an emptiness to the air as I step through the front door, dump my bag in your room and make my way to the kitchen.

I've bought pizza and Frascati from Mr Hakimi's shop.

We only bought that stuff because we were flat broke.

I know, but it's nostalgic somehow. I'm sure it's not as bad as we remember.

It is.

I turn on the oven and put the wine in the freezer. Seconds later, smoke starts billowing from the oven. I throw open the door and find a greasy tray someone hasn't bothered to wash up. Quickly, before the smoke alarm can go off, I unbolt the back door, allowing cold air to sweep through the kitchen. I put the tray by the sink to soak, and just as I'm about to cook my pizza, everything goes dark. Another power cut. Shit!

It's pitch-black. There are no street lights creeping in through the window here. I reach for my alarm before I remember it's in the bottom of my bag, broken and useless.

My phone is in your room, dumped with my bag when I came in because I couldn't be bothered to take it upstairs, and because the moment the pizza is cooked and the wine is cold, I'm planning another night on CamChat looking for you.

I inch slowly forwards, hands out until I touch the wall. The absolute silence rings in my ears. I never realized how much noise the house makes – that soft electrical hum, the clonk of the heating pipes. My fingers find the wall and I pat my way to the door.

My skin tingles; the hair on my arms stands on end. With every short, sharp breath I take, I'm sure someone is going to grab me. Is this part of the game? The back door is standing wide open, and suddenly I feel a presence, a change in the air I wish I could ignore, tell myself I'm imagining – but I can't, because it feels like I'm not alone in the kitchen.

'Hello?' My voice is a faltering whisper that makes me feel stupid and scared and stupid again. 'Is anyone there?'

Silence.

I swallow hard, desperate to run, to scream, but my legs are lead and it's all I can do to creep forward. My hands feel the grooves of the door frame, then the handle. The only noise now is my ragged breath.

The door opens with a long creak that sounds too loud in the darkness. I step through it and find the walls of the hallway.

I take another step as the kitchen door begins to close behind me with another whine of its hinges. And then it stops and I freeze. There was no click, no thud. It didn't shut. Something got in its way. Someone.

Chapter 49

Cleo

Now

The scream lodges in my throat. I hold my breath, straining to listen above the sound of my own hammering pulse.

There'll be another reason the door didn't close, I tell myself. Except there isn't. It's a fire door. It always shuts.

Which means someone was in the kitchen with me. And now that person is right behind me.

Adrenaline ignites inside me – the strike of a match – and I throw myself forwards, no longer caring about the dark or the power cut or finding my phone. All I care about is getting to the front door and the safety of a world outside this house.

My feet pound the carpet – two steps, three, four. I'm almost there, but I can't stop my eyes dragging back, searching into that black ink for who is behind me.

And then I'm colliding with the unmistakable

weight of a body. Hands grab at my arms and I scream, pushing back.

We're scrambling, limbs knocking against each other. It only lasts a second, maybe two, before I hit the wall with an echoing thud that stuns me for long enough to hear the click of the kitchen door closing and I realize that the person in front of me is screaming too.

'Stop,' I shout, and they do.

Neither of us moves for a beat.

'It's OK.' The voice is male and has a strong French accent. 'I'm not going to hurt you.'

'Who are you?'

'My name is Charlie. I live here. On the top floor. Who are you?'

'Cleo,' I reply. 'I'm staying in the room below you.'

My eyes adjust to the soft glow from the street lights. I can make out a shadowy face but nothing else.

It's him. Your other housemate, finally. There are questions I want to ask him about you, but all I can think about right now is the fear pulsing through me, the feeling of someone in the kitchen, the door not closing.

'You scared the life out of me,' Charlie says with a shaky laugh. 'I thought I was the only one home. I scared you too, I think. I'm sorry. I don't have a torch.'

'Hang on.' I feel along the wall, back towards your room, and open the door, patting the top of your dresser until my fingers close around my phone. A moment later, the white light of the torch illuminates around us and I look up at the man in the corridor and yelp. 'You're not Charlie.'

He laughs, running a hand through a mop of black hair. 'Yes, I am.'

'I saw the man who lives in the loft room during the last power cut. He was coming down the stairs. I called after him but he ran off and then came back and pushed me over.'

'What other power cut? What are you talking about?' he frowns.

'Sunday night.'

'Sunday?' he says. 'Oh. My brother was staying in my room. He'd had a fight with his girlfriend. He probably had to get to work. He's like that. Oversleeping and running off. I'm sorry if he scared you.'

'But he didn't stop when I called out to him.'

'He probably thought he was in trouble.'

'And the pushing?'

He makes a face. 'Are you sure it was him? Jacq is a doctor. I can't think why he'd push you. There are lots of kids on this street. Some cause trouble for me.'

'I guess it could've been one of them,' I admit. I'd assumed it was the same person who ran out of the house, but I didn't actually see who did it.

'So, shall we turn on the lights?' he asks.

I nod, wrong-footed. Confused. Everything this man is saying seems perfectly reasonable. But can I trust him?

The question turns over in my mind as I find the fuse box. A moment later, we're standing awkwardly in the hall, the light now too bright around us. I glance at Charlie. He's small, compact and muscular, nothing like the lanky frame of the figure I saw running down the stairs. Charlie's face is open. He's tanned with perfect white teeth.

My eyes move from Charlie to the closed kitchen door. Was someone there? Or did I just freak myself out?

'Were you in the kitchen a minute ago?' I ask.

He shakes his head and a lock of hair falls over his eyes. 'No,' he replies, pushing the hair back into place. 'I came straight downstairs when the lights went out and bumped into you.'

'It's the second power cut in a week.'

'Old house, right? The landlord doesn't care. He's selling soon. He said he was moving in with his girlfriend.'

I nod, wishing I could believe it was that simple. A coincidence.

'You are new?' he asks.

'Sort of. I used to live here. I'm just staying for this week.'

'Ah.' A look of understanding dawns on his face. 'You're staying in the room in the middle on the left?'

I nod.

'I used to stay in that room. I moved up to the loft room a week ago when it became free. It's warmer. The other day I was so jetlagged when I got home, and it was the middle of the night and I hadn't slept for about twenty hours. I forgot I'd moved and tried to open your door.' He laughs, but stops when he sees my face.

'That was you?' I remember the handle moving up and down, the fear pinning me in place and then the steps above me.

'I'm so sorry. Did that scare you?' He looks sheepish for a moment and fidgets his feet, and I realize that whatever else is going on, I believe him. 'I should get back upstairs. I have an early flight tomorrow.'

'Do you mind if I ask you something?'

'Sure.' He shoves his hands into his pockets and leans against the wall.

'You know Rachel, right?'

'Sure. The girl who lives there.'

'Is she your girlfriend?'

He laughs at that. A proper, head back, 'ha ha' kind of laugh. 'I'm gay,' he says, as though the thought of dating women is ludicrous.

'Oh.' And there it is again, that feeling of being wrong-footed. 'She's missing. Did you know?'

He nods. 'I was very sorry to hear it. Simon called me and left a message while I was flying.'

'Another one of your housemates saw you arguing.' The words are out before I can stop myself. I need answers.

Charlie gives a 'pft' and then says, 'The other housemate is wrong. I like Rachel. She's funny. She helped me move my boxes and then we bump into each other sometimes and walk home together. She does more than Simon ever does around here.'

'What stuff?' I narrow my eyes. 'Your room is empty.'

He frowns, amused. 'I didn't say it was a lot of stuff.'

'The door is always open.'

'I lose my keys. All the time,' he adds with a shrug. 'I asked the landlord if I could put a key box on the wall outside – you know, one with a combination lock – but he said no, and so I bought a padlock for the wardrobe and keep my things in there and leave the door open.'

'You keep all of your things in a wardrobe?'

'Come,' he says, motioning for me to follow as he turns to the stairs.

I traipse behind and when we reach the loft room, Charlie throws open the wardrobe and I almost laugh at the absurdity of it. All my fear of Charlie, of this room, disappears as I take in the neatly folded T-shirts, the trousers hanging from the rail. Everything colour-coordinated. He pulls out a duvet and pillow from a shelf at the top. 'You don't become a flight attendant without knowing how to pack well,' he grins.

'But what about the front door?' I ask. 'You must need a key for that.'

Charlie shifts his feet again. 'I have a hiding place.'

I groan, covering my face with my hands. 'This is London, you know. You can't leave keys under door-mats here.'

'I keep it in the back garden in a special stone. It's very safe.'

No, it isn't, I think. Anyone could have been in and out of this house, but another piece of the puzzle makes sense. The noise I heard in the garden that time. The figure. It must have been Charlie.

I have answers at last, and yet none of them are leading to you.

'I hope you find Rachel,' Charlie says. 'She seemed fine when I saw her last.'

'When was that?'

He thinks for a moment. 'The Saturday before last.'

'Saturday? Are you sure?'

'Of course,' he says, like it's no big deal. 'I was fly-ing to New York that day. I was going to ask her if she wanted some Hershey bars. She mentioned once that she likes them. But she was in a hurry and didn't stop to talk. Is there anything else, Inspector Cleo?' he asks with a joking smile.

I shake my head. 'Thanks.'

When I'm back downstairs, I open the door to your room and lock it behind me before pacing up and down. I need to go back to the kitchen and shut the back door and turn off the oven. I'm not hungry any more. But I need to collect my thoughts first.

Charlie says he saw you the day after you disappeared. Do I believe him? It would explain why I found the bag I'm sure you used that night. Maybe Simon just didn't hear you come in on that Friday night, or maybe Charlie is wrong. He's already admitted he gets muddled when he's jetlagged.

My head throbs with frustration and tiredness. The more I search for you, the more I know, the less it makes sense.

Chapter 50

Cleo

Now

Beth calls me on Saturday as I'm leaving the passport office in the shadows of Victoria Station. I'm drained from the hours of queuing, the questions, the waiting. I'm thirsty, half asleep on my feet from lack of sleep last night.

'Hi, Beth,' I say, raising the phone to my ear.

'Are you OK?' Beth asks by way of greeting. 'You didn't text me yesterday.'

'There's not much to say and we're seeing each other tomorrow.' I don't want to tell Beth how wrong I was about Anik and Charlie – about everything, it feels like now.

'What's wrong?' she asks.

'Nothing. It's just I feel like I've been no help this week. I think you'll have better luck waiting for the police. It's only a few more days now. I'm not even sure there's any point in you coming to London tomorrow.'

'Don't say that,' Beth cries out, her voice jumping a few octaves, the same way yours always does when you get cross. 'You sound like you're giving up.'

'I'm not.' It feels like a lie.

'Are you still planning to leave tomorrow night?'

'I . . . I don't know,' I admit. 'There's nothing else I can do.'

'What about CamChat?'

'What about it?'

There's a pause. 'Simon told me he thought Rachel was using it again,' she says a beat later.

'I know.' I bite down on the side of my mouth, fighting the desire to cry. I have one more day now, Rach. My flight to Bermuda leaves tomorrow at seven p.m. I'm torn, ripped down the middle, just like I was that night in the woods. I don't know what to do. I don't know how I can help you.

I know now that the *Enchantress*, my bubble of safety, is a stopgap, a distraction. I meant what I said in the text to Mum. She replied to my text with lots of encouragement, lots of love and kindness that made me ache to see her.

At some point I need to come to terms with what happened to us and move on with my life. Maybe I could try again as a make-up artist. The thought unleashes a whisper of excitement in the pit of my belly.

But can I live with the guilt? It's a scorching flame that leaves my thoughts, my emotions, one big heap of mushy confusion.

'Are you still there, Cleo?' Beth asks.

From behind me there's the low rumble of a train leaving the station.

'Yes, I'm here. I have to go.'

'Cleo, wait. What about CamChat?'

'I'll try, OK?'

'Thank you. I'll see you tomorrow,' Beth says before I hang up.

One more night on CamChat. I can do that for you. On Sunday, I'll meet Beth and tell her everything that's happened this week. Whether I'm here or not, the police will take your disappearance seriously when you don't return from holiday on Monday. They'll do what I couldn't. They'll find you.

Dead or alive?

I don't know.

I'm almost at the front door on Lockton Road when a figure steps out of the doorway.

'Anik?' I frown. 'Were you just inside?' My gaze pulls to the door, but it's shut. Did I hear the latch click?

He makes a face before shaking his head. 'No. I was just knocking. No one answered.'

'What are you doing here?' I ask, folding my arms across my chest.

'It's about Rachel.'

Anik looks different today. His beard is shorter, his face tired but fresher somehow too. 'I haven't been drinking,' he says, as though I'd asked.

'OK.' I shrug, annoyed at myself that I'm pleased for him.

'You've not been answering my calls,' he continues. 'I've got the photo of Richard Gilders to show you.'

I nod, but inside, my heart skips a beat, nerves twist in my gut.

He pulls out a piece of folded A4 paper and holds it out to me. My hand shakes as I fumble to open it and focus on the grainy image of a photocopied driver's licence.

Recognition stabs at my chest. The photo is small, but I'd know his face anywhere. It's him. Richard Gilders is Luke Richards.

I freeze, my mind stalling on this one fact. Luke Richards is dead. I wait for the relief to flood my body but there is nothing – a blank space.

I was so sure Luke was behind this. I know I should be happy he's dead, but it doesn't mean you are safe, does it? Who else would kidnap you? Who else would drag me into this game?

'It's him,' I whisper, pushing the paper back at Anik. It's only as I hear my own voice that it hits me. Tears prick at the corners of my eyes. He's dead. He can't hurt me. I cover my face with my hands and cry.

'I thought so.'

'I can't believe it,' I say, wiping my eyes. 'If not him, then who?'

'There's more than one bad person in the world,' Anik says.

'I guess.' I take a step, moving around him. 'I should go in.'

'Hang on,' he says. 'There's more. I spoke to DC Nicola Jackson from Bethnal Green Police Station. She's new to the unit but she's got a good reputation. She's going to look at Rachel's case, and assuming Rachel hasn't returned from holiday by Monday, she's personally going to raise the risk level and lead the team in Rachel's missing persons case. She's going to call on Monday and talk about the text messages. I've passed all the information on to her, but she'll want to hear it directly from you. And she looked up the mobile number from the texts you got,' Anik adds.

'And?'

'A burner.'

'Thanks for trying,' I say, taking a step away, wishing I didn't feel so defeated.

He nods. 'I'm here for you, Cleo. If anything happens, you can call me. I know I've messed this up. I should have been honest from the start. I was just so happy to see you again. I'd hoped . . .' He trails off.

'Don't worry about it.'

I don't look back as I slide my key into the lock, but I feel Anik's eyes on me right up until I slam the door behind me.

I stand for a moment, wondering if I'm imagining the feeling in the air, like someone was just here.

A noise breaks the silence – a thud from your room. I don't hesitate this time. I've been wrong about so much. I've let my anxiety and paranoia cloud my judgement.

I grab the handle with such force that I almost fly into the room and find Lexy standing by your wardrobe.

'It's not what you think.' The words rush out of her in a hissed whisper and before I can reply, she bursts into tears.

I stay in the doorway and wait. A minute passes before she lifts her face, looking at me with watery eyes. Only then do I speak. 'What are you doing in here really? And don't tell me it's about a hairdryer.'

'I'm returning something,' she sniffs.

'What?'

Her eyes fall to the floor. 'Money.'

'What money?'

'Our rental deposit for our rooms. Rachel took it because Simon was away and said she'd keep hold of it until we left and there wasn't any point paying it into a bank as we're only here for a couple of months, and the thing is, Faye and I – we're flat broke. Like, you wouldn't believe how broke we are.'

I have a good idea, but I don't say anything.

'Then, like, a couple of weeks ago, we found a bag by the front door. Rachel's keys were in it.'

'You found it?'

Lexy gives a furtive nod. 'It was just lying on the carpet by the front door. We took the bag to give back to Rachel the next time we saw her, but then Simon told us that she was missing and asked if we'd seen her, and we hadn't. That's true, I promise. But then we thought about our money and how no one would know if we snuck in and took it.' Lexy pauses, swallowing hard. 'So we threw her bag in the cupboard and used the keys to let ourselves in.

'Except we started feeling really bad about it. It was a really stupid thing to do. We were planning to put the money back, when you showed up and started hanging out in here all the time. The other morning, I was trying to do it then, but I heard you coming and panicked. The money is all here . . .' Lexy pulls out a drawer and points at a white envelope before hugging her arms to her body. 'I'm really sorry.'

'Have you ever been on CamChat?' The question is out before I can stop it. 'Did you study psychology at university?'

Lexy looks startled for a moment. 'No. German and Spanish. What's CamChat?'

'It doesn't matter.' I step aside and Lexy scurries out

of the room. A minute later, the front door slams and I feel the emptiness of the house wrap itself around me.

Another dead end, another thing I was wrong about.

There is nothing left. No one left. Just you and me and that fucking game.

Chapter 51

Cleo

Now

I'm clicking, clicking, clicking. Skipping through chat after chat because I told Beth I would, and because what else is there left to do? My eyes itch with a gritty tiredness, like sand scratching against my pupils. I'm bored too. Mind-numbingly bored. That's a horrible thing to say, isn't it? It's the truth, though. It's late evening and I've been lying on your bed like this for hours now. I want to stop, but I know that when I do, it'll be for the last time.

There is so much I'm certain of.

You're missing.

Click.

Someone has kidnapped you and tied you to a chair.

Click.

It's connected to CamChat and the game we played; a game someone is still playing.

Click.

But it's not Luke Richards because he's dead.

Click.

The screen freezes, the roulette wheel appears. I rub my eyes and stretch.

My hand is out, already resting on the laptop screen, one, two seconds away from closing it and giving up, when the roulette wheel disappears and a new chat loads. I'm barely looking, so used to skipping ahead that I almost shut your laptop. But, out of the corner of my eye, I see something that makes me stop. That empty room. That chair. You!

It's the same room, the same darkness as before.

'Rachel?' I whisper your name, suddenly aware of the silence around me. Relief and panic vie for attention. You're still alive, but you're still tied to that chair.

Your face is a mess of smeared dirt, tears and snot. Your hair is limp and stuck down on your head. The terror in your eyes sends a bolt of ice straight through my heart. It snatches the breath from my lungs and for a second we are both frozen, staring at each other.

You mumble beneath the tape and I lean close to the screen as though I might be able to understand what you're saying. You move then. Raising your shoulder and frantically rubbing the side of your face, pushing and pushing at the tape covering your mouth.

'You've almost got it,' I say as my pulse races, thumping so hard in my ears that I'm not sure I would hear you even if you did get the tape free.

My eyes scan the room, looking for any clue, anything that I can tell the police. There's a window in the background. Black curtains have been drawn across it, but there's a gap in the middle, a slit. I think I can see brickwork. I narrow my eyes and move so close to the screen that everything becomes a pixelated blur. It is. It's bricks. It's a house opposite your window, and the more I stare, the more certain I am that I can see a window, the flickering of a TV.

There are people near by. Lives being led, TV shows being watched, and across the road, you are fighting for your life.

I scramble for my phone and take a flurry of photos to show the police. They're grainy and a little blurred but it's still you on the screen, still tied up and gagged. They have to believe me this time.

There'll be a manhunt. A huge media campaign. They'll find you.

My hands tremble as I tap on the keypad and dial 999, and that's when I hear your voice – a soft, urgent croak. 'Cleo.'

I gasp and look up to see you've done it. The silvery tape is hanging loose from half of your mouth.

'Rachel,' I hiss. 'Where are you?'

'Listen,' she says, coughing suddenly. 'It doesn't matter. He's moving me. Any minute. He's taking me back to the woods.' Her eyes fill with tears and there's a guttural sob that stabs at my very core. 'Don't call the police. He says he'll kill me if he sees them. You've got to come. Please, Cleo. You're the only one who can help me. You know where to go.'

'I can call Anik.'

'No,' she sobs again, almost howling, and shakes her head. 'Just you. Listen, he's tracking you on your phone and watching everything. He'll kill me if he knows the police are on their way. He'll kill me if he hears them coming. He's going to be back any second.' Her shoulders heave. 'Please, Cleo. I need you.'

'Who is doing this?'

She opens her mouth to reply but there's the sound

of a door banging and she yelps, head shaking from side to side. 'No,' she cries. 'Please, no.'

The camera goes dead and all I can hear is my own gasping breath.

I stare at my phone, now shaking in the tight grip of my hand. The three digits of 999 stare back, waiting to be called, and I know I should, I know it's the right thing to do, but I delete the numbers one by one. I won't let you down again.

A hard ball of fear forms in my throat. *'He's tracking you on your phone and watching everything.'*

I switch off my phone and let it drop to the bed, my eyes scanning the room, searching for a hidden camera, a microphone.

The terror, the panic, is pulsing through me so hard, so fast, that I run to the sink and retch two, three, four times. When I'm empty, I run the tap, washing it all away before splashing cold water on to my face.

I know what I have to do. What I should have done five years ago. I have to save you.

My eyes fix on your car keys in the dish and I snatch them up before grabbing my coat and digging in the cupboard under the stairs for the orange torch I saw there earlier this week.

I hesitate a moment in the hallway and then scribble on the Post-it note stuck to Simon's door.

Found Rachel. Gone to Epping Forest.
Call the police! Call DI Saha!

Simon is due home any minute. He'll see it. Or Lexy or Faye or Charlie. Someone will see it.

I'm coming for you, Rach. Hold on.

Chapter 52

Rachel

Now

The tape hangs loose from her mouth and he steps forwards and tugs it off with one sharp movement, stinging her skin with the same force as a slap.

He kneels down and pulls at the rope around her feet and then her hands. The thought of escape flits into her mind. This could be her last chance to change what is coming.

'Take off your clothes.' He's on his feet fast.

Rachel does as she's told and stands before him naked. He's seen her body so many times, so many ways, but she hugs her arms to her chest anyway, aware of the white lines that criss-cross her body – the knife scars from that first attack.

He scoops up her clothes and throws her a pair of jogging bottoms and a jumper. They're brand new with tags still on them, and she dresses quickly, grateful to hide her nakedness.

He swallows hard, Adam's apple juddering in his

throat, and for a moment he looks as terrified as she feels.

'Let's go.' He grabs her arm and pulls her across the room.

Rachel stumbles. Her feet won't obey her commands, let alone his. She wants out of this house so badly, but the thought of those woods has paralysed her.

'We need to move.'

And just like that, the front door is open and he's bundling her towards a car she's never seen before. She can't believe how normal the road looks. After being in one room for so many days, she's lost all sense of reality, and she stares at the rows of houses, the windows into the lives of the people who've been going about their days with no idea what's been happening to her.

Rachel scans the windows and the street for people, for anyone, but it's deadly quiet. It's only a few seconds before the boot is open and she's lying inside. She waits until he slams the boot shut before she cries. She's scared now. She doesn't know what will happen. She closes her eyes as the car starts to move and prays Cleo is on her way.

Chapter 53

Cleo

Five years earlier

My feet slip and skid in the squelchy mud, but I run flat out, arms pumping. Not caring when I slip and fall. I run for ages. I run for so long that doubt creeps into my thoughts. Am I sure I've gone the right way? It's so dark. Have I missed a turning?

There's a break in the clouds above. It's not much, but it's enough to show me a fork in the woodland. Two tracks to choose from. One path bends to the left and looks like it goes back in on itself, the other stretches ahead. I take the latter. It has to be a way out.

I tear down it and run until I sense the path squeezing in around me. Twigs and brambles grab at my jacket from both sides. My foot catches on a tree root and I trip, smacking the ground hard. There's no time to check myself over, no time to register the pain now throbbing in my foot, my knees.

Another sob catches in my throat. It feels like the

dried leaves on the ground are stuck in my airway. It's so dark. The path is narrowing. Every few strides I find myself veering into undergrowth.

This isn't right. The thought pounds in my head in time with my racing pulse. I should be out by now. I should be waving down a car on the road or knocking on someone's door. How am I still in these woods?

And then I hear the scream. It's somewhere close. An animal in pain? A fox? I hold my breath and listen. There's another noise. Soft and muffled. A voice. And then I realize – it's not an animal screaming, it's Rachel.

Oh God, oh God, oh God. I thought the path would lead out of the woods, but I've doubled back on myself. I've found Rachel and Luke.

I crouch down and crawl slowly towards the noise. Every rustle, every snapping twig bounces in my ears and makes me freeze. There's a light up ahead. Some kind of camping lamp on the ground, casting a yellow glow between the trees. My eyes fall to where Rachel is lying, naked and hunched in a foetal position. Luke is standing over her, a blade of some kind in his hand.

'Please,' Rachel sobs. 'Let me go.'

'Where's the fun in that? I thought you liked playing games, *Roxy*. So, let's play.' Luke's voice is harsh, mocking.

'Cleo will be here any minute.' The desperation in Rachel's voice cuts right through me and I have to fight the desire to shout out and tell her I'm here, I'm with her.

'I really hope so.' Luke spins around, his eyes scanning the trees around him. 'Cleo?' He calls out my name, dragging it into two long syllables. 'Clee-oooo, come out, come out wherever you are.'

I bite hard on my lip, trapping the scream inside. Luke falls silent and takes a step towards me. His eyes scan the darkness for a moment before turning back to Rachel. As he moves, I see the mounds of earth. Two piles of darkness on the ground. Two holes. Two graves. One for Rachel and one for me. A sob rises up, desperate to escape.

Luke spins towards Rachel, raising the blade in the air and swiping it down, slicing across her face. I cover my mouth and a stifled cry escapes my lips, the noise drowned out by Rachel's piercing screams, begging him to stop.

A pummelling terror pushes into me from every direction as Luke's attack continues, on and on.

Tears roll down my face as I back away, slowly, silently, feeling for every step first before I move. I can't help Rachel. I can't stop this maniac. I'm too scared. Only when I can't see the light any more do I stand and run again, feeling every bit the coward that I am.

Shame burns through me but I keep running. I can't feel the pain of the twigs as they dig into my feet any more. I'm running for my life.

When I reach the main path, I keep going. It feels endless. I've no idea how much time has passed, but it's enough. Rachel will be dead by now. A sob catches in my throat and I gasp for air. I can't break down yet. Luke could be driving back this way any second.

It's a lifetime of running before the path opens up, the trees thin, lights appear ahead of me. I can hear traffic, life, people. My back screams in pain but I keep moving, barely a run now, pushing forwards until my feet land on the pavement and I find myself on a quiet street.

A car approaches. A 4x4, a monster of a vehicle, and I don't think as I throw myself into the road, waving my arms frantically in the air. The headlights are blinding and I don't even see the driver as they swerve around me and roar down the road.

I cross the street and find myself standing outside a row of large houses, mansions really. Gated and private.

With a shaking hand, I jab the call button on the gate of the nearest house. Seconds drag and I'm about to run to the next house when a woman answers with a fearful 'Hello?'

'Help,' I gasp. 'Please help me. A man has kidnapped my friend. He has her in the woods. I need to call the police.'

'Is this a joke? Because it's not funny, it's sick. Bloody teenagers.'

Desperation squeezes me tight. 'Please,' I beg again. 'It's not a joke. My name is Cleo Thomas. I'm twenty-four years old. I was with my friend in the car but I got away. Please phone the police. Help me.'

There's another stretch of silence and for a moment I think she's gone back to the safety of her locked doors, but then the gates creak open and an outside light switches on. A woman appears at the door, a phone already pressed to her ear, and I fall to the ground, a heap of panic and fear and relief.

It's all come down to this.

Checkmate.

Game over!

Who lives, who dies? It will all end tonight!

Chapter 54

Cleo

Now

It's been well over a decade since I've driven. I learnt the year before we met, when London and make-up school still felt out of reach. I was terrible at it. Too nervous. My legs used to shake so badly I couldn't work the clutch properly, stalling at every traffic light, crunching every gear change. God knows how I passed my test. But at least your rust bucket, Pete the Peugeot, is an automatic.

There's a tremor in my hands as I buckle my seat-belt and start the engine, but by the time I'm out of Bethnal Green and driving north-east, I'm not think-ing about the car or what I'm doing, I'm thinking only of you.

Five years ago, I chose to run away. Twice. The first time, when I fell out of the car, I chose to run for help instead of going after you. But I didn't. I got lost. I found you anyway. I could have run into that clearing. I could have thrown myself at Luke and together we could have got away. But I was scared. A coward. I thought he'd kill us both.

The shame of what I did judders through me with the racing of my heart.

I won't run away this time.

Forty-five minutes later, I pull into a quiet street, houses on the right, the start of the six thousand acres of Epping Forest's woodland on the left. I park outside the same house with the wrought-iron gates that I called on all those years ago, half mad with fear. It's so familiar, this road, so raw, and for a moment my body won't move.

Memories clog my thoughts, the nightmares too. I'm frozen. Unable to move.

It takes every last drop of my strength to leave the car and run into the pitch-black woods, but I do it. I do it for you. I ran away from you five years ago and I haven't stopped running since. I won't be that person any more.

The track is slippery with thick mud puddles that splat up my legs, but I don't care. I point the torch a metre ahead of me and start to run, praying I'm not too late, praying I'm doing the right thing coming on foot. The car would be quicker, but I can't risk the noise of the engine. Surprise is all I have. Surprise and a desperate hope that Simon sees my note.

There's a dampness hanging in the air, lifting the smell of the woodland. Pine and undergrowth, a freshness that at any other time would be inviting, but there is nothing alluring about the dark and the reason I'm here.

I run until my lungs burn with cold air and I'm sweating under my coat. And then I stop, breathless from panic as much as the exertion. The path ahead of me splits in two and I don't know which way to go.

I turn in a slow circle with the torch, but all I see is

forest. The road, the houses, safety – it's all gone. I've never felt so utterly alone.

Then I see something on the ground by the other path. It glints in the light of the torch and when I step closer I see it's a trainer – a white Converse pump with metal lace holes, exactly the type you love.

I know exactly what this is: it's an arrow telling me which way to go.

Every few steps I find something else of yours and the fear, the urgency, pounds through me until I'm wound so tight I could scream. Is this a trail? Am I supposed to follow? Did you leave these things, or did someone else? Either way, I forge ahead into the darkness. I find the top you were wearing in the video hanging from the branch of a tree. Jeans flung over a log. Knickers in a muddy puddle, then a bra, all leading me deeper into something.

With every item I find, my pace slows. I know it shouldn't. I know I should be running full pelt to your side, but I can't. Each careful step I take seems to echo around me, the noise amplified as though I'm wearing a hundred microphones. The slopping water of the puddles, the rustle of the branches I push aside, my own breath – it's all so loud.

I wish I had my phone. I picture it lying on the bed in your room. Is there a tracking app on it? Some kind of hidden spyware? I think of the night I fell asleep in your room. That click of the door. The night I'm sure someone tampered with my alarm.

Questions spin in my thoughts, but I keep coming back to the same one – who? Who is doing this?

Another step and I freeze. There's a noise coming from somewhere ahead of me. A rhythmic clunk followed by a softer whomp.

A voice is screaming in my head to turn and run. Escape like last time. But I won't.

The path bends to the right and as I reach the corner I see a VW Golf parked between the trees. The engine is off but the headlights are on – two spotlights illuminating the ground ahead and a figure dressed in black, a shadowy outline of a man. He's driving a spade into the dirt, hitting the hard earth with a clunk and throwing it into a pile.

I switch off my torch and drop slowly to the ground, breathing hard and fast. My heart is leaping, jumping against my rib cage like a trapped animal desperate to escape.

Am I too late?

The spade stops. No clunk, no whomp. And as the silence wraps itself around me, I hear something else. It's soft, a barely there sound, a muffled cry. It's you. And suddenly I'm moving again, scrambling to my feet and sprinting forwards, faster and faster, around the car and straight at the hooded figure.

He's facing away from me, staring at the hole he's dug, and I lift the torch in the air and it's swinging down, aiming right for his head, but already he's moving, turning, and I catch the profile of his face in the headlights, and my arm falters, I lose momentum and the strike as it hits is pathetic.

'You?' I gasp the word.

'Hello, Cleo.'

Chapter 55

Cleo

Now

I stumble back, away from the man now standing over me, his face showing the same impenetrable calm I've seen so many times before. My left foot steps on a fallen branch. It's wet and I slip, my ankle twisting hard as I fall, hitting the ground with a yelp. For a second, I'm stuck again, fixated on the pain throbbing across my foot.

'Simon.' I whisper his name under my breath as though I can't quite believe it, but, just like my body, my mind is frantic too, and I'm leaping from one question, one unknown to another, and it all starts to make sense. All this time, I've been searching for the link between the before and the now. I thought it was Luke Richards, or a madman. I've suspected everyone, but not Simon. And yet, he's the constant. He was there five years ago and he's been here ever since.

I try to make the pieces fit and it's sickening how easily they do. Simon contacted Beth and reported you missing. I don't know what his job is, except it's something in computers. I'm sure he could easily have sent emails from your work account to your colleagues. He told Beth that you'd been on CamChat again. He mentioned me, planting the seed for Beth to get in contact. He did just enough to lure me here, but not enough for the police to take it seriously.

I think about that first time I saw you on the screen and how only hours earlier I'd told Simon I was planning to leave. Is that why he tied you up and shoved you in front of the camera – to stop me going? This is just as much about me as it is about you. And every step of the way I was telling him my thoughts, my plans. He has always been one step ahead.

Everything in the house – the power cuts, the night I fell asleep in your room and someone tampered with my attack alarm. Simon had access to everything. He planned it all. The realization sends a nausea burning in the back of my throat. I believed him. Everything he said – I believed it all.

'Where's Rachel?'

'She's here.' He throws a look towards the car before picking up the spade and surveying the hole and then me, as though measuring me against it.

'Rachel?' I scream your name, my voice hoarse, ringing with a grating, unstoppable fear. I can still get us out of this.

I pull myself to my feet, standing on shaking legs as pain shoots out from my ankle. I cry out again and the world threatens to tip. It takes everything in me to stay upright.

My throat closes. It's hard to speak but I force myself to look at him. 'Why?'

He gives a mirthless laugh. 'It started after you left.

You missed my big breakdown. All the work pressure got to me and I lost it. Even tried to kill myself. Rachel was the one who saved me,' Simon says, as if that explains why he's kidnapped her, why he's tormented me this week. He lifts the spade and steps closer.

'What about Liz?' I ask. 'And your plans?'

He laughs, hollow and empty. 'You mean the random woman I convinced to take a selfie with me? Wake up, Cleo. Everything was all part of the game.'

'I don't understand. Why are you doing this?'

He pauses as though considering my question. 'I never meant for things to go this far.'

'Then stop,' I croak.

'It's too late.' He shakes his head and I realize he's insane. Completely and utterly nuts. How did I miss this? I limp back. One step, two steps. Every tiny movement is matched by a long stride from Simon, and then he's on me and I cower. My ankle gives way and I collapse back to the cold ground.

'I don't understand. Why are we here? Why are you doing this?' A sob shudders through me and I feel that same defeat, that same understanding I felt five years ago. If I stay in these woods, if I try to help you, I'll die. Except this time, there is nowhere to run.

Simon's eyes flick to the grave.

'Simon, please. You don't have to do this.' Tears stream down my face. Wave after wave of realization crashes over me. No one is coming. No one even knows we're here. That note. That fucking note I put on Simon's door. Will the other housemates have seen it?

He glances at the car as ice chases through my blood. I'm running out of time.

I stare at the treeline again, thinking of escape, of

darting into the night, but my ankle – I'll barely make it two metres before Simon catches me. Plus, there's you. I've come this far. I can't leave you this time.

If I can keep him talking, maybe someone will come, maybe between us we can overpower him.

Simon turns back towards me and something shifts in his expression. His eyes widen with a sense of something impending. Excitement. He lifts the spade, holding it in both hands. I cry out, blubbering and pleading.

I gasp, a sharp intake of breath, and wonder if it will be my last. The blow comes hard and fast. There's a sickening crack in my left ear and then I disappear into the black.

Chapter 56

Rachel

Five years earlier

Rachel pulls her arms and legs close to her body, hugging them tight – a naked cocoon – wishing she could make herself smaller somehow.

'Shall we play another little game?' Luke's voice rings with excitement and malice, and she tightens her ball of protection.

'Please.' Her voice is croaky from the screams, the pleading. It's pointless, but Rachel can't stop herself. Sharp, stinging pain throbs from her cheek where Luke has already cut her. She can smell her own sweat, her fear, mixed in with the damp forest ground. She's so cold.

'Now, now,' he says, waving the knife one way then the other, as though shaking his head with it. 'Don't spoil the game now. You wanted this.'

'I didn't.' More tears fall from her eyes. Her shoulders shake. 'Please let me go.'

He laughs. 'I saw you on CamChat, you know? A

chat loaded while you were having a little heart-to-heart with Cleo and you didn't know I was there. I heard what you were doing – playing games with people, pretending to be people you weren't – and I thought, hey, I like playing games. You enjoyed it, didn't you?'

'No . . . it was stupid.'

'Don't lie to me.' His voice is loud and makes her jolt.

'You're right,' she half sobs. 'I did. I liked being someone else, but I didn't want to hurt anyone.'

'You liked playing games with people, didn't you?'

'Yes.'

'Me too,' he says, and she can hear the smile in his voice.

'Was any of it true?' The question is out before she can stop it. Hurt stretches across Rachel's chest. She thought she loved him. She thought he was the one. The knowledge burns a fiery path of humiliation through her.

He laughs, ending in a wolf howl as he tips his head up to the sky.

'But the hotels,' she sobs, desperate to keep him talking.

'A friend of mine works at a hotel and doesn't mind me popping in now and again. And in case you haven't noticed, I'm not actually American, either.' He swoops down, pushing his face into hers, stroking her skin with the cold blade of the knife.

Something snaps inside her. A bolt of adrenaline spurs her into action. Rachel kicks out, hitting one of his legs with everything she has. He yells with pain, stumbling away, and then she's up and running, sprinting for her life.

Rachel doesn't look back. This is her only chance.

And then it's snatched away from her. Her head yanks back; pain explodes from every direction. He's on her, holding her by her hair, throwing her to the ground.

She screams, landing in a heap by one of the holes. The knowledge of what is to come is far worse than the pain now. 'Please stop.'

There is no mocking taunt now, just the sharp pain of the blade slicing across her skin again and again until every part of her hurts and her body is slick with blood.

The frenzy stops as quickly as it starts. The smell of damp earth is gone, replaced with something else – blood and urine. Luke is still standing over her. Rachel can hear him panting, the noise distant somehow. He kicks her hard and she tumbles into the hole.

She lies still, too weak to fight. There is nothing she can do to stop the earth piling on top of her.

She's not going to die, Rachel tells herself.

Cleo will save me, Cleo will save me, she chants over and over in her head as the world turns dark.

Chapter 57

Rachel

Now

She's shivery. Freezing from the inside.

She has no shoes. He took them. Numb toes push into the cold ground.

There's shouting. A cry Rachel recognizes as Cleo. God, she's here. She really came. Fear and relief are a hand squeezing her throat. She draws in a ragged breath.

Cleo is here because of her. And it's up to her to do something.

Rachel creeps forwards, her heart thumping siren-loud.

A silence settles over the woods. There's no more shouting.

She's scared. More scared than last time. Last time there was no choice, no time to think. This is worse.

Rachel inches closer and sees a hole. A black mouth in the ground.

She has to do something. Simon is just there. Standing over Cleo in the darkness.

Now or never.

Then her toes touch something cold and she looks down, her gaze landing on a spade. It's small but sturdy. She picks it up and swings it through the air.

Chapter 58

Cleo

Now

I don't remember coming round. There is no slow awakening. No jolt. It's as though my thoughts are flying outside my body and slowly they land on the top of my head, sinking into me.

It's cold. That's the first thing I realize – the first thought that makes sense. A penetrating force. It's everywhere. Outside, all around, but inside me too, like I'm submerged in ice water. It pushes into every corner.

The next is the pain, sharp and shooting from my ankle, a hammer knocking against the side of my skull.

I don't know how long these two thoughts swoop and soar, dancing in my empty head.

My eyes are closed. The thought, the realization, lands on me with an 'oh' feeling, like I'm being silly. I need to open my eyes. Except it's hard. There's something on my face that's getting in the way.

The hammer keeps pounding the side of my head. Bang. Bang. Bang. Except now, every bang wakes me up that bit more.

Bang. I'm freezing cold.

Bang. I can't open my eyes.

Bang. There's something on my face. Something on my body. A weight. Dead. Heavy. Unmoving.

Bang. I can't move.

Bang. I remember where I was just before it went dark. I was in the woods.

There was a grave.

Instantly, I realize why I can't move. I'm in the ground, the grave. The something on me, that dead weight, is earth. Lots and lots of damp, cold dirt.

My eyes fight to open, to prove me wrong. But the moment they do, I scrunch them shut again. Tiny specks of dirt scratch my eyeballs. I move my hand instinctively to rub at them, but of course I can't. I'm trapped. Buried alive. It's every single one of the thousand nightmares I've had, but worse. This is real. There is no waking up in a heap of covers this time.

Every breath is short and sharp. The dirt is everywhere. In my mouth, my ears, my hair; it's in every corner of me. The back of my throat burns with panic, with the knowledge that I'm going to throw up. I swallow and swallow again, fighting to gain control. I can't be sick. I'll drown in it.

I swallow again and try to wiggle my fingers. Back and forth they go, wriggling worms. The movement calms me. My breathing slows a little. I keep wiggling until there's a little circle of space around my hands.

Slowly, very slowly, pressing my hands close to my body, I move them up, up, up, until finally they're by my face.

I don't need to think about what's next. I've read the article on the survivalist website a hundred times, a thousand times. Using just my fingers at first, I wiggle a space around my face and immediately the air feels easier to breathe. My head doesn't spin quite so fast. And then I begin to push the earth downwards. The movements are tiny and the second my fingers move forwards, more earth drops on to my face. It feels utterly pointless, but I keep going. I remind myself how cold the earth is, how hard it would have been to dig a grave, and how even though I didn't consciously look into the hole, a tiny part of my peripheral vision must have done, because I don't think it's that deep.

I picture the deck of the *Enchantress* in my mind; I try to remember the warmth of the sun. Then I think of my lovely mum waiting so patiently for me to come home.

I push another tiny mound of earth away from my face and again more arrives, except it's softer, as though there's less of it, and wetter too.

Panic and hope and desperation surge so fast through my body that before I can think, before I can stop myself, one of my hands is punching upwards. Dirt and mud and wetness fall all around me and the air completely disappears, and I realize too late that I can't breathe.

It's my nightmare again. It's every single panic attack that has paralysed my body. I know it was you who was buried alive and me who escaped. I know it should be you with this anxiety, but I can't help it, Rach. Lying in those bushes, watching it happen to you – it did something to me. I'm not strong like you are. I couldn't just carry on.

Chapter 59

Cleo

Now

My lungs burn. The hope and desperation disappear, leaving only panic. And yet, my hand – it's not touching anything, I realize. I can feel the wind on the tips of my fingers. I'm almost there. The surface is in reach.

I pull my hand back and return to moving the dirt, the mud, the earth. Faster this time, scooping desperately, until the dirt stops coming and my face is free. I breathe – great gulps of air. Tears of relief slide from the corners of my eyes as I open them and see a light. I think it's the sun at first, but the angle is wrong. It's bright and yet the sky above me is still black. Headlights, I realize. The car Simon used. It's still here.

For a moment I consider shouting for help. Screaming. Crying. But who would come? It's late; I'm in the middle of a secluded woodland in January. The only person likely to hear me is Simon. And if the car is still here, then he can't be far away.

The thought sends fresh terror through my body

and I clamp the scream inside and focus on shifting the earth until I try to sit up, but I move too fast and have to lie back down as my head pounds in protest. Carefully, gently, I touch the side of my head where I guess Simon hit me with the spade. The memory is blurred. It all happened so fast. I can feel a lump and the crusts of blood-matted hair.

When I sit up again, it's slower, yet still the inside of my head feels like it's being spun in a blender. I throw up. No warning this time. Just a heaving retch.

I look around me. One side and then the other, and that's when I see a body.

I cry out, the sound suddenly loud in the silence.

It's a lump on the ground, limbs splayed out. Unnatural. Unmoving. Even in the glow from the headlights I can see the grey tinge to the skin, rusty-red blood on the head, and cold, staring eyes. Simon is dead.

I start scooping again, my movements frantic as I heave breath after breath, desperate to get away from the body, the grave, these awful woods.

It takes an age to uncover the rest of me. I've lost all sense of time. Then I'm free and dragging myself out, clambering on all fours, and for the first time since I came round, I think properly of you.

'Rachel?' My voice is weak, barely a croak, as I call your name. 'Rachel?'

Silence.

I can't stand. Not yet. My head, my ankle – it's too much. So I crawl towards the car. I'm shaking all over. Shivering and sobbing all at once. It's a fight not to curl up on the ground and wait for help to come. But you're still missing.

I check the boot, but the car is empty. The key is in the ignition and I climb in and lock the doors, my eyes fixed on Simon. He still doesn't move, and even though a big part of me is sure he'll never move again, I keep staring. Waiting.

I'm not sure how long I stay there for, panting, crying, shaking so badly my limbs jerk, a violent tremor. It's you that finally makes me start the car. We need help. I don't know where you are, but we need the police and we need medical care.

I drive slowly, barely scraping five miles per hour. A fog is starting to creep over my mind, my eyes. I'm dizzy and so tired. It's a fight to stay awake. I can feel the car slowing down, rolling towards a stop. The path has disappeared. All I see is trees. I know I should brake, but my legs are ignoring me.

I'm vaguely aware of a bump, a jolt and then nothing until the tapping. It's a light rat-a-tat-tat. Rat-a-tat-tat. Where is it coming from? It's only when I open my eyes that I realize they were closed. I'm still in the car. There's a huge tree trunk dead ahead of me and a dent to the bonnet.

Rat-a-tat-tat.

I follow the noise to the window and burst into tears at the sight of the fluorescent-yellow jacket, and the reassuring worry on the police officer's face.

'Cleo Thomas?' he asks.

The relief that he knows my name, that help is here, makes me nod too fast. The edges of my vision cloud and I'm hit by a wave of nausea.

What happens next is a fuzzy blur. There are lots of police cars, lights flashing, hurting my eyes. I lie in the back of an ambulance, a blanket covering my body as a paramedic cleans the cuts on my arms I didn't know I had. I give them Anik's name and ask them to call him, but mostly I ask about you.

'My friend Rachel was here. Have you seen her?'

'Where's Rachel? Rachel Winslow?'

'My friend is lost. Please find her. Have you found her?'

I think I shout. A lot. And cry. No one has an answer, just more questions for me to answer. Question, question, question. A barrage of when, what, how, why. I tell them everything. The whole story. From that first text from Beth all the way to climbing into the car and locking the doors. I'm not sure how much sense I make. By the end, my teeth are chattering and I'm so thirsty and sleepy.

Then the rocking of the ambulance, and sinking, sinking into a nothing sleep.

When I wake again I'm in a hospital ward with five other beds. All empty. It's morning. Outside the window, the sun is a faded yellow ball. I have a vague memory of being wheeled through the hospital. A doctor talking to me. Some kind of scan.

I shift in the bed, aching all over. My ankle doesn't hurt as much, nor my head. Painkillers, I guess. My mouth is still dry. I can feel tiny grains of dirt rubbing against the back of my teeth.

A nurse steps over to me. Her smile is the same welcoming one I use on board the *Enchantress*. She looks at the machine by my bed and pinches the skin on the back of my hand. I want to tell her I'm OK, but I can't find my voice.

'Water,' I whisper. The one word has a tremor to it.

The nurse gives me a sympathetic pat on the arm and returns a few moments later with a jug of water and a cup. This time, she's not alone.

'Anik?' Just the sight of him makes me cry. Relief

and humiliation and shock pooling inside me and rolling in two lines down my cheeks.

'How are you?' he asks.

'OK.' I hear my own croaked answer and wonder if it's true. I gulp down the cup of water. It does nothing to ease the rawness in my throat.

'Sounds like it was a close call.' Anik pulls a plastic chair up to the bed and sits down.

'Again.' I mean it to be light-hearted. I mean to smile, but my voice is flat.

He frowns, and I know I can't put it off and nor can he.

'Where's Rachel?' I ask.

'Did no one tell you?' he asks.

I live and die a lifetime in the pause that follows.

'She's all right, Cleo.'

I cover my face with my hands and sob with relief until I'm too weak to cry any more.

You're OK.

'Where is she? Can I see her?'

'A PC drove her home last night to get some clothes.'

'She's not here?'

'No. She's fine, Cleo. Shaken but all right.'

I thought you were dead. I'd convinced myself. Told myself we couldn't get lucky twice.

'No one is telling me anything.' I give a shuddering gasp.

He nods. 'You've got a concussion, Cleo. You got a nasty whack to the side of your head and a sprained ankle. I've just spoken to the detective in charge. He said he tried to explain everything last night and tell you about Rachel, but you were confused. Rachel has told them what happened.'

'What did she say?'

'It looks as though your old landlord, Simon,

developed a troubling fixation with Rachel and what happened to you both. According to Rachel, she dated Simon on and off for some time, but broke it off when he started asking a lot of questions about what happened with Luke Richards.'

'I just can't believe it was Simon. In the woods he mentioned having a breakdown and Rachel helping him, but he seemed fine. I had no idea.' I shudder before rubbing my hands over my arms and wondering if I'll ever feel warm again.

'There are a lot of loose ends right now,' Anik continues. 'It may take a while to get all the answers.'

But Anik is wrong. All the pieces have fallen into place. It was Simon. He knew me. He knew our history. It would have been so easy for him to text you, pretending to be me.

I picture the man with the grey hair and horrible smile. *'Are you ready?'* I don't know where he fits in yet. Did Simon use CamChat too? Did he ask that man to scare me? Did he pay him?

'Officers are searching his apartment for evidence now. I expect they'll find a second phone.'

'I just . . . I can't see why he dragged me into this. Why text Rachel pretending to be me in the first place? Why tell her sister she was missing?'

Anik shrugs. 'To mess with her. To mess with you. Sometimes all the evidence lines up and we know the where, the when, the who, but the why is often trickier to understand.'

The side of my head starts to throb. A slow, pounding whomp of the hammer. Everything is lining up, neat and tidy. It was Simon. And yet, something nags in the shadows of my thoughts.

'Where's Rachel?' I ask.

'You just asked me that.' Anik frowns.

I shake my head and immediately regret it. The room spins. 'I mean, what happened to her last night?'

'Simon had her in the boot of the car he'd hired when you found him. She was able to get free and hit Simon with the spade before running for help. She didn't know he was dead until the police told her.'

The lights in the ward are suddenly too bright. I close my eyes and feel that queasy, too-much-wine, the-world-is-spinning feeling. I force them open. Bright lights are better than throwing up.

'But it doesn't explain why Rachel was using Cam-Chat again.'

'You'll be able to ask Rachel that when you see her tomorrow.'

'Tomorrow?'

'You have a nasty concussion and you need to rest. Rachel is shaken and resting at home.'

Anik stands and takes my hand. 'I'll come see you again tomorrow too.'

I lay my head on the pillow and close my eyes.

Tomorrow.

You are fine and I'll see you tomorrow.

'What day is it?' I ask.

'Sunday,' Anik replies.

I repeat the day in my head as I hear him leave the room. Sunday. Today is Sunday. My flight to Bermuda leaves at seven p.m.

I open my eyes again. After everything that's happened, the *Enchantress* is the only place I'll ever feel safe again. I thought I was ready to get help, to start living, but after last night, I know I need more time. A lot more time. I don't care how bruised and battered I am, I have to be on that flight.

The floor shifts beneath my feet as I slide out of bed and stand barefoot beside it. Pain sears across my ankle and my legs almost buckle. I hobble to the cabinet by the bed. My clothes are gone, stashed in an evidence bag somewhere, but there's a faded blue tracksuit someone has tucked in the cabinet for me. It takes forever to dress. Every movement is slow and causes a fresh wave of dizzying nausea to tornado through my body.

I don't try to discharge myself. It will take too long. The nurse will get a doctor and they'll try to talk me out of it and bully me back to bed, and I'm too tired to argue. So I leave a note explaining that I've gone home. It feels wrong, but I'm not breaking the law. It's my life. I can leave if I want to. And I do.

I need to see you today, Rach. Now.

I need to catch my flight.

Chapter 60

Cleo

Now

I find a taxi rank, give the address for Lockton Road and fall asleep in the back seat. I only wake up, cold and confused, when the driver shakes my shoulder and I realize we're outside the house. *Simon's* house.

The fear is a flame held to my skin, burning and raw. I'm scared. Terrified.

He's dead, I tell myself. But there's a disconnect, a broken circuit between my mind and my body, my emotions. There's something stopping me from breathing properly, from accepting that it's over.

Every limping step towards the house feels like a gigantic effort, a marathon. Tears stream down my face as I open the front door, catching the smell of the carpets and something else – burning dust. For the first time ever, the hallway is warm, the radiator hot.

I shut the front door and when I turn around your door is open and you're standing there and it feels like a dream, like I've wished it so much that my mind is playing tricks on me. But then you're moving and so am I.

We meet in the middle, arms wrapping around each other in a tight hug that feels like a million memories.

'I'm sorry,' you whisper in my ear and then we're both crying. 'I didn't think you'd be out today. I was going to come visit later.'

'I had to see you.'

We hold each other tighter and I cry with relief and sadness too. I've missed you so much.

'You need a hot shower,' you say a while later, pulling away. 'Come on.'

You step back and I see the gleam of your skin, the damp kink to your hair. My eyes travel to the scar. It's exactly as I imagined, but worse too. A long, jagged and bumping line. I look away, but you notice, of course.

'You get used to it,' you say, voice soft. You help me upstairs and I let you take over, turning on the shower and making me lean on you as I undress. I stand under the hot spray until my skin is red, my fingers wrinkling, until you hand me a towel and some clean clothes from my room.

'Rachel,' I say as you turn to go. 'Are you all right? These last few weeks. Simon . . .'

Tears fill your eyes, cutting to my core, but you nod. 'I thought he was going to kill me. Every day I thought I was going to die. Seeing you on the computer – it was the only thing that kept me going. I knew you wouldn't give up.'

I close my eyes. I didn't give up, but I wanted to. I tried to.

'Get dressed,' you say. 'I'll make us toast and tea and we can sit in my bed like old times.'

And that's exactly what we do. It's like the years have melted away. Disappeared. Gone.

'So, how—' you ask at the same moment I say, 'What on earth—'

We laugh. 'You first,' I say.

'How come you came back to London?'

'Beth texted me and told me you were missing. I called Simon and he said you were playing on Cam-Chat again.'

'Oh.' You frown. 'I mean, yeah, I was chatting on CamChat. I wasn't playing a game or anything. I was just talking to people, that's all.'

'But you called yourself Roxy?'

'I like the name.' You shrug as colour glows in your cheeks. 'I was lonely, that's all, but I stopped when I saw Simon on it too. It was then that I realized something was really off with him.'

'What happened?'

Your face falls. 'He had this breakdown not long after you left. His job was really stressful. You remember how much he worked.'

I nod.

'It all came crashing down and he tried to kill himself. I was lonely and not in a great place myself. I was taking some rubbish out and happened to look in his window and saw him on the floor. I called an ambulance and they pumped his stomach. It was touch-and-go. Another half an hour and he'd probably have died. After that, we got close. Friends with benefits, sort of, but never anything serious. We were on and off for a while and then, like I said, I saw him on CamChat and it gave me the creeps.

'Then DI Saha came to see me in early December to

tell me Luke Richards was called Richard Gilders and he was dead.'

'But you didn't believe him?'

'Not at first. But I looked up his brother and dug around on social media and found some photos and realized it was him.

'I told Simon about Luke being dead and that's when he started asking all these questions about what happened to us. It freaked me out. That was why I texted you last month. To tell you Luke was dead. I thought you'd want to know.'

'I'm so sorry. The signal on the—' I stop myself. 'I found it hard to stay in contact. I'm a terrible friend. I'm sorry, Rach.'

'Hey, you came when I needed you. I'd be dead twice if it weren't for you.'

You look at me then, your gaze unwavering. Nausea burns the back of my throat. 'I need to tell you something.' Memories of the past fill my head.

'It's OK,' you say. 'Rest first. We've got plenty of time.'

I nod, glad of my reprieve from the confession I know I need to make. 'So, what happened with Simon?'

'I told Simon I'd tried to contact you and the next thing I know I'm getting these texts from you on a new number. I was so happy to be talking again that I didn't even question it until Simon told me last week it was him.'

'How did he—'

'Kidnap me? I was an idiot. He slipped some sleeping pills into my cup of tea on a Friday after I got back from a night out, and the next thing I know I'm trapped in a skanky old bathroom in some run-down house.'

'Where was it?'

'I don't know. He kept visiting me and then he tied me up and put me in front of his laptop. He told me he'd hacked my laptop and he could see everything you were doing. And when he saw you were on Cam-Chat, he took over the screen, showing me in front of the camera to make you think it was on CamChat.'

I try to think back. The two times I saw you. The first time, it cut right through a chat, and then – nothing. Both times, the screen froze. Loading. I thought it was just CamChat connecting me to another chat.

Tears build in your eyes. 'I don't know how I'd have survived if I hadn't seen you.'

'I didn't do much.'

'That's not true.' You throw an arm around me and pull me close. 'I'm so glad you're here, Cleo. It's the best thing ever to be back together, isn't it?'

I nod, but something you've said niggles in my thoughts.

'Simon took you on the Friday night?' I ask.

'What about it?'

'Nothing.' I push the thought away. Charlie must've been wrong about seeing you on that Saturday, that's all.

My phone is on the nightstand, still switched off. A shiver races down my body thinking of whatever spyware Simon put on it. But it doesn't matter now. He's gone. It's over. I pick it up and hold down the power button until the screen lights up.

'I should call Beth,' I say. 'She's been so worried about you. She's supposed to be coming today. She'll want to know you're OK.'

'Oh, don't worry about that now. I've spoken to her and Mum. I told Beth not to come today. I said we needed a bit of time together. She wasn't happy, but she's going to come tomorrow instead.'

You fall silent and all I feel is the bang of my headache throbbing in my temples.

'You ran for help?' I ask suddenly, memories of last night hitting like a slap. 'Why didn't you take Simon's car?'

'I guess I didn't stop to think. I just panicked and ran. There was a shovel on the floor and I just grabbed it and swung it at his head and ran.'

'I was buried.'

Tears glisten in your eyes. 'I know. I wanted to help you but I thought Simon would kill us both. I just legged it through the woods and found a house and called the police.'

What can I say to that? You did exactly what I did to you, minus the getting-lost part.

We fall silent and I sip my tea. It tastes delicious. Hot and milky and sweet, just how I used to drink it. You always did make a good cup of tea. My head is still throbbing, but I'm warm and I feel safe beside you.

'So, what are you going to do now?' you ask. 'We're looking for someone to do some marketing stuff at work. You'd be so great at it!'

'Me?'

'Of course.'

'Do you ever miss working in make-up?' I ask, hoping you don't notice that I've not answered your question. The thump in my head is getting faster. My tea is finished and the taste of the earth is back in my mouth, dry and gritty.

'Every damn day,' you reply, looking suddenly sad and lost in the same way you did that day at the hospital when you begged me for that mirror and I tried to say no.

'Why didn't you—'

'The same as you, I guess,' you say. 'I stopped believing that dreams could come true.'

The comment is so utterly sad that I stop for a moment, trying to think. Is that what I did?

I'm so thirsty. I rub my hands over my face.

'Cleo, are you OK?'

'Yeah. I just can't get the taste of the earth out of my mouth.'

You're on your feet in an instant and heading for the door.

'I'll get you some juice. And hey, we could look on Rightmove for a place together. I can cover the rent while you get a job. We totally need to get out of this place.'

You laugh but stop when your eyes land on mine. 'What?'

'I . . . I'm not staying. My flight is tonight.' The words catch in my throat and I realize in that second that I don't mean it.

I've been deluding myself. I can't go back to the *Enchantress*. My bubble of safety shattered that day in Southampton and there's no way I'll find it again, on the *Enchantress* or anywhere else. I need to face my problems.

I'm about to take the words right back and explain all this to you, but you're already halfway out the door.

Chapter 61

Rachel

Now

Disappointment slides over her skin and into her body, oily and slick. Rachel knew Cleo wanted to leave, but she'd hoped, prayed, wished that being together again would be enough to change her mind.

Rachel takes her time in the kitchen, washing up a glass and pulling out the nice squash she keeps hidden at the back of the cupboard by the back door. She runs the tap for ages so it's extra cold. It tastes better that way. Rachel wants Cleo's drink to be perfect, but she also wants the time to gather herself. She doesn't want Cleo to see her sadness. Rachel was prepared for this. She can't stop Cleo wanting to leave, but she doesn't have to make it easy for her.

The smile feels tight on Rachel's face as she steps back into the room and hands Cleo the drink. 'I think this will help,' she says, taking in Cleo's frail body. She's been through so much, and Rachel doesn't just mean this past week. Guilt niggles. Everything has been her fault, her doing.

'Thank you.' Cleo takes a long sip and then another and it's a fight to hold back the tears as Rachel slides into bed next to her.

Cleo cradles the glass in her hands and rests her head on the pillow. Her eyes glaze, terror marks her face and Rachel can almost see her replaying what happened over and over in her mind.

Rachel reaches her hand out to comfort her, but Cleo is already picking up her phone and fiddling with the lock screen.

Rachel's heart is suddenly racing. 'Do you need anything?'

Cleo shakes her head, looking from Rachel to the phone, and there's something in her eyes, a silent question she's asking.

'Who are you calling?' Rachel asks, keeping her voice light. She wishes so badly Cleo would stay, but if this is the last time they talk, then Rachel wants it to be just the two of them. 'Honestly, if you're worried about calling Beth, you really don't need to.'

'I know.' Cleo bites her lip. 'It won't hurt though, will it? I'm sure she'll be relieved to know I'm with you.' There's something in her voice, that silent question again, and before Rachel can say another word, before she can stop the train wreck that's happening right in front of her eyes, Cleo is pressing 'call' and holding the phone to her ear.

Rachel jumps up, tears forming in her eyes. So this is how it ends. Was it really too much to ask that they have this one moment to themselves? Cleo will be gone soon and she'll be alone again.

She reaches the door just as the phone in her pocket starts to ring. She should've turned it off, but maybe it's better this way.

Cleo frowns. 'What?' She hasn't twigged yet.

'That's the thing about you, Cleo,' Rachel says, locking the door before turning to face her. 'You can travel to the other side of the world. You can change your make-up, your hair, you can lose so much weight that you look like a skeleton, but you can't change that one thing about yourself, can you?'

'What do you mean?' Cleo's voice is shaking. She reaches for her glass and takes another long gulp.

'You're a coward.' Rachel has to bite back a peal of laughter as she sees the reality dawn with comical slowness on Cleo's face.

'I don't . . . I don't understand.'

'Yes, you do.'

'Why have you got Beth's phone?'

'She gave it to me at Christmas,' Rachel says. 'She got a new one and wanted a new number, so I took this one.'

Cleo slumps on the bed and Rachel can see her turning it over in her thoughts. That first call when Rachel really wasn't sure Cleo would buy it. All the times she pretended to be Beth, waited for Cleo to recognize something in her voice, but she never did. Rachel laid on the guilt in that first call, but she wasn't sure it would be enough until Cleo called Simon.

The timing wasn't great. Rachel had just paid the deposit for the surgery, but it had been so hard to keep track of Cleo's movements. She was hardly ever in the country. But Rachel knew when the *Enchantress* was leaving from Southampton. She knew Cleo would be on board, and Rachel took her chance. She'd waited five years for the surgery. Another few weeks wouldn't make any difference.

'You were Beth this whole time?' Cleo says.

'Oh, she's getting it at last.' There's a nastiness to her voice that she can't hide any more.

'But . . . I spoke to you. On CamChat, when you were tied to that chair.'

Rachel can't help the faint smile that flickers across her mouth.

'You weren't really tied up, were you? I mean you were, but it wasn't real. It was all a game. All this has been some insane game to get me here, to punish me for leaving?'

'No.' A horrible sadness wraps itself around Rachel. 'I never wanted any of this.'

'How can you say that?' Cleo pauses, thinking. 'Did Simon take it too far? Jan told me your boyfriend was scaring you.'

'Jan? Oh, the widow. Poor cow. I did wonder who you'd end up speaking to. I knew you'd go on Cam-Chat, so I left lots of breadcrumbs for you to follow. I even got that nutter, Larry – the one with that awful grey hair – to talk to you about our game. I knew that would freak you out. He's harmless, really. All talk.'

'I don't understand.'

Rachel turns away and fiddles with one of her make-up brushes, running the soft bristles over her hand. She's wanted to say this for so long. 'You cut me out of your life. After everything we went through. And I don't mean what happened that night, I mean all the nights we spent in this room, our friendship – it was everything to me. And you just dropped it like it meant nothing. You threw me under the bus, just like everyone else.' Her throat aches and she can't stop the tears from falling.

'You have no idea what I was going through,' Rachel continues. 'I pushed you away because I couldn't cope with what that bastard did to me, I get that, but I didn't think you'd leave me.'

'I had to—'

'Yeah, I know. You had to get away. You said. And I tried to understand, but then you didn't come home, did you? You didn't answer a single text, you didn't pick up when I called. You got to run away, Cleo, but I didn't. I couldn't run away from my face, from reliving what that bastard did to me every single time I looked in a mirror or caught sight of my reflection.

'I let you have your time, but I really wanted to reconnect with you. It's been five years, for fuck's sake. And you still wouldn't answer my calls. And I knew that the only way I could get you back was if you thought I was in trouble.'

'So you faked your own kidnap? That's insane, Rach.'

Rachel nods. It was actually pretty easy. Simon had argued with her about the police angle, though. He understood how desperate she was to see Cleo, and he wanted to help like the obedient dog that he was after his breakdown, but reporting her missing to the police was a step too far for him – at first, anyway. Rachel had to convince him that it was the only way to make Cleo believe it was real.

It was surprisingly simple to research police procedure and make sure they didn't take it too seriously. To be fair to Simon, he played his part to perfection, even mugging Cleo and taking her passport. He did everything Rachel asked right up to the end.

Poor Simon. He was so weak after his breakdown. So desperate to make her happy. He tried to tell her no when she asked him to do just one more little thing, and then another and another. But he was in too deep to refuse and he knew it.

Of course, he didn't know the full plan at the end. He thought luring Cleo to the woods was about the two of them – her and Cleo – having it out at last, facing up to what had happened to them. Rachel convinced him it was the only way they could ever move on, right down to digging that grave.

'How did you know I'd come back?' Cleo asks, and Rachel wonders if she realizes her words are slurring a little.

'Because of the guilt. That's the reason you left, isn't it? You blamed yourself for what happened to me,' Rachel continues, her words coming fast. It's a relief to finally say it. 'I never did, by the way. I mean, come on. Luke Richards was all my fault. But then Anik came to see me last month and he let slip a few things I didn't know about that night Luke tried to kill me.'

Cleo's mouth drops open. 'You know?'

'About you being in the woods? Oh yes. Anik told me about how you found your way to that clearing and watched Luke try to kill me and then ran away instead of saving me. And then pretending you couldn't remember. A complete blank, you said. And it all clicked. I knew then why you'd run away. It wasn't because you needed to escape what happened, it was because you needed to escape your own guilt, and I realized it really was your fault I was left in that grave.

'I finally understood your silence all these years. For what it's worth, I forgave you at first. I thought if I could just get you back, you'd remember how close we were and see that I'm fine, that I didn't think it was your fault. You still got to the police on time, didn't you? If you'd tried to confront Luke, we might both have been killed. I understood that.

'That's why I pretended to be missing – to get you back here. The plan had been to turn up after the first weekend you were here and we'd have had a laugh about it all, but then you were going to leave too soon, weren't you? One day, you gave. One! You told Simon you were going after talking to the police and I realized no matter what I did, you'd always run away from me. So I expanded the story. It wasn't even hard. I was hiding in a house around the corner anyway.'

Rachel shudders. It was harder than she'd thought, being shut away in that one room. Simon didn't get why she wouldn't use the whole house, but she wanted it to look authentic when they set up the camera. She needed to look like someone in trouble. Besides, Rachel wasn't sure how it was going to end with Simon. She knew there was only so far she could take it with him. She knew if the police got involved, and of course they would, then they'd find the house she'd asked Simon to rent for them – and Rachel had to make it look realistic, as though Simon really was behind it all.

'And Simon?'

Rachel clenches her jaw. The last few weeks with him were tough. She needed to keep him in the game, but faking their relationship at the end, having sex on the mattress that had been left at the house by the old occupants, was not fun.

Cleo's eyes glaze again. Off she goes. It's nearly over now. Rachel looks at the empty glass and can't resist a triumphant smile playing on her lips.

Chapter 62

Cleo

Now

My head is pounding. It's a fight to keep my eyes open. An image flashes across my mind. The woods, the dark, the cold ground. Simon standing over me, raising the shovel.

'*I never meant for things to go this far.*'

Then the look of surprise on his face just before the world went black. He was raising his spade but he wasn't swinging it at me. I touch the lump on the side of my head. The left side of my head. I picture Simon again, standing before me, the spade in his left hand as he lifted it up. I thought he was going to hit me with it, but he didn't, because if he had done, it would have been on my right side, not my left.

'You hit me. You buried me alive.' My voice is a whisper as a weak sob shudders through my body.

'Well, it seemed only fair.'

'And Simon? Why did you kill him?'

'He was weak. He'd have caved eventually and I

couldn't risk it being his word against mine. Besides, you'll be gone soon, and with Simon gone too, I'll have a fresh start. It's for the best. I was never going to let you die in the woods, by the way. I just wanted you to see what it felt like to be in that grave. The plan was always to bury you and run for help. Well, when I say run . . . I mean, I was going to take my sweet time about it, that's for sure. I was in that grave Luke dug for . . . what, two hours?'

'So what was all this?' I throw an arm around the room. I'm so tired. It's a fight to keep my eyes open. The room is spinning. 'Why bother?'

A sadness takes over your features. 'I wanted to give you one last chance to stay, to be the friend you promised you'd be.'

'I . . .' There are no words. The guilt I've tried to bury is now ripped raw and standing before me, twisted and evil. 'So what happens now? Are you going to kill me?'

You shake your head with a sad acceptance. 'I don't need to kill you. You've done that for yourself. You couldn't cope with what happened last night. The trauma of it, when you were already struggling so much with your mental health. Thanks for going to visit that therapist, by the way. That really adds believability to the story, don't you think? You came into my room after I fell asleep on your bed. You found the sleeping pills I was prescribed years ago. You took too many.'

'No.' I shake my head and the room moves with me. My eyes drag from you to the empty glass.

'On top of the concussion, you won't feel a thing.'

Panic rises up inside me, but it's muffled beneath the thickest of blankets. I know I need to do something, but I can't. My voice is distant, my mouth no longer responding. 'I was going to stay.'

I watch the surprise register on your face – a flash of regret – and for one moment I think you'll change your mind and stop this madness.

'We can live together.' The words blend in to each other, mumbled, incoherent. I'm sinking.

You shake your head and the hope disappears. 'I know you, Cleo. You might stay for a month or two, but not forever. You'll always run away in the end, because you'll always be a coward. It's better this way.'

My phone is still clasped in my hand. There's no time to press the three digits, to call 999 and explain what's happening, but Anik's name is just below Beth's on the call register and I press it as the world folds in on itself. Cold nothingness seeps into every cell, a sinking ship being pulled beneath the surface of a pitch-black sea.

Chapter 63

Roxy

Eight months later

A wide smile stretches across Roxy's face as she pushes through the glass doors of the BBC studios. *The BBC!* For the longest of times, this dream has been dead, but there's something about a fresh start that makes a person want to shake things up, to really start living.

There's a woman in tight jeans and a turquoise blouse hurrying towards her. The woman is in her forties and her hair is tied in a messy bun on the top of her head. There's a make-up brush stuck through the middle of her bun and she looks every bit the harassed make-up artist Roxy has imagined.

'Roxy?' She holds her hand out for Roxy to shake. 'I'm Tania Locke. Thanks for coming in at short notice. As you can imagine, we've got *Strictly* fever here this week ahead of the first live shows. Tom Phillips got a black eye in training this week thanks to an unfortunate knee in the face, and so we've had to do some extra scenes around that. The public love that kind of thing. Then one of our junior make-up artists fell down some stairs on a night out, so we're absolutely desperate for the help.'

'No problem at all.' Roxy watches Tania's eyes flick across her face before she motions her forwards. 'Come on, we're in the back studio today.'

Roxy still can't get used to how little people stare now. She still gets a lot of looks, but it's different. Being blonde turns a lot of heads. And her face is unrecognizable. She hardly believes it herself. The lumpy red scar is a barely-there line, thanks to a skin graft and an amazing plastic surgeon. Roxy had fillers in her cheeks and got her nose done at the same time; it seemed silly not to. Gone is the flat, piggy look she's always hated, and it's hello to the cutest little button.

After the face and the nose and the hair, she didn't want to be Rachel any more. She's not sure she's been Rachel for a long time. So she changed her name and officially became Roxy Winslow. It was the only way to finally move on from what had happened to her. She still has flashes sometimes, still wakes in the night screaming once in a while, but she can live with that.

She has a new flat on the other side of London. A whole new life. It's only Anik who won't let it go, pestering her every few weeks. He will not accept Cleo's attempted suicide. Roxy has told him time and again that Cleo probably leant on her phone by accident as she passed out. But he swears he heard movement on the line, a door closing.

He's still asking questions about what happened that night in the woods. It's annoying, but Roxy isn't worried. He can ask questions for the rest of his pathetic life if he wants to. All the evidence points to Simon. She made sure of that. Poor Simon. He was so weak after his breakdown, so easy to manipulate. His IT skills certainly came in useful for keeping tabs on Cleo and loading software on to Roxy's laptop so they could hijack it anytime they liked, loading a live feed when they knew Cleo was on CamChat so Roxy tied to that stupid chair looked like any other chat.

But Simon was her weak link. He had to go. Roxy couldn't risk that at some point he might change his mind and go to the police.

It hasn't been quite the ending Roxy had planned. Anik ruined that when he called an ambulance and rushed to the house. Cleo was already dead. No heartbeat. Roxy thinks her screams of horror and disbelief were pretty convincing. But the paramedics did CPR and rushed Cleo off to The Royal London. They brought her back to life. Sort of.

A heart beating. Lungs that draw in air. Brain activity too. Although no one will know how much is going on in that head of hers until she wakes from her coma. If she wakes. Roxy's heart flutters at the thought. How much will Cleo remember? Roxy has come too far, risked too much, for it all to be over, but it's Cleo's move now, her turn in the game they're playing.

Tania leads Roxy through a maze of corridors and she hurries to keep up. It's an effort not to stop and stare at all the pictures on the walls, the history that she is going to be part of.

Tania opens a door and Roxy sees straight away that they're in a backstage area. Rails of costumes and props line both walls and she has to duck under the leaf of a fake palm tree.

It's everything Roxy has ever dreamt of. And she

knows immediately that this is where she's meant to be.

'We're in here.' Tania waves her into a dressing room with a long row of mirrors and chairs. 'I just loved your portfolio. So diverse. Anyway, I'm going to call one of the runners in to be the model today, but please don't worry. I love you already. You'll be a perfect fit here, I'm sure.'

'I'm sure I will too.'

'I warn you now that it is always a mad rush, but everyone who works on the show is amazing and we love it.'

Roxy grins and she knows with her whole heart that she's finally where she's supposed to be. She'll do anything to keep it that way.

Sometimes she wishes it could've been different. Not a day goes by that she doesn't feel a stab of regret. But what Cleo did, leaving her like that all those years ago – it hurt. Their whole friendship, the time they spent together, was just a game to Cleo.

In every game, there can only be one winner – and as long as Cleo stays in that coma, that winner is Roxy.

Acknowledgements

My first thanks are to my readers. It can be hard to remember when I'm putting words on a page, cutting, deleting, and rewriting in a hundred different ways, why I'm doing it. And then I'll get a tweet, an email or a review from a reader who has enjoyed my books and it reminds me that I love writing stories, but I also love how those stories become yours when my jumble of words jump into your head. So thank you for reading this book. I really hope you enjoyed reading it as much as I did writing it.

I was a bit nervous when I had the idea for this one. This is my first psychological suspense novel without an anxious mother, and I knew the moment the idea formed that it would be a little darker too. So thank you to Tash Barsby for seeing my vision and for your unwavering belief that I could write it. I'm so grateful to everyone at Transworld for the continued support and championing they give me, especially Imogen Nelson. You have been a massive cheerleader to me in both my career goals and your wizard editing skills in making my books the best they can be. Also, Hayley

Barnes and Holly Minter for the amazing work you do in getting my books into the hands of readers. There are many more at Transworld working behind the scenes too, so a huge thank you to them as well.

To Tanera Simons, my fantastic agent. We've been together from the start and I'm beyond grateful for the continued support, guidance and encouragement you give me, and for never saying no when I suggest yet another book idea I'd like to write. Thank you for everything you do for me! And thanks also to everyone at Darley Anderson Literary Agency.

Day to day, writing can be a lonely profession. I'm so lucky to have three kind, generous and amazing friends to share not just the highs and lows with, but all the little things that mean nothing to anyone but us. They are Zoe Lea, Nikki Smith and Laura Pearson. I'd be lost without your support.

I feel very lucky to have made too many author friends to mention here, but I would like to say thanks to Lesley Kara, another fantastic friend, for her wonderful advice and the fun she brings to my life with our podcast, *In Suspense*. Maybe one day we'll feel like we know what we're doing.

Social media is a place of both connection and procrastination. Thank you to all the book bloggers who shout out, review and champion books every single day. You are amazing people and I'm so grateful. I'm often posting little requests, and I'm grateful to Sarah Bennett, Shelly Wilson, Helen Edwards, and Donna and Luke Adams who are always on hand with a saying or a word I need.

Huge thanks also to Kathryn Jones for being one of my first readers and for getting me out of the house on dog walks, listening to me ramble on about made-up people and always making me laugh and feel human. And also Sarah Perrin, Catherine Malkin and Carol Halsall for dragging me out of my writing cave for cocktails and treats.

I'd like to give a short mention to my dad, Steve Tomlin. He passed away in July 2021 as I was writing this book. He was a writer too, but he'll be remembered best as captivating the room with a story (even if we'd heard it before). He'll be remembered fondly and his life celebrated often.

I normally only give a passing mention to my husband, Andy, but on this occasion, I'll go a little further. The cruelness of death is the sheer volume of admin and jobs to do on top of grief, and Andy has taken everything on, as well as being a rock of support, allowing me to grieve and find my way back to my writing desk and the stories I love so much. You'll probably never read this, but it's here anyway. Thank you isn't enough.

And finally to Tommy and Lottie for distracting me with games of Monopoly, dog walks and shopping trips, and understanding all the times I'm at my desk. I love that you're old enough to share and understand this roller-coaster career of mine and even help with brainstorming my book ideas.

After the sudden death of her husband, **Tess** is drowning in grief. All she has left is her son, **Jamie**, and she'll do anything to protect him – but she's struggling to cope.

When grief counsellor **Shelley** knocks on their door, everything changes. Shelley is understanding and kind, and promises she can help Tess through the hardest time of her life.

But when a string of unsettling events happens and questions arise over her husband's death, Tess starts to suspect that Shelley may have an ulterior motive. Tess knows she must do everything she can to keep Jamie safe – but she's at her most vulnerable, and that's a dangerous place to be . . .

*****

'A captivating, suspenseful thriller that draws you in – with a twist that will take your breath away.'

T. M. Logan, bestselling author of *The Holiday*

OUT NOW

Jenna is a wife, a mother, a doctor. She's also the victim of a stalker.

Every time she leaves her house, she sees him. Disturbing gifts are left at her door. Cruel emails are sent to her colleagues. She has no idea who this man is but she feels powerless against him.

Until the day he is brought into her hospital after a serious accident, and Jenna is given the chance to find out once and for all why this man is tormenting her. Now, the power is all hers.

But how many lines is she willing to cross to take back control of her life?

*****

'A gripping psychological thriller that pulls the reader through the story at a terrific pace, not giving them a moment to draw breath.'

Nikki Smith, author of *All in Her Head*

OUT NOW

What if you left your child alone, and something
terrible happened?

Anna James is an anxious mother. So when she
has to leave eleven-year-old Harrie home alone
one evening, she can't stop worrying about her
daughter. But nothing bad ever happens in the
sleepy village of Barton St Martin.

Except something goes wrong that night, and Anna
returns to find Harrie with bruises she won't explain.
The next morning a local businessman is reported
missing and the village is sparking with gossip.

Anna is convinced there's a connection and
that Harrie is in trouble.

But how can she protect her daughter if she doesn't
know where the danger is coming from?

* * * * *

'Addictive, tense and pacy, *Safe at Home* kept me
constantly guessing'

B A Paris, bestselling author of *Behind Closed
Doors* and *The Therapist*

OUT NOW

And now read on for an early look
at Lauren's next book . . .

THE UGLY TRUTH

L.C. North

Melanie Lange has disappeared.

Her father, Sir Peter Lange, says she is a danger to
herself and has been admitted to a private mental
health clinic.

Her ex-husband Finn and best friend Nell say
she has been kidnapped.

The media will say whichever gets them
the most views.

But whose side are **you** on?

#SaveMelanie   #HelpPeter

'Totally fresh and very clever.'
Emily Edwards, author of *The Herd*

**COMING SOON AND AVAILABLE
TO PRE-ORDER NOW**

Melanie Lange video 1/9
Published on Melanie Lange YouTube channel on 2 August 2022

I'm Melanie Lange. Today's date is the seventeenth of June 2022. I can't give you any proof because I have no access to the news. The only reason I have a phone is because it was smuggled to me earlier this week.

I'm recording this video from the bathroom of the house I've been locked in for the last four months. I've got the shower running and I'm whispering but I need to be quick. There's a guard in the next room. No lock. This is the only room in the house with a door. This is the only time I'm ever alone.

[Pause]

[Crying] I'm a prisoner. I'm not allowed to leave. There is someone watching me every minute of the day.

[Gasping] I don't know where I am but I believe it's somewhere in England. It's a private estate with no escape and no other houses anywhere nearby. The house is modern, newly built and on the coast somewhere. There's a cliff that leads down to a small private beach. I'm trapped. I can't leave. I've not seen or spoken to my . . . [crying] . . . my beautiful, precious boys for four months. I miss them so much. All I want is to hold them in my arms.

My father, Peter Lange, brought me here on the fourteenth of February. He tricked me into recording a video for my YouTube channel, telling people that I was taking some time away from the public eye. I thought it was for a few days. Not this . . . this hell. Please help me!

Extract from National Newspaper, 3 August 2022

MELANIE LANGE: MY FATHER IS KEEPING ME PRISONER

Former model and businesswoman Melanie Lange (34) has appeared in secret video recordings claiming she is being held prisoner by her father, billionaire business tycoon Sir Peter Lange, in a 'private estate with no escape'.

The two videos, which have now been released, show a distressed Melanie begging for help. 'I've not seen or spoken to my beautiful, precious boys for four months.' Her two sons, Sebastian (6) and William (5), currently live with their father, entrepreneur Finn Parker.

The first video was allegedly recorded on 17 June of this year and sent to close friend and personal assistant Nell Stevens, who kept the videos private following Melanie's instructions. Posting her own video to Melanie Lange's YouTube channel, Nell said: 'Melanie wanted to find a way to free herself that didn't involve the media. These videos were her safety net should all else fail. She asked me to keep them safe and only publish them if contact between us stopped. And it has. I'm deeply concerned for her safety.'

Melanie has not been seen publicly since her birthday celebrations ended in chaos in February.

Sir Peter Lange, who made his money in a global hotel chain (Lange Hotels) in the nineties, was not available for comment.

Statement from Sir Peter Lange, 6 August 2022
Read by a spokesperson for Lange Hotels

Following a breakdown earlier this year, my daughter, Melanie Lange, is currently being treated at a private mental health facility supported by medical professionals. She is safe and healthy and grows stronger every day. She will return to public life as soon as she is able.

The media reports released this week are not reflective of the actual situation, but we would like to thank everyone who has raised concerns for her safety and reassure all of her fans that Melanie is being well cared for by people who have her best interests at heart.

Extract from National Newspaper, 18 August 2022

NETFLIX COMMISSIONS DOCUMENTARY ON MELANIE LANGE STORY

Netflix has announced today that it has commissioned a documentary on Melanie Lange's disappearance which will start filming next month and be aired in October. This tell-all three-part documentary series, titled *The Ugly Truth*, will delve into Melanie's rise to fame and promises to uncover the truth behind Melanie Lange's reported imprisonment by her father. No one from the Lange family is thought to be taking part.

Twitter
18 August 2022

Connie Rose @Wannabeawritergirl
#SaveMelanie I love ya girl!

James Hilton @James_T_Hilton
Who actually cares about #TheUglyTruth?? This is just another stunt by an attention-seeking woman! #MelanieLangeHoax

> **Tahlia J @TahliaJenkins55**
> YES!!! Next week they'll be launching a new product for sure! #MelanieLangeHoax

Kaitlyn M Davids @Mummyrulestheroost
OMFG how is this woman still a prisoner? Let's finally get #TheUglyTruth #SaveMelanie

Jane Godfellow @WorldofCats2002
I knew there was something off about Melanie's last YouTube video! It had a really bad vibe. She's been imprisoned by her father for 6 MONTHS!!!!! #SaveMelanie

Lucie Bolton @LucieBoltonOfficial
Is it any wonder #MelanieLange went totally off the rails with the way the British media have hounded her her whole life? Her dad is clearly looking out for her #HelpPeter

Richard T Maloney @Richard&LesleyM
This is a private family matter surrounding a woman's mental health problems. Why can't everyone just leave this family alone? #HelpPeter

Jessie W @Jessiebakescakes4U
This would never have happened to a man! #SaveMelanie

Amy B @GirlAboutTownBlog
Guys!!!!! Who else is excited about #TheUglyTruth???? I'm #SaveMelanie
ALL THE WAY!

> **Kaitlyn M Davids @Mummyrulestheroost**
> You are such a hypocrite @GirlAboutTownBlog! How can you be
> #SaveMelanie after everything you've said about her?

dead good

Looking for more gripping must-reads?

Head over to Dead Good –
the home of killer crime books,
TV and film.

Whether you're on the hunt for an intriguing
mystery, an action-packed thriller
or a creepy psychological drama,
we're here to keep you in the loop.

Get recommendations and reviews from
crime fans, grab discounted books at bargain
prices and enter exclusive giveaways
for the chance to read brand-new releases
before they hit the shelves.

Sign up for the free newsletter:
www.deadgoodbooks.co.uk/newsletter